Irish Ghosts and Hauntings

Also by Michael Scott

A CELTIC ODYSSEY
IRISH FOLK AND FAIRY TALES OMNIBUS
IRISH MYTHS AND LEGENDS
IMAGE
REFLECTION
IMP

Irish Ghosts and Hauntings

♣

Michael Scott

WARNER BOOKS

A *Warner* Book

First published in Great Britain
by Warner Books in 1994

Copyright © Michael Scott 1994

A CIP catalogue record for this book
is available from the British Library

ISBN 0 7515 0154 9

Photoset in North Wales by
Derek Doyle & Associates, Mold, Clwyd.
Printed and bound in Great Britain by
Clays Ltd, St Ives plc

Warner Books
A Division of
Little, Brown and Company (UK) Limited
Brettenham House
Lancaster Place
London WC2E 7EN

Contents

✣

For Morgan Llywelyn – thank you

Acknowledgments

♣

I am indebted to all of those people who were so generous with their time and memories in the summers of 1989–1993, when these stories were collected. I am particularly grateful to Morgan Llywelyn, who allowed me access to her extraordinary library, with its wealth of invaluable research material. Barbara Boote of Little, Brown deserves special thanks for her remarkable patience and understanding.

CHAPTER ONE

The Saint and the Devil's Mother

——————— ♣ ———————

The early-morning mist hung low over the broad river, blanketing it in gauze. There was no breeze to disturb it, and yet still it moved, currents and eddies shifting sinuously through the mist in serpentine shapes. The air was chill and deathly still, tainted with a foulness that spoke of death and disease and utter desolation. No sound broke the silence that enclosed this blighted place close to the source of the river, for no creature lived within a thousand paces of the water, no birds flew over its scummed waters, no insect hummed across its surface.

Two men crouched in tall grass on a knoll overlooking the river. They had spent most of the night there and their rough-spun brown robes were shining silver with dew, the moisture beading their beards and tangled hair. Neither man spoke. They had spent enough time in the countryside to know how sounds carried, especially so early in the morning and particularly so close to water.

As the sun climbed higher into the heavens, the mist

1

that clung stubbornly to the river thinned out and slowly burned off, revealing the murky water beneath. The older of the two men strained forward to look at the water, a frown on his long, narrow face, his thin lips drawing into a line. He remembered this river from his youth. Before he had become a monk, he had spent many years as a slave of the local chieftain, herding sheep on a nearby hillside. He had often slaked his thirst in the clear waters. But he wouldn't even consider drinking the water now: it was scummed and filthy, an oily, rainbow-hued stain curling lazily across the surface, white-bellied fish floating amongst the clotted debris, the partially decomposed skeleton of an enormous water rat rotting on the bank. The water was dead, polluted. Nothing lived in it now – but as he watched, the surface of the water was briefly broken by what looked like a flipper. Turgid ripples lapped across the stained and blackened banks.

When he had seen enough, the older man tapped his companion on the arm, then slid back down the knoll, moving away from the river. At the foot of the incline he scrambled to his feet, then turned and walked away in absolute silence, his leather-soled sandals making no sound on the soft, damp earth. His younger companion hurried to catch up.

When they were a thousand paces from the polluted water, the older man stopped. He slid his arms into the brown sleeves of his robes and turned to look back in the direction of the river. He tilted his chin upwards. 'Tell me about the river.'

'It began no more than a season ago, Brother Patrick,' the younger man said softly. He turned and pointed to the left, where a dozen wisps of grey smoke twisted up into still air. 'The villagers reported seeing an enormous cloud moving quickly across the sky. They remarked upon the cloud because it was a greenish yellow in colour and was constantly in motion, as if something twisted *within* it. It befouled the air with a reek, like that of rotten eggs, and for days after its passing, every place was covered with a yellow, gritty ash. They thought that it had come to earth close to the source of the river.'

The man known as Patrick nodded. He had heard similar stories across the land of Erin, and he had come across similar occurrences in his homeland, in the land of the Britons.

'The villagers assumed it had passed on,' the younger monk continued. 'Two or three days later some of the villagers fell ill, vomiting and soiling themselves, blood in their waters. Cattle, too, were similarly affected. No one connected it with the curious cloud until the local headman noticed that those villagers who lived closest to the river were the worst affected, while those who drew their water from the well had suffered no ill effects. He followed the river to its source, suspecting that it had been the cause of the villagers' illness. However, he wasn't unduly concerned, indeed, he didn't even consider it unusual; stomach sicknesses like this are not uncommon, and dirty water is nearly always the cause.'

'I've seen that happen all too often,' the small dark man said. 'An animal will fall and die in a stream and its decaying corpse will taint the waters.'

'That was what the headman expected to find, brother,' the younger monk nodded. He was still very much in awe of this man, whom some of the converted were already calling a saint. Most holy men he knew, whether they were Christian or druid, were unworldly, preferring the realm of the spirits and gods to the real world. But it was

Brother Patrick's practicality that convinced the younger monk that here, at last, was the man who would convert the pagan Irish.

'Tell me what the headman found in the stream,' Patrick said.

'The village lies yonder, through the trees. Perhaps it would be better if he were to tell you himself.'

Patrick followed the younger monk through the trees, his head ducked low, eyes roving across the uneven ground for roots or holes that could trap and snap a man's ankle. He was surprised by how easily the skills he had learned as a slave boy herding pigs on Slemish Mountain just to the north had returned to him. When he finally escaped his terrible ordeal, he thought he would never return to this savage land. When he returned to civilised Britain, he would take up his father's occupation as the local decurion – the tax collector.

He had been wrong on both counts.

The monk had been born Magonus Succatus Patricus in the town of Clannaventa on the west coast of Britain. Taken as a slave to Erin, he had been called Patrick or, more often, simply 'boy'. When he had escaped back to Britain, he was once again Magonus Succatus Patricus, the son of the Roman tax collector; but instead, he found that he was still Patrick. And he discovered that the faith that had kept him strong through the long, hard years on the mountain in Erin had grown and intensified, and he knew he was going to devote his life to God. In time the same faith urged him to return to the pagan land of Erin and convert its people to the one true God.

In the four seasons since his return to Erin, Patrick had converted many from the old ways. He had achieved his first great victory when he had stood up to the king himself and faced down his druids on the sacred hill of Tara. Angras, the queen, had given up her pagan ways to follow the one true God, and many had followed her example. The druids and most of the chieftains were still ranged against him, however, but he knew that if he concentrated on converting the ordinary villagers then the rest would follow in time. And the simplest way to convert them was to defeat their enemies – especially their non-human foes. The people called them devils and demons and foul spirits, and while Patrick didn't disagree with them, he had enough education to know that some were probably the last remnants of the ancient peoples who had occupied Erin in times past.

But he had also lived long enough in Erin to know that wild magic survived in its dark forests, in its deep pools and rivers, and to dismiss blithely or ignore the manifestations was tantamount to suicide.

There was evil in the world.

Paradoxically, he was glad of that, for without evil, there could be no good, much as night differs from the day. But he had faced evil before – evil men, evil circumstances and pure evil – and faced them all down. He would do it again.

And now he suspected that what had befouled the river was evil – ancient and deadly.

The village headman was tall and grizzled, and held himself with the assurance of a warrior. He met Patrick, bowing gravely to him, as one equal to another, and stood back, indicating that the other man should precede him into the wood and wattle hut and take his place at the table. The two men sat on either side of a glowing fire and sipped mead from wooden beakers. Finally, the headman spoke, breaking the long silence. 'The young brown-robe tells me that you can help us.' He made the statement into a question.

'I can try. I make no promises.'

'A man should not make rash promises.'

Patrick bowed, waiting for the older man to continue. He was aware how difficult it must be for this man to have to ask aid of one of the followers of the new god. The very fact of doing so forced him to acknowledge that his own faith had failed him.

'There is a creature in the river. A demon,' the headman said eventually.

'Have you see this demon?'

The old man shook his head. 'I have never seen it. No one has. But we have all heard it, seen its spoor, smelt its stench. It is there.'

'Its presence has poisoned the water,' Patrick said gently.

'There have been deaths,' the headman continued. 'The old, the young and the sick – both human and animal – have died from drinking the water, or eating the flesh of creatures which have drunk the water. Now the vegetation that borders the upper reaches of the river is beginning to die.' His eyes met the holy man's. 'This village has been here for generations.' He paused and added, 'I have instructed the villagers to make preparations to move.'

'Where will you go?'

'East, along the river. We will warn others about the foulness in the water.'

Patrick nodded. 'When do you intend to leave?'

'In a day or two.'

'Can you wait any longer?'

'A day, but not more. Why?' the headman asked simply.

'Let me use that day to see what I can do.'

'Are your gods strong, holy man?'

'I worship but one god,' Patrick said softly, 'and yes, He is strong.'

'There is no shame in worshipping a strong god,' the headman said slowly and Patrick, looking into his eyes, nodded in understanding.

The stench of bitter decay grew stronger as the small, dark man approached the source of the River Lagan. The air stank of rotten eggs, rancid fruit and fetid meat.

The grass close to the river bank was seared and yellowed, and the trees that clustered close to the waters were already dying, their leaves limp, flakes of bark hanging from their trunks. Scores of dead fish were tangled in their roots and the bloated bodies of birds lay snagged amongst the matted reeds.

Patrick dampened a cloth with the flask of water he'd brought and pressed it to his mouth. He could already taste the foulness on his lips. But he knew the taste, recognised the smell: he had seen this destruction before, though never on such a scale. Usually these creatures settled in pools or small, landlocked lakes, where the devastation they wrought was contained. It was easy then for the local people to declare that the lake was cursed, and shun it. In some of the wilder parts of the country, Patrick knew that the locals sacrificed to the lake, feeding it with cattle and sometimes humans, and he had also heard the stories of monsters birthed to human women who lived near these stricken pools. Obviously whatever inhabited these lakes crept forth at night and mated with humans.

Patrick spent the rest of the day watching the pool, but he saw nothing, except the indistinct flicker of movement beneath its surface.

The holy man returned to the river at noon the following

day. Standing on a knoll, he looked down over the area of desolation that bordered the river. The young brother had told him that it had doubled and then doubled again over the past few days. If it continued to grow at this rate, then it would soon cover the entire valley. Where would it go then? Would it continue, until it covered the entire countryside?

Turning his back on the river, Patrick filled his lungs with comparatively clean air and then, holding his breath, a damp cloth pressed across his mouth and nose, he walked down to the water's edge. The grass was brittle underfoot and he knew he would have to burn his sandals and robes afterwards. The water itself was scummed with thick, yellow-white froth; in the few places where the water showed through, it was marred by an oily discoloration. Squinting into the dead water, he thought he saw the coil of a tentacle.

Standing at the river's edge, Patrick bowed his head in prayer.

This was not one of the peists that inhabited many Irish rivers and lakes. The peist was a serpent, rather like an eel, though often three times longer than a man. They were relatively harmless, though the bigger creatures were perfectly capable of taking humans or cattle swimming in the water.

The old man suspected that this was one of the fabled Fomor, half-humans from the icy northlands. They had appeared in many guises in Irish lore, before being defeated by the equally legendary Tuatha De Danann.

The filthy surface of the water rippled and a leathery fin appeared.

They were creatures of death and destruction: one of the Fomor kings, Balor, was reputed to be able to turn humans to stone simply by looking at them. Perhaps there was more than a grain of truth in the old story; Patrick had seen the remains of humans who had lived near similarly polluted lakes: their skins had been hard and grey, flaking like old stone.

The dome of a scaled head broke the surface. Flat, yellow, slit-pupilled eyes regarded the human unblinkingly.

So what were they: the remnants of a long-dead non-human race . . . or demons? His education advised him that the former was correct, but his faith dictated the latter. These creatures had been in the world since God had created Adam. Therefore, these were the spawn of Lilith, Adam's first wife. When she had been cast forth from the Garden of Eden into the wasteland, she had given birth to the demons who now troubled the world.

Smoothly, silently, the creature rose up out of the water.

The stench alone was enough to send the holy man staggering backwards. He opened his eyes and looked into the face of absolute evil.

He had seen these demons before: but never one so big. The serpentine Fomor was vaguely manlike. It stood twice as tall as a human and was broad in proportion. It was covered in iridescent scales that leaked a pale, yellowish bile that the holy man was convinced was poisoning the water. Its snout jutted forward and a forked tongue tasted the air; when it opened its mouth, Patrick caught a glimpse of rows of triangular teeth. Its long, sinuous arms ended in three slablike claws, and the tail that lashed the water to a froth was ridged with triangular fins. It spat at Patrick, the gob of yellow venom catching him on the sleeve of his robe. The thick wool immediately curled and blackened.

The holy man's lungs reached bursting point and he

breathed out in a great gulp, tasting sulphur and noxious gases in his mouth and on his tongue. His stomach roiled in protest.

'Spawn of Satan,' Patrick intoned, 'I banish you in the name of the one true God, the Lord Jesus Christ. In the name of the Father and of His Son and the Holy Spirit . . .'

The creature howled. Its mouth worked and it spat at the human again. This time Patrick managed to scramble back and the venom fell harmlessly on the ground before his feet. The already seared grass darkened and crisped.

And then the holy man raised his hand and made the sign of the Cross.

The young monk who had been hiding further up the river took his cue and ran forward, a blazing torch held high, the breeze fanning it to a flame. The saint's instructions had been specific: while the creature's attention was directed towards him, the young monk was to creep up from behind, plunge the torch into the river . . . and then run.

The monk came as close as he dared to the water's edge. Planting his feet firmly, he spun his arm in an underarm throw, sending the torch flaming high into the air. The Fomor turned at the dull, roaring sound. It caught sight of the blazing torch falling towards the water and launched itself in a desperate twisting lunge for the brand. Its claws nicked the edge of the falling torch, but it plunged head first into the fouled water.

And died in a hissing sputter of grey smoke.

There was a moment of absolute stillness while the two humans and the reptilian creature looked at one another, and then the Fomor threw back its serpent's head and hissed aloud its triumph. It turned back to the small, dark-skinned humankind, claws flexing . . .

And the river erupted in flame.

The detonation lifted Patrick and the young monk off the ground, and flung them forward, away from the inferno that smothered the water. The river bank looked like a scene from hell. The seared and withered grass snapped alight and the blighted trees closest to the water crackled to a blaze, sap boiling, the trees exploding in long detonations of sound.

The Fomor was caught in the centre of the conflagration. Its hissing rose to screeched howls as its oily scales ran with liquid fire, its yellow eyes turning milky and opaque, the venom that drooled from its lips burning as it dripped to the water. The creature attempted to escape the flames by diving beneath the water, but it was burning so fiercely now that the very water was billowing off in steam.

The young monk staggered up to Patrick and helped him to his feet. The soles of both their sandals were burning where they had stood on the polluted earth.

'What was that?' he demanded.

'The mother of all demons,' Patrick said grimly.

'And you have slain her,' the monk breathed.

'This creature yes, but there will be others like her. I think I will meet her like again,' Patrick said prophetically.

'*An Catoranach*,' the monk said excitedly, '*an Catoranach*, the Devil's mother! You have slain the Devil's mother!'

CHAPTER TWO

The Crow Goddess

--- ♣ ---

There is no pain now, so the end must be very close indeed.

I have been told that there is a kind of peace that claims the human body before death, but I saw too many men scream their throats bloody before death took them to believe such superstitious rubbish. But I have to admit that I feel . . . at peace now. Waiting.

This is the day the priests call Good Friday, the day the Lord Jesus Christ gave up His life on a wooden cross to save this world. I'm not sure He succeeded. Before we went out to battle this morning, the priests told us that our cause was just, that this was a good day to die, and that those who die today will join the Lord in heaven. But there is never a good day to die. Dying is hard and bloody, death is never easy.

There are dead all around me now, but the moans and cries and whimpers of the wounded and injured have mostly faded away. We fought the invaders to a standstill on this hillock and the tide was turning when I was struck down. Since they haven't returned, I can only assume that they have been pushed back, and that the army of King Brian Borouma, the High King, has swept away the Norsemen.

I saw the king just before we went out to battle. He was shorter than I thought he would be, his hair and beard white, his face lined, but his eyes still blazed with the fire of youth. I have been told that he is seventy and two years old, but I find that hard to believe. And when he spoke, I knew that here indeed was a man to follow, a great leader of men. He spoke to us about our country, and the greatness of our people, he likened us to the ancient heroes of old: Cuchulain, Oscar, Oisin, Fionn MacCumhal, Fergus and even Bishop Patrick, who had endured much to free this land from its paganism. The king reminded us that if we failed today, we would be failing the heroes of old, failing Saint Patrick, allowing the ancient evil to take this land once again.

In this year of Our Lord, One Thousand and Fourteen, all the men of Erin profess to follow Christ, but Christ was a man of peace, and not a warrior's god. Warriors still pay homage to the ancient gods of Erin, the Dagda and Danu, the Morrigan, Macha and the Badb, the goddess of battles, wife of Net, the battle god.

The priests dismiss such beliefs, of course, claiming that warriors who fail to honour the one true God will suffer the punishment of eternal fire in the next life.

In another few moments, I shall know the truth of it. Is the Christian God the one true God, or do the priests of the old religion who now wander the roads of Erin speak the truth?

I was baptised into the Christian faith and though my mother was a great believer, my father paid only lip service to what he called the new religion. When I was five summers old, I remember being taken to a place of stones, two days' ride from our settlement. This was one of the old places, the weathered stones marked with the ancient whorls and twisting spirals of long-dead craftsmen. There was an old man in the midst of the circle of standing stones before a blazing fire of wood and dung. The shifting shadows on his face made it impossible to read his age, but I saw his hands once and they were wrinkled and mottled, the flesh sagging with great age, the tattooed lines and circles on his flesh faded to the colour of veins. His fingernails were long and black.

I have little memory of the ceremony that followed. I think I knew then – and if I didn't, then realisation came quickly afterwards – that the old man was a druid, or if not a druid then one of the followers of the old faith. An animal was sacrificed, a chicken perhaps, I don't remember. I squeezed my eyes shut as it screamed its last, but the memory that is most vivid is the hot blood splashing across my face. A droplet touched my lips, and I licked it instinctively: the blood was hot, salty and bitter. The druid and my father considered this a good sign: the old man prophesied that I would be a great warrior, whose name would be remembered for future generations. He lied.

That night I was dedicated to the Badb.

I am ten and nine summers now. And I know I will never see my twentieth.

The light begins to dim. The noises of battle have almost entirely faded now; Brian's warriors or Murchadh, his sons, must have driven the invaders back towards the town of the Black Pool, Dubh Linn.

There is smoke on the cool evening air. It almost, but not quite, disguises the myriad smells of death and dying.

Perhaps I should have listened to the rumours that

circulated through the camp last night; perhaps then I would not have gone out to battle. I could have slipped away in the middle of the night and none would have been the wiser . . . except me. The talk was all of the allies and mercenaries that Sitric, the Norse king of Dubh Linn, had managed to gather together. First he had allied himself with Brian Boru's old and bitter enemy, Maol Mordha, the king of the province of Leinster, and then he had enticed Sigurd, the Viking king of the Orkneys, and Brodar, the king of Denmark, with promises of land and pillage. Our cause had been dealt a severe blow because Maol Seachlainn, Brian's ally, had refused to join in the battle, and none knew the reasons. There were also rumours that the army that Donnchadh, Brian's younger son, had raised would not arrive for another two days.

A wise man would have heeded the rumours. Wise men live longer than fools.

And this very morning, when I rose, a cloud the shape of a large black raven flew across the sun, briefly blotting it out, casting Brian's army into shadow.

I should have heeded that warning too. My head told me to flee, my heart wanted to fight.

Perhaps if I had listened to my head I would not be lying here, with a Norse spear through my belly.

Night is coming on. The sky has darkened, the wind has grown chill and I can see clouds gathering on the horizon. The noises are clearer now: the snapping of burning wood, the distant shouts of victory – I can hear 'Boruboruboru' carried on the wind. And something else . . .

Something moving close by.

Cloth is flapping, cracking in the breeze, as something heavy moves through the bodies. Leather creaks, harness jingles, metal clinks, but I cannot turn my head to see.

Scavengers? Camp followers stealing the jewels and ornaments off the dead . . . dealing death with a knife to the wounded clinging stubbornly to life. Was this to be my fate: to die at the hands of a woman or child thieving the rings off my fingers?

The wind gusts, wafting a foul odour over me, dry and bitter and musty. A tiny, grey-tipped black feather settles on my bloody hand.

There is movement behind me. I try to tilt my head to see, but I have not the strength. Another feather settles on my chest.

And I know . . .

As a child, I was dedicated to the Badb. The crow goddess haunts the battlefields, claiming those who have been given to her, first plucking their eyes, before savouring the softer flesh.

But the Badb was legend . . . is legend!

My fingers are numb, but I cross myself. 'In the name of the Father . . .'

A shadow rears, black wings flapping open, enclosing the night. The voice is a harsh caw. 'Pray to your mother!'

CHAPTER THREE

The Legend of the Banshee

———— ♣ ————

This river gives me life. Its waters sustain me. While it flows, I live. I feed not on flesh and water, but memories and emotions.

I was once human; now I am legend.

The humankind have a name for me and my kind. They call us the Sidhe, the fairy folk. Sometimes they whisper, *'Fairy woman, bean sidhe, banshee.'*

I am the banshee.

My people were the Tuatha De Danann, the people of the goddess, sacred to fair Danu. Once we ruled this world from the De Danann Isle in the midst of the Great Ocean. Our empire encompassed the lands to the west, the country of the copper-skinned folk and east to the lands of the black-skinned races. But my people destroyed the isle, fouling the earth, leeching the soil, despoiling the waters, drawing the very power of life from the land, but giving nothing in return. And when the isle twisted and shuddered in its final spasms, torn apart by fire and molten rock, those who survived went in search of a new homeland. In our ships of gold and silver we crossed the

17

sea, some of our peoples sailing into the west, where the copper-skinned folk worshipped them as gods and called them Aztec. Others sailed to the east where the black-skinned races worshipped them as the white gods. One craft sailed deep into the Middle Sea and settled in the lands around the long river, the Nile. Some of my people settled on Lyonesse . . . but Lyonesse is no more, sunk beneath the waves for that same reason that the De Danann Isle sank. Had they not learned their lesson? Perhaps those who settled there were just especially stupid, but more likely the arrogance that destroyed our own race still drove them to believe they were invincible.

It matters little now: what matters is that they did not learn the lesson of our own land. On Lyonesse, they used their magic to raise buildings, palaces, observatories and theatres in a day and a night. The wild, uncontrolled magic stripped the earth of much of its power and allowed the sea to encroach. It was the tragedy of our own land all over again, but whereas it took centuries to overwhelm the De Dannan Isle – though the end came in a day and a night – with Lyonesse it was only a matter of decades, and the end, when it came, was sudden and cataclysmic. Now only the water-folk inhabit its sunken streets and swim through the once-proud towers.

I was amongst the group which came to the land which would one day be known as Erin. This was a wild and mysterious place then, and the mantle of ancient power lay heavy across the hills and valleys. When the world was young, an ancient priestess had used the old high magic from the land of the Egyptians to make the island grow from little more than a rock to something approaching its present size. That same magic had permeated the very rocks and soil, creating a land in harmony with the men and beasts who walked its fields: a country sensitive to the moods of its people.

When the metal ships hove up onto the deserted beaches, the last of the De Danann folk swore an oath never to abuse our power again, and to abide with the natural law, to take only what we needed and to return to the land what we had taken. Even the beasts replenish the fields which nourish them, and what is man but a beast? So, when we used our magic to make the land grow, we were always careful to return to the earth what we had drawn from it. When the first harvest was reaped, we gave the best part back to the land; when the first mead was drunk, portions were spilled back into the earth. If a tree was felled, another was planted in its place; when a field was turned, another was allowed to lie fallow. We learned our lesson – too late – with our own island. We would not make the same mistakes again.

But this is not to say that we were gentle folk: once the De Danann armies ruled the known world. Men – the Fir Bolg – had claimed this land before we came to it. We fought them for possession of the land and we defeated them, though they were fierce and fearsome warriors, and cost us dearly in men and leaders. But once we had defeated the Fir Bolg, we set about making the land of Erin something like our magical homeland.

For generations, we ruled this place, until the sons of Mil came in their ships of wood and leather. They were primitives – barbarians – and so we laughed at them. What could they do to us?

Our laughter was shortlived when we discovered that the Milesians had brought with them a fearsome weapon, something we could not hold, could not even bear to look upon: the metal, iron.

We resisted the invaders for many seasons, but the end was inevitable. The Milesians' iron tools and artifacts slowly poisoned the land, tainting the rivers, befouling the very air we breathed, and so the Tuatha De Dannan slowly retreated from the world of men. Perhaps some of us would have lingered in the land we had come to worship . . . except that now a new invader came to Erin. These were the brown-robed followers of the white Christ and, in truth, they were even more dangerous than the Milesians because they turned people from us, gave them a new god to believe in, a new magic to worship. There were few of us left by that time, though; most had already gone and even then, even before the last of the De Danann folk had left Erin, the settlers were beginning to call us Sidhe, fairy folk, magical folk.

The last remnants of the once-proud De Danann folk left the land of Erin on the morning when the world turned and the seasons changed. Some of us went into valleys that were hidden from human sight by magical spells; others retreated beneath the ground into the hills and mounds. Still more went to the magical islands – Tir na Nog, Tir Tairnigiri, Hy Brasil – or the land beneath the waves, the Tir Faoi Thuinn.

I came to this river.

During the years when my people held the sovereignty of the land, I lived in a fort close to the river's source. Its metallic tinkling awakened me every morning, lulled me to sleep in the evenings. I drank its sweet waters, bathed in its icy chillness; its moods and rhythms matched my own. It became such a part of my life that I saw no reason to leave it. But in accordance with the decision laid down by the elders of the De Danann – and through necessity, too – I moved *apart* from the world of men, slipping slightly into the Otherworld, into whose borders this river flows.

Existing partly in the Otherworld, partly in the physical world of men, I now wander the banks of the river that had been such a friend in life. This is not a life as the humankind know life, nor is it death: but something between. I have no need to eat, no desire to drink. Now the emotions of the humans sustain me, keep me alive. I share their pain and passion, their fear and loathing, feeding off their love and fear.

I find death the hardest emotion of all to bear. Perhaps it is because the humans fear death so much. There is always so much pain then, so much agony. There are times when I fear that it will overwhelm me. Emotions are always so acute at the time of death.

There is no time in the Otherworld; here I can see what was, what is and what will be. I watch the humankind and I know when one of them has been marked for death. I can see dark Macha spread her invisible crow wings and enwrap her next victim. Once death has put her mark on the humankind, they are doomed . . . and sometimes I cry aloud, venting my despair and agony.

And those unfortunate enough to hear me, those with a little of the Sidhe blood in them, they will stop and listen and then whisper, '*Banshee . . . bean sidhe . . . fairy woman.*'

My cry has become a portent of death.

Those few amongst the humankind who possess a little of the Sight have seen me too. Occasionally, they chance upon me as I sit on the river bank, combing my hair. When I am at ease the spell that cloaks me sometimes slips, rendering me visible. Others have stumbled upon me as I wash my robes in the river's pure water. They might see me as a young maid or a matron, but more often a crone. But they are not seeing me, they are seeing a reflection of their own desires. They have all come to fear me . . . and without cause too. The banshee heralds a death, she does not cause it.

The humankind have nothing to fear from the last remnants of a once-proud race.

Even now my power wanes. I wander the banks of this mighty river, seeking, searching, waiting . . . for one of the humankind to spare me a kindly word. I have been waiting for centuries: I doubt if it will happen now. Soon I will be gone, and only the legend will remain.

Perhaps some day, one of the humankind will lie on the banks of this river and listen . . . listen. Then they will hear my legend in the rattle of the water over the stones, in the whisper of the river through the reeds, in the murmur of the water against the banks.

Banshee . . . Banshee . . . Bansheeeeeee . . .

CHAPTER FOUR

The Wolf Reared

───────── ♣ ─────────

Legend credits Patrick with converting the pagan Irish, but five centuries before he came to the island, native priests were already spreading the word of God.

Saint David of Wales, who was born of an Irish mother, is said to have been baptised by the most famous of these early pioneers of Christianity – Ailbhe, Bishop of Emly, the wolf reared.

The cry sliced through the late afternoon, long, undulating . . . and terrifying.

The woodcutter stopped, the axe poised in mid-air, and the woman with him straightened, the bundle of sticks in her hands tumbling to the forest floor.

The cry came again, the unmistakable howling of a wolf. The beasts called a third time, and now the sound was closer. Wood snapped in the long silence that followed; leaves rustled.

And when the wolves cried for a fourth time, the sound enclosed the couple. Without thinking, they turned and ran, blundering through the undergrowth, branches gouging flesh, thorns scraping skin . . . and it wasn't until later, much later, that they realised that they had left the year-old babe behind.

Alone in the forest, the baby lay on a nest of moss, waving his fat little arms and legs and crooning to himself. Tiny, perfect fingers grasped at the disc of the sun that appeared, then disappeared through the canopy of leaves.

Then the warm, yellow light was blotted out by a monstrous head. Jaws gaped, razor teeth glinted . . . but did not close on the child's head.

The child fell silent, staring solemnly at the head of the beast.

The wolf moved closer to the child, head swaying from side to side, nostrils flaring, tasting the forest scents. The odour of the child was strong, rich and fresh. An ice-cold nose brushed across the babe's cheek. There was something about the smell of the child . . . something familiar, something which stirred memories.

Memories of a time when it did not walk on four legs . . . memories of a time when it wore the form of a human . . . memories of a time when it had been a woman.

The wolf dropped to her belly beside the child, her heavy dugs dragging. Her own cubs had recently died; she ached with milk.

Ailbhe was too young to be afraid. He reached up and grabbed the wolf by her furry neck. A moment later his hungry mouth was fixed on her teat.

And when the rest of the pack closed in, she snarled them away.

Night was falling when Ailbhe's father returned to the forest with his brothers to look for the remains of his son. They soon found the clearing where he had left the babe, the scattering of sticks where they had dropped them, their footprints clearly marked in the soft earth . . . and over them, around them, the palm-sized prints of the wolf-pack.

But they found no trace of Ailbhe, no splashes of blood on the earth, no shreds of cloth or bone. And they knew what had happened then: the child had been carried off to be devoured in the wolf's den.

The seasons passed.

And with the passage of time came the rumours, the whispered tales of a beast-man, a creature who wore the form of a man but crawled and ran and howled like a wolf. The villagers, wary of witchcraft and with the full knowledge that shape-changing was not unknown, sent an envoy to their lord, Turlough the Red.

Although an old man, who had not ridden to hounds for many seasons, Turlough ordered his hunting pack to be prepared. He knew the dangers of gossip and speculation, knew too what would happen if the rumour was not quashed. Today it was but a single beast-man; tomorrow the peasants would be talking of a dozen, then a hundred. Soon, they would flee the district, leaving the harvest to rot in the field.

With a troop of archers, his wolf-hounds, and trackers, Turlough rode in search of the beast-man, though privately he doubted the creature's existence.

But in the shadowless noonday hour, they spotted a wolf-pack . . . and a small, naked, human form running with them. It took all Turlough and the dog-handlers' skill to keep the hounds from attacking both wolves and child and ripping them to pieces, but eventually, when the sun was sinking into the west, Turlough managed to ride in amongst the beasts and snatch the struggling child.

Back at the fort, the story of the boy's capture spread and people gathered to marvel at him. Aside from being lean, scratched and incredibly grimy, he seemed quite unharmed. Although without a language other than grunts, whines and howls, he appeared to be advanced mentally beyond his years, the result of having to use his wits to survive with the wolves. At first he fought his captors with unrestrained savagery, but he soon realised they meant him no harm and accepted their care, though he preferred to go naked, and persisted in sleeping on the cold floor.

And when the moon was full, he grew restless, and would raise his head to stare at the silver orb, and then he would throw back his head and howl, and all who heard it agreed that the sound was one of absolute despair and loneliness.

Word of the beast-child soon reached the ears of the woodcutter and his wife. They made the long and arduous journey in the vague hope that it might be their lost son, Ailbhe, though in their hearts neither expected it.

But when they looked upon the boy, the mother fell into a dead faint. It was Ailbhe. He was easy enough to identify; he was growing into the image of his father, tall and broad-shouldered, with fire-red hair and brilliant green eyes. One look at the almost identical features satisfied Turlough that he had found the child's true parents and he turned the boy over to them.

Everyone agreed that Ailbhe's survival was a miracle.

The term 'miracle' was being heard more frequently in Ireland as the first intimations reached that island of the new religion growing in the east. Christianity, it was called, and it centred around a man who was able to work miracles, to cure the sick and blind, to bring the dead back to life, and even raise himself from the dead.

Ailbhe's parents decided the hand of God had surely touched their son, and as the boy grew he came to share their opinion. He spoke to Turlough, who retained an interest in the child he had snatched from the wolves, and the aged warrior advised him to follow his heart. He bore the cost of sending him to Rome to learn about this new religion, this Christianity, at first hand. Like most Irish nobility, Turlough considered himself both an educated man and an enlightened one, and wanted to know more about this strange new faith, where men worshipped not many gods, but one. It was a religion he thought he might be able to understand: he was a lord of his land, but he in turn paid homage to the Ard-Ri, the High King. He imagined this single god in that light.

In Rome and later in the lands to the east where the man-god had walked, Ailbhe studied the new religion. When he was convinced of its merit, he became one of Ireland's earliest converts, and then a priest. When he returned to his native land, he was determined to convert the people to the one true religion.

And to those who doubted the power of his God, he would remind them of the miracle of the wolves who had spared him, and the bitch who had suckled him.

It was something he could never forget either. On moonlit nights he sometimes felt the old, sweet longing take him, and he yearned to throw back his head and sing with the pack, sing to the moon, to howl aloud his joy at being alive . . . to give thanks to the Lord.

Then one autumn, as Ailbhe and his few followers were harvesting the crop upon which the small religious community depended for sustenance, they heard a hunting horn.

A few minutes later a band of hunters appeared on the horizon, accompanied by wolf-hounds. In front of them ran a single huge wolf.

Panting hard, its huge chest heaving, spittle flecking its muzzle, eyes glazed with exhaustion and fright, the creature fled down the hill and straight into the bishop's vegetable patch. It shuddered to a stop at his feet.

His followers fled, screaming. But Ailbhe crouched down beside the wolf and spoke to it in a soft voice.

As the hunting party rode up, they were astonished to see their quarry with the holy man, and more astonished when the wolf lifted its great head and deliberately rested it upon the bishop's knee.

Ailbhe gazed at the hunters with his cold green eyes. 'When I was helpless, the wolves showed me mercy,' he said calmly. 'I demand that mercy be returned now.'

The hunters exchanged glances, uncertain what to do next. They itched for the kill, but were reluctant to defy a holy man, especially this one who had once run with the beasts. But they were young and impetuous, they had ridden hard in pursuit of their quarry and none was a member of Ailbhe's faith.

The monk sensed the gathering danger.

Bending over the exhausted wolf as it lay on the ground, he wrapped the wide sleeves of his homespun robe around the animal, covering it with his body. Any spear hurled at the wolf would hit the man.

The hunters hesitated.

Ailbhe waited.

At last the leader of the hunters grinned. 'Very well, holy man. If you want to hug that savage animal to your bosom and let it eat your heart out, go ahead.' He reined his horse in a circle and began to ride away, followed by his men.

But at the last moment he glanced back. He saw Ailbhe lifting his arms from the wolf he had been cradling . . . he saw the wolf's form shuddering, twisting, pink flesh showing through matted fur . . .

The warrior turned back, his hunting spear clutched in a white-knuckled grip.

Ailbhe looked up from the aged woman he cradled in his arms.

'There was a wolf . . .' the warrior began.

'There was. But no longer. Once there was a woman, changed by foul magic into the shape of a wolf. The wolf found an abandoned child in the forest, suckled and protected it, and because of that, the child was able to bring the Word of God to this island. God has now repaid that woman.'

The warrior plunged his spear into the earth and slid off his mount. Kneeling on the ground before the priest and the old woman, he said, 'Perhaps you would teach me about this god of yours . . .'

CHAPTER FIVE

The Merrow

———— ♣ ————

Memories.

All it retains now are its memories.

Memories of the time when it walked with feet in the world above. Memories of vast cities of stone and gold, ships of wood and metal . . . and the mountains that belched flame and skies that rained clinging soot and poisonous dust.

But the memories are dim. It recalls the emotions with greater clarity: the fear and terror as they fled the sinking isle in a huge fleet, the days of waiting, watching the featureless horizon . . . and then the rejoicing that had swept through the crew and passengers as the small, green land appeared over the horizon. A hundred ships had left the sinking isle; less than one-tenth reached the new homeland, the island that would one day be known as Erin. There was a time of happiness then, until that too faded as newcomers invaded the land, bringing with them the terrible weapon: iron.

Its people could not stand against the cold metal and so retreated from this world of men. And in time they died, and the few who remained forgot what they were, what they had been.

For a long time now, there had only been sensations: the chill of the water, the ebb and flow of the currents against its smooth skin, the dim awareness of the passage of time, of light and dark

off the surface of the water far above its head.
And the hunger. Always the hunger.
Once, there had been so much . . . now there was only the river.
Now, this was its world, its domain.

Cormac was convinced that there was something in the river, something sleek and slender and fascinating. A salmon or a seal.

He had first glimpsed the creature in the early part of the year, shortly after the last snows had disappeared and the new growth had appeared on the upland slopes. It usually took at least three days to drive the sheep from the valleys to the higher pastures, though he had done it in two when he had been in a hurry. But he'd been in no hurry on that day, enjoying the new season's crisp, cold air. He had been following the route his father had taught him, the same route his grandfather and his father before him had used, along the banks of the river known as the Black Water. It wasn't the quickest route, and when he'd been younger, he'd bitterly resented the extra time spent on the trip. As he'd grown older, however, he'd come to appreciate the beauty of the longer journey, and at this time of year – and again, when the year turned and it was time to bring the sheep home – the river sang with an almost magical sound.

An irregular splash in the water – a break in the rhythm – disturbed him, and he turned and looked into the water in time to see an iridescent flipper disappear beneath the surface. He walked back to where he'd seen the disturbance, crouched and stared into the river. But, with the sun shimmering off the surface, turning it metallic, it was impossible to make out anything beneath in the depths.

A salmon. . .?

Maybe a seal. Sometimes the seals came upriver from the sea. . .

The young shepherd thought no more about it and continued on up into the hills, driving the flock of sheep before him. It was slow, exhausting and sometimes frustrating work, and it was close to evening before he finally reached the upland pastures. Leaving the sheep in the field, he made his way across to an outcrop of stones, high on the mountainside. Perhaps it had once been a natural configuration of stones, but generations of his family had shaped it into a primitive, but comfortable stone hut. Sitting in the mouth of the hut, Cormac basked in the last rays of the sinking sun and allowed taut muscles to relax. From his vantage point, he could see across the entire mountainside, down over the valley to the haze that shimmered above the large town of Yew Wood, where the river flowed into the sea. The Black Water curled below him, a sheet of silver metal.

As he watched something disturbed the water. Long and sleek, it rippled across the width of the river and then appeared to lurch up onto the bank, where it remained for a few moments, lying flat on a stone, before it finally slid back into the water.

The shepherd nodded, convinced. A seal. The young man's lips twisted in a cruel smile. If it was still there when he went down into the valley, he would catch it. Either its pelt or its flesh were sure to be worth something.

This is its world. This is its domain.

It knows this river from its pure, ice-cold source to the tart salt of its destination. It feeds off the flesh of the creatures that swarm in its cool waters and sometimes — when the sun is low in the sky and the air is soft and hazy, not unlike in its own domain — it comes up out of the water and sits briefly in the world of men. The memories come then and they are stronger, clearer: of places and times long gone, of faces, both human and non-human . . . and the boy.

It remembers the boy clearly. One of the humankind, he had been tall and lithe, dark-haired and dark-eyed. They had met once – a long time ago – and their meeting had been all too brief, but it remembers everything about that meeting. The emotion sustained it for many moons: the passion and the pain . . . and the love, terrifying in its intensity.

It remembers the love.

On days when the sun lies low in the heavens, and the air is cool and the light is soft, it comes up from its own world and wonders if it would ever experience that emotion again.

Cormac crouched on the banks of the river and stared deep into its depths. He had been watching the creature for days now; it appeared late in the afternoon, shortly before sunset, and lay on the same flat stone for a few moments before slipping back into the water. He was convinced it was a seal . . . or an otter. And a giant, too, judging by its size. He touched the heavy wooden club that hung from his belt. The pelt of a creature like that would bring in a handsome dividend.

The young man glanced up into the heavens, gauging the time: the sun was sinking in the west. The creature would come up out of the water soon.

And he would be waiting.

It was lonely, but it was not alone.

There were others like it, others who had chosen to escape the world of men in the rivers and lakes.

When it penetrated the saltiness of the river's mouth, it came in contact with the Ron, the seal folk, shy, gentle creatures, little of the magic left in them. In the wild Atlantic Ocean, close to the west coast of this land, there was the Tir Faoi Thuinn, the land beneath the waves, which swarmed with others like it who had changed. However, they preferred the safety of their undersea kingdom and rarely ventured to the surface. The years had made them savage, however, and they delighted in the flesh of drowned sailors.

And while it was not alone . . . it was lonely, truly lonely.

Cormac lay in the long grass and watched the shadows lengthen along the ground as the sun dipped lower in the skies. A dozen paces directly in front of him was the flat stone on which he'd seen the otter. He had convinced himself that it was an otter. They were wily and cunning creatures; he knew he'd only have one chance to get close to it. If it saw him and escaped, it would never again return to this place and he'd lose it altogether.

But he wasn't going to lose it.

Cormac watched the sun. At the precise moment it touched the distant mountains, the waters parted and the creature's head appeared. Smooth-skinned and hairless, its skin a rich golden-brown, the creature turned in the water, large brown eyes surveying the surroundings. . .

Cormac blinked the sun's glowing-red after-images from his retina. Wiping his streaming eyes, he looked at the creature, seeing it clearly for the first time . . . and almost choked with fright: this was no otter . . . this was a woman!

Ancient and primeval, the creature rose up out of the water. And even before she heaved herself up onto the broad flat stone, the young man knew that she would have the tail of a fish in place of her legs. She was a merrow. Perfectly formed, her head, face and neck looked human, except for the slitted gills in the slender column of her throat. Her breasts were small and without nipples, her arms long and slender, and he noticed that she had no navel.

Did a pattern of scales appear on her skin when the sunlight touched it? Were the creature's fingers joined together by membranes?

Cormac watched the merrow lie down on the broad, flat stone, her tail dipping in the water, flicking droplets back over her naked body. This was the Black Water merrow. He had heard stories about this creature; his father and grandfather had told him some of the legends that spoke of her. Some stories said that she was a princess of the ancient Tuatha De Danann, who had been cast under a spell by an evil witch; others spoke of how the young princess had assumed a merrow's form to play a prank and had never been able to return to her human shape. The most popular story told of the time when the Tuatha De Danann were leaving the world of men, and how some of the De Danann folk chose to remain behind in the world they loved, but changed and altered so that they could live in new environments: beneath the ground, under the water.

The young man shook his head quickly. The truth was of no interest here: whatever she was – merrow, mermaid, freak of nature, cursed woman – she was valuable. Taking a deep breath, he gripped his cudgel and crept from the concealment of the grasses.

The watery world is timeless.

The river knows no time; it flows, is renewed and flows again. The life that lives in its heart is timeless too, though often the individual life-spans are short. Fish and vegetation live and die in their watery environment, and their dying enriches it, forging the chain that allows the next generation to thrive.

The creature is old now, so old, so tired. There are times when it would be so easy simply to stop moving, to allow the river to claim its soul, absorb it into the flow, become part of the life cycle.

But it couldn't even begin to consider that: it had once belonged to a race which worshipped the goddess Danu, the goddess of life . . . and on some spiritual, emotive level, it knew that while it still lived, then so too did the ancient goddess.

It cannot – will not – die.

Cormac was almost on top of the creature when she suddenly opened her eyes. They were huge and a deep, rich brown: they caught and held his gaze, unblinkingly. He pushed the heavy cudgel behind his leg, hoping the merrow wouldn't see it. He didn't want to use it; he didn't want to mark her in any way, but he would if he had to: she wasn't going to escape him. She was too valuable. Some men might look on the creature and see a thing of beauty, others might consider her a monster, but he saw only fame and fortune.

'Can you speak?' he asked.

The creature stared at him.

Now that he was close he could see how completely alien she was. When she had risen out of the water, he had thought she was a woman with the tail of a fish . . . now that he was beside her, he realised that she was more animal than he had first suspected. Indeed, the resemblance to the otter was marked. Maybe this was nothing more than an unusual breed of the reclusive creatures, or a giant amongst its own creatures . . . or should that be a giantess, he wondered, leering at her breasts: they were female enough.

'Come with me,' he commanded, pointing back across the fields behind him. The tail continued tapping the water. 'You're coming with me,' he snapped, using the same tone he used for commanding dogs.

Its eyes – huge and round – never blinked, but a shudder ran through the creature, and suddenly Cormac realised that it was rippling back into the water.

The shepherd grabbed for it, but his hand ran along slick, oily flesh. He raised his club when a web-fingered hand closed over his left wrist, jerking him forward . . . and down.

It remembers a boy.

One of the humankind, tall and lithe, dark-haired, dark-eyed. And it remembers the emotion of their encounter: the passion and the pain . . . it remembers the love.

Was it this boy?

It was so long ago now that the features have become lost in a blur . . . but there are similarities certainly. This boy is tall, dark-haired, dark-eyed. Maybe it is the same boy.

It reaches for him, catching hold of him, his flesh soft and smooth and dry, pulling him forward . . . and down.

It is the boy. It is her human lover returned once again. After this great time. . .

See how he struggles, wriggles, twists like an eel, like a salmon joyously returning to the place of its spawning. It is the same boy, and he is happy, so happy to be coming home. . .

His eyes are wide with desire, mouth open, bubbles streaming upwards as he speaks to her, professing his love. His hands touch her, beating at her passionately, his legs entwine lustfully around her tail.

She lost him once before, she will not lose him again. She will take him down, down, down to the very depths of her river, and there they will swim and play and love together. When she tires of him, she will lay him to rest amongst the silt and soft sands . . . amongst the countless bones of his predecessors.

CHAPTER SIX

The Beasts of Ossory

♣

The storm, which had been threatening all morning, finally rolled in just before the sun sank over the treetops. Lightning cracked, a jagged spear striking deep into the heart of the ancient forest. Moments later a tall plume of dark smoke, shot through with angry flames, rose up into the lowering sky.

The old priest ducked beneath the nearest tree, crossing himself quickly, murmuring a quick prayer that this wouldn't be the next tree to be struck. As if in answer to his prayer, thunder boomed and the lightning struck again, but further away this time, on the other side of the forest. He actually saw the ragged, clawlike fork of lightning bite into the treetops. Flames immediately spat red and orange into the grey sky. When the thunder rolled again, it took several seconds for the lightning to brighten the sky, and the priest relaxed. A brother priest, who had studied in Castile and learned a little of the Moorish ways, once told him that it was possible to gauge the proximity of the storm by counting the distance between the thunder roll and the lightning flash. Father John wasn't so sure, but he took some comfort from that fact that he could count to ten between the flash and the boom. Perhaps the storm was fading. Now would come the rain, he guessed.

As if on cue, the heavens opened and the rain came down in a heavy, solid downpour that churned the earth to mud before his eyes.

The old priest slumped down with his back to the gnarled oak tree and resigned himself to spending another night in the open, without hot food or a fire to warm himself by. The priest sighed: he was getting too old for this. And he was beginning to think that this mission was cursed, doomed to failure. Perhaps he had failed his Lord; perhaps this was a punishment for some sin . . . He shook his head; he hadn't committed any unusual sin, and he had made a full confession before he left the city.

Father John had set out three days ago on the long road to the city of Limerick. A priest there had been caught indulging in (according to the letter from the bishop) unnatural practices – which could be anything the bishop either didn't understand or approve of. The cleric had begged that Father John, as the representative of King John in Ireland, pass judgment on the wretch. Reading between the lines, the old priest guessed that politics were involved; the local priest was either well connected or from a powerful family, and the local bishop didn't wish to get involved.

Although he knew the dangers of venturing beyond the relatively safe confines of the Pale, the area of land around the city of Dublin that the crown controlled, Father John felt he couldn't refuse the bishop's request.

From the start there were intimations that this expedition was ill-fated. His small band was ambushed almost in sight of Dublin city walls, and four of the men, including his page, were slain. He fled southwards with two surviving soldiers, pursued by the wild Irish brigands. When they finally managed to outrun their pursuers, they reined in . . . and one of the soldiers simply slid from his horse. When Father John examined the man, he discovered that the soldier had taken a sword cut in the leg in the skirmish. The great vein along the inner thigh had been severed; the man simply bled to death as he rode along.

The remaining soldier died late the previous evening, as they rode into the first fringes of the great forest that covered much of the heart of Ireland. In the fading light, the man rode straight on to a projecting branch that had taken him through the throat. He was dead before he hit the ground. His mount, carrying much of the supplies, galloped off into the gloom and, no doubt, some Irish peasant was even now enjoying what must seem miraculous bounty.

When he lost his own horse in an equally bizarre accident – it had caught its foot in a rabbit hole and shattered its leg – Father John began to suspect the presence of the Evil One. Since coming to Ireland, he had evidence aplenty that the Devil was abroad in this land. It was a wild and savage place, where the people, though they worshipped the Christian God, still paid homage to the older, darker gods. The pagan festivals of Lughnasadh and Samhain were still honoured, and were occasions for debauchery and licentiousness, and the old priest had even heard rumours of human sacrifices on the western shores.

Before he came to the land the natives called Erin, Father John looked at the island on one of the great maritime charts in the library in Canterbury: there, on the heavy parchment maps, it was called Hibernia, but in the margins, a scribe had written 'The Isle at the Edge of the World'. The world ended in the western ocean that pounded Erin's dark cliffs. The sea foamed over the edge of the world into limitless space . . . and who knew what demons of the dark might crawl up out of the icy chill of space or the flames of hell? And hadn't Patrick, who brought the Word of God to this pagan place, actually fought with a creature that legend had named *an Catoranach*, the Devil's mother?

Was the Devil stalking him? Father John smiled; what use would the Devil have for a tired old priest? The smile broadened as he suddenly wondered if that was a sin of false pride. Probably.

Straightening, pressing his hands to his aching back, the priest squinted up into the lowering sky. He had spent thirty of his fifty years here in Erin, and if he had learned nothing else in that time, it was how to read the weather. The rain was down for the night. With a sigh of resignation, he moved deeper into the forest, looking for the driest – and safest – spot.

The old priest was trembling with fatigue before he stumbled across a small hollow, ringed on three sides by high thorn bushes. Staggering into the hollow, he used his belt knife to cut branches from the bushes, and wove them across the entrance. It wasn't much, but it would keep out the inquisitive animals. Scraping a flat stone clean, Father John piled twigs and dried moss on it. It took several attempts before he finally managed to coax a spark to drop onto the moss. The moss caught. A thin wisp of iron grey smoke twisted straight up into the canopy of leaves. The priest sighed with relief; he knew if he hadn't lit it, then he would be effectively blind in the heart of the forest.

Leaning forward, the old man blew on the tiny spark, bringing it to life. A yellow flame appeared, and quickly spread, crisping the moss to grey, ashy threads. With infinite care and patience, the priest fed the tiny flame pieces of dried wood until he had a sizable fire going. The fire was a double-edged sword, he knew. It would keep him warm, and protect him from even the most dangerous of beasts; but the same flames would be visible for many miles, and the scents of burning wood and moss would carry far in the damp forest air.

Right now he was too tired, too hungry even to care. Relaxing in the warm glow of the fire, feeling its gentle heat salve his aching muscles, he chewed on a crust of hard bread – glad for the darkness that prevented him from seeing the weevils and maggots in it.

He must have slept. . .

One moment the fire was blazing high, crackling and spitting sparks to the heavens . . . and the next it was a nest of glowing, ash-coated sticks.

Father John blinked awake, rubbing the sleep from his eyes with the heels of his hands. He'd been dreaming of . . . of eyes.

As he looked around, he could see that the trees and bushes were alive with scores – no, hundreds – of glowing red eyes, reflecting the fire's embers. He crossed himself automatically, immediately thinking of demons . . . until he recognised an owl's round, unblinking stare, and then a rat's jewellike glare. The forest animals, attracted by the fire, had gathered to look curiously at this intruder.

The priest was smiling at the image when, one by one, the eyes disappeared, winking out of existence. Instinct warned the priest and he'd pulled his knife free even before wood snapped nearby, driving the birds off the branches, sending the smaller creatures scuttling through the bushes.

Something large was moving through the forest.

Wolf? Boar?

Wood snapped again, and Father John knew that only man was that clumsy. He plunged a long stick into the heart of the dying fire, coaxing it back to life. Sparks and glowing embers flowed upwards, and then the length of wood in his hand snapped alight. The priest waved it to and fro in the air before him, and then held it high, shedding a wavering yellow light over the bushes.

'I am a priest,' he said immediately, hoping that whoever was moving around in the darkness wouldn't shoot him down with spear or arrow. He kept turning around, trying to follow the sounds. 'I was on my way to Limerick, but my horse broke its leg and now I am on foot and alone.' A branch cracked behind him and he spun round. 'I have no coins, no jewels, no food, save some hard crusts, and only the clothes I stand up in,' he added. But he knew some of the brigands would kill him for the clothes, and the sandals on his feet. Only the Lord would protect him now.

Red eyes winked in the darkness.

Father John turned to look at them. They were about at the level of his waist . . . and then as he watched, they rose to head height. He raised the burning stick high. He had the briefest impressions of light on a heavy-furred cloak, before the man stepped back into the deeper shadow.

'I will not harm you, priest.' The words were rough and harsh, rasping from a throat that had either been damaged or was not used to shaping words. A forest hermit? A charcoal burner? 'I will not harm you,' the voice rasped.

'Who are you?' Father John demanded.

'I am of the Clan Allta. Like you, a traveller. Like you, a believer in the Lord God, Our Lord Jesus Christ and the Blessed Trinity.'

The priest was taken aback. 'You are a true believer then?' he said.

'We are.'

'We?' the priest said. 'You said "we".'

'My wife is also a believer.'

Father John moved closer to the edge of the clearing, but he had the distinct impression that the man in the woods moved back out of the light.

'Father, my wife is sorely afflicted. She wishes the comfort of a priest in her last hours.' The voice had become even more ragged, barely above a whisper.

'My son, if you take me to her . . .' the priest began.

'Father, you should know that our appearance is . . . unusual.'

The priest bent his head to hide a smile. Since he had come to this land, he had become used to seeing the natives in all manner of clothing, and he knew it was the custom for many – both male and female – to wear nothing but a cloak thrown over their shoulders. Disease was commonplace and lepers were not unknown.

'Are you diseased?' the priest asked cautiously.

'Some would say that,' the voice replied, 'but it is an affliction only of my clan.'

The priest nodded; he had seen diseases, birthmarks, disfigurements, pockmarks that had been passed down from father to son. Such disfigurements were far more common in the small, isolated communities.

'You will find my appearance startling,' the voice in the shadows said slowly, 'but you must believe me when I tell you that I will do you no harm.'

'My son, I have been a priest for all of my adult life; I have seen much and heard more than you will ever understand. Little shocks me now.'

There was movement in the shadow, and a huge, green-eyed wolf, walking on its hind legs, stepped into the light. The wolf's jaws moved, strands of ropey saliva dribbling onto the matted fur on its chest. 'There is a man beneath this skin. A man who believes in the one true God,' the beast said urgently.

Father John crossed himself. His heart was thundering in his chest, and his breath was coming in great heaving gasps.

The beast awkwardly mimicked the priest's movement and crossed himself.

'Have you been sent by the evil one to torment me?' the old priest whispered.

'No. I have only come to ask your help and blessing.'

Father John backed away from the creature. Even though it was standing on the other side of the thorn bushes, he knew it could easily vault them. The creature was enormous, standing half the height again of a tall man, its fur shimmering red and gold in the firelight, but matted and tangled with twigs and leaves. Its head was enormous. While the features were those of a wolf, there was something about the planes and angles of the face, the sloping jaws, the cheekbones, that suggested the human beneath. The eyes were cold green, firelight winking in the pupils, and the teeth – long and razor sharp – were those of a meat eater.

'What do you want?' the priest asked, unable to keep the tremble from his voice. He had heard of such creatures, of course. Cursed men who wore the shapes of beasts and beasts who walked like men during the hours of darkness had been reported from the remoter parts of the island, and Father John had read of similar accounts of the creatures known as werewolves in the writings of the ancients.

'I need your help, Father,' the creature said hoarsely.

'Why?' Father John asked. This was a trick, it had to be, some plan to lure him into the heart of the forest and devour him – or worse, infect him with the terrifying curse that would turn him from a human into a beast in the light of the full moon.

'My wife lies not far from here, father. She is ill, and close to death. She wants the consolation of a priest before she dies.'

Father John shook his head firmly. He wasn't about to leave the safety of the fire; he was convinced that the flames were all that kept the creature at bay.

'Please,' the creature whispered. The priest stepped closer to the fire. 'Do you fear me so much?' the beast asked. 'Am I so terrifying?' It paused and then answered its own question. 'Yes, I suppose I am. But Father, I have told you, beneath this skin of fur and hair, I am human, and a believer.' He paused and added bitterly. 'And I wear this fleshy form because of the curse of a holy man.'

'Who?' Father John demanded.

'The Abbot Natalis!'

Father John stopped. He had heard of Natalis, even read some of the abbot's learned writings. The holy man had come to Ireland shortly after Bishop Patrick had first brought the Word of God to a pagan land.

'The Abbot Natalis cursed my clan. That is why we wear the wolf-shapes,' the beast continued. 'We wear the clothing of the beast as a penance for a long-forgotten sin. Help us, father. Do not deny my wife the consolation of her faith.'

The priest turned and looked into the fire. Despite the creature's physical appearance, it spoke with a human tongue and its belief in God seemed genuine. Dropping his dying torch on to the fire, he plucked another long branch from the flame. Holding it aloft, flickering light washing over the beast, he said, 'Take me to your wife.'

The trek through the woods took on a nightmarish quality. Father John was not sure which parts were real and which the products of his imagination.

The beast moved silently through the thick undergrowth, convincing the old man that the noises it had made earlier had been deliberate, to alert him to its presence in the woods. Occasionally, it vanished, leaving him alone in a pool of light shed by the burning branch. Just when he was beginning to panic, the beast would loom up out of the shadows, walking on either two or four feet. Curiously, the priest found it less frightening when it walked on two legs; then it was truly alien, a creature of myth. But when it walked on four legs, its canine body and almost human head gave it an incredibly evil appearance.

'Almost there,' the beast grunted.

The priest heard the musical trickle of running water nearby and took some consolation from it. The creatures of evil find it almost impossible to cross pure running water.

The creature led the old man to the base of an ancient oak tree that overhung the stream. Its huge roots coiled and twisted up out of the ground like writhing serpents and with the firelight dancing over them, the effect was truly terrifying. The second werewolf was nestled deep in the roots. It raised its head, torchlight turning its eyes amber.

'This is my wife,' the beast said, dropping down beside the obviously injured animal, nuzzling it with his snout.

The priest cautiously approached the couple. He could see where the female wolf's hindquarters were caked with dried, crusted blood. The tip of an arrow protruded from its haunch.

The smaller wolf raised its head and looked at the old man. Its mouth worked, forming words. 'When we smelt the smoke, we feared that the hunters had returned.'

'There is a price on wolf-pelts,' the male wolf said. 'The local people know the legend; they know we're living here. Pelts like ours would bring a handsome reward.'

'Who are you?' Father John asked. 'What are you?'

'We are the Werewolves of Ossory,' the male said simply.

'We are neither human nor wolf – but something in between,' the female added. Blood, bright and red-black in the torchlight, bubbled on her lips. 'And now, I beg you, hear my confession and your blessing.'

The priest drew back, suddenly unsure again. This could be a trick of the Evil One; surely the soul of a priest would be doomed if he were to bless an animal – and especially an enchanted beast.

'You think we are evil,' the female said quickly. 'You think that this is some trick of the Devil to tempt you.' Father John nodded. 'What would it take to convince you?' she asked. 'We are both believers. We can say the name of the Lord God, of Jesus Christ, His Son and the Virgin, His Blessed Mother. Surely no thing of evil could do that?'

The priest nodded, still unsure.

The male werewolf rose up on his hind legs, towering over the priest. 'What would it take to convince you?'

'You say you are human . . .' the priest began. 'But I can only see the animal. I can hear your voices, but they are rough, beast-like grunts.'

'If you could see the human beneath the skin?' the male asked.

Father John nodded.

The female wolf straightened painfully. She brought her right forepaw to her jaws and began to bite and gnaw at her flesh. Crimson spurted and the moist forest air was tainted with the metallic odour of fresh blood. As the priest looked on in horror, glints of white bones showed through the bloody gristle ... and then Father John realised that it was not bone he was looking at: it was a human finger.

There was a sound of cloth tearing, but this wasn't cloth which tore: it was skin and muscle, hair and sinew. A human hand, small, delicate, long-fingered and coated in blood and fluid, appeared where the werewolf's claw had been.

'Jesu!' the priest breathed, falling to his knees, crossing himself repeatedly.

The female used its human hand to pull away at the fur on its left forepaw, peeling back the skin, tearing off the fur as if it were a piece of clothing. Another human hand appeared. Then it raised its hands to its face. Its bloody fingers caught at the loose skin behind its jaws, long nails gouging deep into the flesh, catching and pulling it forward over its face. The wolf's head came off like a leather mask, revealing the small human face beneath. The flesh was bloody, dark red hair plastered close to the woman's skull.

'Beneath this wolf's body we wear, we are human,' the woman whispered tiredly, the effort of pulling off the wolf's skin having exhausted her.

The terrified priest looked up as the male werewolf stepped into the pool of light. He too had pulled off the fur around his hands and the wolf's mask, leaving it dangling on his chest like a woollen scarf. He had carried water from the nearby stream on a broad leaf, which he used to clean his wife's face.

'Do you believe us, Father?'

The priest nodded. 'But how came you to this state?'

'Five hundred and more years ago,' the male said, 'our cian mortally insulted the blessed Abbot Natalis. Our clan followed the old ways, honouring the ancient gods, offering sacrifice to them in the traditional way. Natalis was bringing the Word of God to the tribes when he was captured by our forefathers, and forced to defend himself and his God against our clan's druid and his magic. They fought – the old faith against the new religion . . . and the new religion triumphed. As a last desperate effort, the druid called forth the clan's totem and set it against the Abbot Natalis. The totem was the wolf,' he added.

The woman raised her head. 'But the abbot turned the spell back on the druid – and in that instant our entire clan was afflicted with this curse. We became wolves, though those of us who had been born human retained our powers of speech and thought. But the children born to us in our wolf-shape knew only beasthood. Towards the end of his long life, the Abbot Natalis relented the spell that had changed us into animals. He said that it was not right for one of God's greatest creatures to wear the skin of an animal.' The woman's voice died in a hoarse whisper.

'So now, every seven years, a couple from the Clan Allta take on the wolf-shape and wear it for seven years, as a reminder of how we once doubted the Word of God,' the male continued. 'If we survive for the seven years, we are welcomed back into our village, and another couple will take our place.'

'Will this curse never end?' the priest asked.

The werewolves shook their heads. 'Never.'

'And now, Father,' the male continued, 'having listened to our tale, and knowing that we are true believers, will you listen to my wife's confession and give her the last rites?'

Father John nodded slowly. Somewhere – at the very back of his mind – there were doubts. They could still be Satan's creatures, but . . . what if they were not? He found it hard to credit the story about the Abbot Natalis, but he knew that the priests and bishops who had brought the faith to this savage land had often been as powerful as their druidical counterparts. And some of them – even including blessed Patrick, whom men now universally acknowledged as a saint – had a foul and bitter temper. They were men first, and holy second.

'I will hear your confession,' he said to the woman.

The male werewolf moved away to stand at the river bank while the priest came closer to the woman. He listened to her confession, nodding and bowing, and then made the sign of the Cross over her. When he pressed the blessed oil onto her forehead, she shuddered with its touch.

When he was finished, the priest cleaned and bathed the woman's wound, gently easing the shaft of the arrow out of her haunch, washing out the deep wound with cold water mixed with a little of the blessed wine. Using a strip of linen torn from his undershirt, he bound up the cut.

Dawn was lightening the trees by the time he finished and the first of the birdsongs were beginning to echo through the forest.

The woman smiled gratefully, but the effect was marred by the dried crust of blood that still coated portions of her cheeks and chin. 'Not only have you saved my immortal soul, but you have saved my life,' she whispered.

'What will happen to you now?' Father John asked.

'We will wear this beast-form for another three years. Then at the end of that time, if we have survived, we will return to our own village.' Lifting her hands, she pulled at the flapping wolf's mask, drawing it back up on to her face.

'To spend seven years in the body of a beast,' the priest said slowly, 'must be a terrifying penance.'

'It is, Father,' the male werewolf said, padding up behind the priest. With the onset of the dawn, he too had fitted the wolf's head back and drawn the wolf's claws onto his hands. 'Why should we suffer for the sins of our fathers?' he asked.

'The sins of the fathers shall be visited upon the sons,' the priest quoted.

Long shafts of early-morning sunlight slanted through the trees, dappling the ground in a speckled pattern. The priest could see the creature's footprints bitten deeply into the soft earth at the side of the river. Even though the man wore the wolf-shape, his footprints were those of a naked human foot. However, as soon as the sun touched him, the footsteps became smaller, rounder – the shape of a wolf-print.

The female werewolf rose unsteadily to her feet. She was still shaded by the tree. 'During the hours of darkness, when God's clean light does not shine upon us, we regain what little of our human selves remains. But during the hours of daylight . . .' – her voice cracked – '. . . we become truly wolves.' Her voice vanished into a bark.

Father John was backing away from the river as the woman's words sank in and he understood what she was saying. He turned to run . . . but the wolves brought him down before he had taken a dozen steps. He flung up an arm to protect himself, but razor-sharp teeth bit through cloth and flesh, striking off bone, numbing the entire side of his body.

'May God forgive them . . .' he whispered. The smaller wolf bit into the fleshy part of his thigh. ' . . . for they know not what they do.'

CHAPTER SEVEN

Beneath the Lake

♣

Extracted from the manuscript of Brother Mo Laisse, the words written as he directed, without addition or alteration.

They come forth at night to haunt me, to torment and tempt me. But I will not be tempted away from this work, for I know these are the Devil's children, these creatures of the lake, and I know the work I am doing – illuminating the Word of God – is hurtful to them.

I will persevere. I know they fear me and soon I will teach them to loathe the name of Mo Laisse.

I think they sleep during the day, or perhaps, like all creatures of evil, the night is their true domain and the sun is hurtful to them. I can work on the Gospels then, shaping the letters and script in the pure light of Our Lord's sunshine. The sunlight gives the inks and pigments a life of their own, imbuing them with a vibrant presence on the page, and the vellum takes on the texture of silken flesh. There is no greater way to pay homage to Our Lord Jesus Christ than by recreating His Words in crimson and gold, decorated with all the imagination with which He has gifted man.

Many of the brothers who toil with me work during the hours of daylight and sleep when darkness falls. However, I have also discovered the advantages that the softer light of candle and oil actually benefit the preparation and painting of the gentler colours, and gold leaf does not shimmer so blindingly in candlelight.

So, while the brothers sleep, I work on.

I hear them then.

In the beginning I thought it was just the waters of the ancient lake, lapping against the rocky beach of this tiny island, rattling the stones, hissing over the sands. Then, when I listened again, I thought it was the wind soughing through the stunted trees, rasping branches and leaves, whispering through the stones.

I ignored the sounds . . . until I started to hear the words.

At first they were nonsense sounds, fragments of words, half-heard phrases, snatches of sentences. Convinced that the noises I was hearing were nothing more than my own imagination – for at night even the most trivial of sounds can assume a significance – I ignored them and took refuge in my faith and my work.

The voices persisted all through the summer, gradually becoming louder, clearer, until at times I found myself straining to catch the meaning. My work suffered; my letters were no longer as perfect as they had once been, my pigments no longer had the same consistency as before, the fine detail of faces were blurred – though the devils and demons that curled around the initial letters were hideously vivid. I think I began to suspect then that I was being tempted.

And yet I was reluctant to share my fears with my brothers: where was my proof? Was I hearing sounds from the lake or was it nothing more than my imagination? And what would my brothers say? I was afraid that they might think me mad: too often some of the brothers, unable to endure the regime of poor food, little sleep and mortification, are touched by the hand of God and slip into madness. What would happen to me then? This community is my life, illumination is my life's work, I could not bear to be sent away and set to work on some menial task.

As the winter rolled in, hard and sharp across the island, the voices became clearer, more distinct, until there was no longer any doubt that they were calling to me . . . speaking to me.

They knew my name. They knew my weaknesses.

They talked to me.

And I listened.

I am listening now. I can hear them.

Whispering. Whispering. Whispering.

I recognise some of the voices; I can hear my mother calling to me, and my father's strong voice. Often – too often – I heard the voice of Searc, to whom I was betrothed before I took holy orders. I can still remember the pain in her eyes when I told her that we would never be wed. She cursed me then: cursed me with a woman's venom. She swore vengeance on me for the disgrace I had brought down on her. She felt that by taking orders, I was bringing shame down on her and her family. On the day I joined the brothers on this isle, she threw herself into the lake and drowned.

It wasn't until I recognised her voice amongst the countless others that I realised that I was listening to the ghosts of my past.

And the only way to exorcise a ghost is to face it.

Tonight is the shortest night of the year. Tonight is the night when the doors between this and the Otherworld swing wide. Tonight, men will walk in the realm of the Sidhe, and the creatures of the Otherworld will stride through ours.

And I am resolved that I will rid myself of these cursed voices.

Tonight I will face my demons.

Looking across the broad expanse of Lough Erne, it is easy to believe that demons live beneath its dark waters. The lake is dotted with islands, all of which are ancient and bear the traces of their pagan past. Even the name of this island – the Isle of the Scald Crow – indicates its terrifyingly pagan origin when the old gods were worshipped here. Most of the local people and my fellow brothers call it Boa Isle.

Tonight, the sky is cloudless, thousands of tiny white star-points shining high in the heavens. I wonder if they are really the souls of the faithful looking down on the world they once lived in. I once read an ancient mathematical text which suggested that there were pictures and images in the heavens but, though I have often looked long and hard, I have never discovered any images.

The black waters of the lake are silent now. But I am patient. I know they will come at the dark of the night. The whispers will herald their presence.

Listen . . . listen, do you hear them? They are coming.

Their voice is the sound of the wind rustling through the trees, the hiss of the waters against the sands, the rattle of pebbles on the beach.

Their voice is the voice of the serpent.

Mo Laisse . . . Mo Laisse . . . Mo Laisse . . .

Their voices whisper in with the tide.

Mo Laisse . . . Mo Laisse . . . Mo Laisse . . .

There is hate in their voices, and fear also. Standing on the rocky beach, I call to them. 'Come forth, face me,' but the wind whips my voice away, shredding the sound.

Mo Laisse . . . Mo Laisse . . . Mo Laisse . . .

The waters shiver and break apart. And the creatures appear.

There are scores of them. Tall, grey-skinned with broad faces that narrow to pointed chins; their eyes wide and staring, they come up out of the water in a long line and move silently in towards the beach. I make the sign of the Cross in the night air and the creatures stop. I know then for certain that they are demons, fearful of the sign of God.

'What do you want with me?'

The creatures stare at me, saying nothing.

'Why do you torment me so?' I demand. 'I am a simple man of God. I have done nothing to you.'

One of the demons moves forward in the water. I can smell its sweat, the odour of spices and dead meat. I can hear its voice, though its mouth is not working.

'You have destroyed us.'

I shake my head. 'I have done nothing to harm you.'

The creature moves forward, sending waves lapping almost at my feet. 'You create the Words of Power . . .' it begins. Its speech is strange, archaic and heavily accented, and the words form in my head slowly, clumsily, as if the creature is choosing them with great difficulty. 'You have destroyed us.'

I shake my head again. 'I am a simple monk; I inscribe the Gospels . . .'

The creature raises its head to look at me. 'With every letter you etch, with every colour you lay, you destroy us.'

'I do not know what you mean.'

'We are the last of the old ones,' the figure whispers. 'You call us demons or devils, but we are neither. We are the last of the people of the goddess. Our ancestors ruled this island in the centuries before the White Christ was sacrificed on a cross of wood. Now we are nothing.'

A second figure appears behind the speaker. This one is naked, recognisably female. Sent to tempt me. She stares at me with large, circular eyes.

'I have never harmed you intentionally,' I tell them, glancing up into the heavens, gauging the time. Although it feels as if little more than a few heartbeats have passed since the figures have come up out of the water, the stars have shifted in the heavens and some of them have vanished. Dawn is close.

'We were once gods,' the demon continues. 'We were worshipped by the people of this land, and while they worshipped us, we remained strong. The gods depend on the humankind for their strength; it is that belief which keeps us alive. Their faith lent us substance.

'When the sons of Mil arrived with their weapons of iron, we retreated from this world, though we still survived in people's imaginations, and their faith – and fear – kept us strong.

'Until you and the others like you arrived.

'The man known as Palladius came first with word of this new god. We ignored him as he spread his faith to a few, but even then, we were not worried: what could one old man do against us?

'Ailbhe was next, but his converts were few. The small dark man, Patrick, came next. His was a mighty power, a terrifying strength. He worked a few minor magics – he called them miracles – but it was not this which turned the people from us. The man defied the druids – and prevailed! He faced them down at Tara and they were unable to overthrow him. We – the gods of Erin – were shown to be weak and ineffectual in our people's eyes . . . and the men of Erin are a proud race, who worship strong, proud gods. They started to turn against us then.

'And so we began to die, little by little, piece by piece.' The figure turns awkwardly, indicating scores of figures standing in the dark water behind him. 'We were once considered beautiful: the Shining Folk, the local people called us. But look at us now. We are hideous even in our own eyes.'

'But what has this to do with me?' I ask.

'We retreated to this lake long before the White Christ came to Erin,' the figure continues, its voice rasping. 'And all was well until you brown-robed ones settled on this isle. Even then perhaps we could have survived . . . until you began transcribing your book of power.'

'My book of . . . Oh, you mean the Gospel.'

'Every letter you form, every word you write scars us, deforms us, kills us a little. You must stop.'

The creature's anger is a physical thing, pushing against me, sending me staggering back. 'I will not.'

'Then you have killed us.'

The female figure leans forward, her round eyes fixed on me with a terrifying intensity, and she places a hand on the speaker's shoulder. If she speaks to him, it is in their own demon tongue which is inaudible to human ears.

'But if anything were to happen to you, then the work on the book would stop,' the demon says.

'There are other monks.'

'Do they have your skill, your artistry?'

'My work is poor when compared with other brothers.'

'False modesty is as much a sin as pride,' the creature says. It shuffles forwards, moving higher out of the water. 'Your work is considered to be amongst the finest in Erin at this time. No,' he shakes his head, 'if anything were to happen to you, if you were to drown this night, then your work would cease for a time . . . perhaps long enough for us to regain our strength.'

'There will always be others.'

The figure starts up the beach. 'All we need is time. If you will not give us that time, then we will have to make it ourselves.'

Stumbling backwards on the slick stones, I fall heavily on my side. I look upwards, offering my soul to God . . . and my God does not fail me. 'You are already out of time,' I point heavenward, to where the thin line of the dawn is streaking the horizon to the east. 'God's own pure light has claimed you.'

The figure turns to look at the dawn. It cries aloud, a long, slow, grating sound. When it turns back to look at me, the transformation has begun, the skin hardening to a solid, grey mask.

One by one the score of figures who have remained in the water simply slip back beneath its dark surface. The female remains above the water, her gaze fixed on me, washing me with her hate, until her greying skin begins to steam and then she, too, slides beneath the lapping water.

The transformation continues on the lone figure. A grey shell forms on the hard skin, splitting it, cracking it. Its clear eyes cloud over, a thin, milky film covering them. But the creature is still moving, coming towards me. I can hear the crackling of its flesh, smell its stench. It is reaching out, its stone fingers touching me . . .

*

Brother Mo Laisse was unable to continue past this point. The following text is in another hand:

The screams drew us from our cells. We found Mo Laisse crouched on the beach before a stone idol. He was babbling incoherently about the beasts that lived beneath the isle: the stone demons, he called them.

For the rest of his long life, the monk was haunted by the image of the stone creature. He abandoned calligraphy and turned instead to stonework, creating wondrous images of saints and holy men, and his carving was renowned. It was only after this death that we discovered the carvings he had been working on in secret, dark, bizarre images, creatures that could only be demons, and chief amongst these was the powerful image of the Sheila-na-Gig.

Mo Laisse's carvings remain, mute testimony to his terrifying encounter with the last of the Shining Folk on the isles in Lough Erne.

CHAPTER EIGHT

The Seventh Husband

♣

I am old, old, old.

So old that I do not even number my years anymore. My breath is blue with frost that lies chillingly in my bones. When I pass by in the night, men shiver and huddle closer to their hearthfires, children whimper fretfully in their sleep and the howling dogs fall silent. For the beasts know me. Know me for what I am, and fear me.

I know what it is to be hated.

And I know what it is to be loved.

Seeing me in the guise I customarily wear, no one would believe that I have loved and been loved in return. The humankind love only beauty – and I am not beautiful. In this guise I am a monster. I am the Thing in the Night, the Shape in the Mist.

I am the Hag of Beara.

My name is spoken in whispers, with crossed fingers, or a quick blessing and sometimes the more ancient Sign of Horns, with index and little fingers extended to ward off evil. I am the Hag of Beara and it is a name not lightly given. It suits me, for the flesh I wear is ancient and hideous and as scored with wrinkles as dried mud. My scanty hair is straggly and thin, my burning eyes sunk deep in their sockets. A reaper's scythe is the contour of my nose and a gnarled and broken branch the shape of my body. One of my forefingers is so long and misshapen, the nail black and razor sharp, that the sight of it can freeze a human heart – or pluck it out!

The Hag of Beara: I am a legend.

I know what it is to be feared, to be shunned and spurned, and hated.

And loved too.

For only those who have hated can love, and only those who have been hated can truly appreciate love.

Even to such as me, spring comes. Not every year, or every dozen years, perhaps no more than once a century, but when a misty circle forms around the moon and blackbirds change the song they sing, and the summers are cold, the winters warm, then I am allowed one more springtime by the gods that shaped me, one more warming of my frozen heart.

Then it is that I can walk unrecognised among men, to choose myself another husband.

Six have I had, over more than twenty centuries. And I can truly say that I loved all of them, and they in turn loved me, deeply and passionately. Six is not a great number, but it is enough. I can make one husband last me a very long time before, like the deadly female spider, I devour the withered sac which is all that remains of my mate.

This is my curse, my doom.

I was not always thus. I am the last of a vanished race. My people were not the sons of men, but the Children of the Goddess, Danu. Here in this land of Erin, they were called the Tuatha De Danann, and they have become legend. They are remembered as the Good People, the Little People, the Shining Folk, the Fairy Folk. Such pretty, gentle names . . . but ill-matched to the true nature of my people. I have listened to the charming and whimsical folktales told about my race, and have longed to rend the talespinners limb from limb. The Tuatha De Danann were conquerors; they once ruled the known world with fire and sword and old magic; now they exist only in children's stories.

It is true that many of my race were noble and shining and generous, and their bright spirits have melted into the trees and stones or sunk beneath the waters and found for themselves an immortality in the land of Erin itself. But these were the De Danann folk of the last days, when my race was weak and effete.

The very memory of them sours my stomach.

The majority of my race were strong and powerful, selfish and greedy. We were accustomed to rule, we were born to conquer. When the De Danann island sank beneath the waves in the vast western ocean, we set out on our ships of metal to conquer the world . . . and we did. From the deep forests of the western continent to the sandy deserts of the east, my people brought civilisation to the savages. And when those savages resisted us, we destroyed them.

I was selfish and greedy always, a creature who wielded her magical powers like a club. For we were magical, we of the Tuatha De Danann. The savages called us gods, but we were not gods, though we possessed some of the lesser gifts of godhood, the power over the elements of earth and air, fire and water. I like to think that my people were an intermediary step between the immortals and mortal man.

The ancients of my race claimed that such gifts as we had were entrusted to us by the gods themselves to use wisely.

Some did. Most did not.

I did not.

I used the humankind as slaves, as fodder, as entertainment, treating them little better than beasts. When my crimes became such that even my own people could not countenance what I had done, they cruelly punished me.

When the De Danann vanished from the landscape, I was not allowed to fade with them. I was entrapped in the ancient body of the Hag and left to roam Ireland, hated, feared and spurned by mortal man.

And my greatest punishment: I cannot die. I can only grow older and older, and suck the warmth out of the earth wherever I walk.

But because the gods, the true gods, have mercy in them as well as justice, I am occasionally allowed my springtime. A ghost of my old power returns to me, and I can take upon myself the appearance of youth. And now it has come around again, and I seek a seventh husband, to comfort me for a little while.

I walk the streets of Limerick city wearing the face of a young girl. My hair is yellow and curling, and my eyes are as blue as summer skies. Men turn their heads as I pass, their eyes wide with lust, their lips wet with desire. Women watch me warily, perhaps instinctively recognising me for the predator that I am, possibly even seeing a shadow of the crone that lurks beneath the pale, unblemished skin. I flaunt myself in front of them, taunting them, delighting in this pretty face, these supple limbs, this youth. But keeping up this glamour, this appearance, requires much of the remains of my power, and if I do not find a mate soon, then the magic will be exhausted, the glossy façade will crumble and I will become the Hag again.

I must find my seventh husband.

Strolling past a shop window, I gaze at fashions designed for the lithe bodies of the female humankind. One in particular attracts me: a white dress in some soft fabric that the De Danann folk could never have made, sprigged with little flowers and with a blue sash of satiny ribbon. I long for the feel of good cloth on my body, not the harshness of the unbleached wool I usually wear. A casual observer might think that I was wearing a fine cotton dress now, in russet and gold, with brocade along the bodice, but this too is nothing more than a spell. If that observer were to glance at my reflection in the shop window, they might catch of a glimpse of the lice-ridden rag that barely covers my nakedness.

The shop is bright with cloths and materials, the air scented with flowers and perfumes. I adore the smells of fresh flowers, the scent of newly mown hay, the sweet freshness of fruit: the smells disguise the odour of putrefaction which clings to my flesh.

The dress is taken from the mannequin in the window and folded across a shopgirl's arm. When I am ushered into a small booth, I strip off the simple peasant's dress I stole from a clothes line and pull the dress over my head, the cloth rustling and whispering over my soft skin.

I look into the mirror.

And smile, teeth small and white and even against my red lips. The yellow-haired girl in the mirror smiles back at me. We are young, she and I.

We will stay young for a while.

Adding shoes, gloves and hat to my purchases, I give

the shopgirl a handful of pebbles in payment for the dress; she sees them as a handful of coins in the proper currency of the day.

Wearing my new clothes, I go back out into the street. When I pass the next reflective window I notice with approval that the blue sash has made my waist look very small and slim, emphasising the curve of my bosom. Then I meet the eyes of a young man who is also looking at my image in the shop window. I twist my mouth into the curve the humankind call a smile.

He is embarrassed, he ducks his head shyly, looking away. His shyness attracts me, and I turn to look at his form and face. He is tall and fair, eyebrows almost invisible against his skin, a sprinkling of freckles across his straight nose. There is warmth in his grey eyes, and the curve of his lips.

Warmth. Life and heat.

'This is the first new dress I've had in a long time,' I tell him softly, taking care not to say anything that might frighten him away, allowing him to pity me. 'Do you like it?'

'It's a very pretty dress,' he says softly, his voice hoarse, 'but I think you are prettier,' he adds boldly, and then, because he is so young, so fresh, he blushes. Hot blood stains his cheeks beneath his freckles.

Hot blood. Salt and meat.

Ah yes, this one will do.

Falling into step beside him, we talk inconsequentially . . . what the humankind call chat, a peculiar habit where nothing is said. I have not forgotten how to chat, how to lead and draw him out, and make him feel strong and interesting, and quite delighted to find himself talking with such a beautiful young woman. In his voice I hear a trace of a stammer which tells me he does not have great self-confidence, so I flatter him gently, teasingly until somehow – he will never know how – we find ourselves seated on opposite sides of a tiny table in a quayside café, sipping tea. He does not notice that I do not drink the tepid liquid or eat a morsel of the tiny seed cakes. Giving him my full attention, I encourage him to talk of his plans and dreams and his problems, and I listen as no woman has listened to him before.

He is lonely.

I understand loneliness.

They are always lonely, the young men I select. Lonely and immature. They have outgrown their mothers and are subconsciously looking for a replacement. I catch them in the exact moment when they are most vulnerable, before they become mature enough to recognise the danger I represent, before they become mature enough to know what they really need is a sweetheart, or lover. Once they have a companion, a mate, I would not be able to call to them.

We spend time together, myself and this sturdy, energetic, lonely young man. I allow him to walk me home, my hand upon his arm, and through magic I let him believe the house he takes me to is my home. Standing at the iron gate, he thinks he sees me go through the doorway and wave to him from the window. When he leaves me, he walks off down the road with a bounce in his step, trailing his emotions in his wake, like rich smoke. I can taste his curiosity, his self-satisfaction, the warm glow of confidence in the centre of his being. I have made him feel like a man, a real man . . . for the first time in his life.

It is enough for the first day.

Other days together follow. As the days pass I begin

drawing the warmth from him into myself. I must, to have enough energy to sustain the illusion of my youth. He begins to realise that I am older than he thought, but that works in my favour, making me more of an authority figure. He allows me to mother him, to scold and chastise him, and reward him. With infinite care, I gnaw away his independence . . . and his youth.

Once I am certain he is the one I want, it is simplicity itself to allow him to believe that he is in love with me. The men I choose are always looking for someone to love. He mistakes the curious feelings in his body and soul for being in love. A man who has ever really been in love would not make such a mistake, but this one does, for he has never truly been in love. He knows no better. They never do, my young ones.

I do not encourage great physical passion. I do not want his valuable energies wasted on passion . . . and there is always the fear that at the height of passion, I will allow the illusion to slip and reveal myself in my true form. The sight would blast his eyes and senses. It has happened before.

Soon he is boasting of his conquest to his friends and family: a woman of beauty and intelligence, a hinted fortune and perhaps even a title; older, of course, but mature, not flighty. They disapprove and try to discourage him, but that only serves to make him more stubborn. He defends our relationship loudly, volubly, committing himself even more deeply. We must marry, he tells me, thinking it is his decision. Thinking no one understands him as I do.

And I do understand him.

I understand him so well.

Subtly, discreetly, I manipulate him, letting him think he

needs me more than I need him. He proposes marriage and, with some reluctance, I agree, allowing him to believe that he has achieved a great victory. Our wedding is a small, private affair, because he has alienated most of his family and many of his friends. So he becomes my seventh husband and binds himself to me in the vows of his religion, while I entangle him with bonds far stronger: those of magic and lust.

But the true victory is mine. This one is a prize indeed: strong and innocent, and so deliciously young. How long will he last? I wonder.

Some of them last longer than others. Eventually, however, they all age and sicken and wither as I draw the very essence of life from their souls to maintain myself.

But this one is strong. So strong. How good it feels to take the heat into me, to draw it out of the very air that surrounds him.

Time passes. I have no concept of it, but I can see it etched into the flesh and soul of my seventh husband.

He shivers often. We attribute it to his health. He is becoming rather delicate, his eyes growing dim, his hair greying and thinning. Sometimes, I catch him looking at me strangely, when he thinks I am not watching, as if he does not recognise in me the pretty girl he married.

I bear him children to keep him bound to me, though I ensure that none survives past infancy. My people can mate with the humankind, and we have often done so. Children keep one young, they say . . . and sometimes the smaller ones make tasty eating.

My husband is no longer young. His friends and family notice, so I try to keep them away from him as much as possible. Still, I am not worried. No one will come to rescue him. And even if they did, who could stand against me, now that I am whole and strong again?

He is frail and grey. His sight has grown dim, his hearing faded, his limbs tremble. He has not long left.

The day will come when this one realises that he has grown old too soon, while I have remained youthful. Perhaps he will realise that I have fattened on his youth, and he will look at me with shock and horror. Possibly, he will hate me, and his hate will allow him to see me as I truly am. But by then it will be too late.

However, I do not hate him. I love him, as much as I can love. I love the warmth and the life I am taking from him. I love him for the spring he has given me, to warm, however transiently, the cold winter of my existence.

When he is sucked dry and dead and gone, I will continue to enjoy life using the residue of his strength – for a time, at least. Then, I will begin to change. To age, to shrivel, my face collapsing upon itself until I become once more the Hag of Beara. I will flee Limerick before this happens, however. I will return to my homeland, to the fretted coasts of Cork and Kerry, and wail my terrible hunger on the winter wind that blows in off the sea.

And perhaps in a hundred years, or two or three, there will be a certain sort of ring around the moon and the blackbirds will change the song they sing, and then I will be permitted to go and seek an eighth husband.

CHAPTER NINE

The Black Dog

———— ♣ ————

The road that ran past the cottage was a road in name only, really little more than a meandering pathway amidst strands of nettles, baked hard and dusty in summer, a muddy quagmire in the winter rains. Like the cottage it led to, it had a woeful and deserted look. A casual passerby would have thought that no one ever came this way.

For many years, few did.

The only regular travellers on the road were the local farmers, taking the short cut across the glen, and the old couple who lived in the cottage. They made occasional trips as far as Tulla for their few meagre needs, and they rarely missed Mass. But they had no visitors, except for the parish priest, who dutifully ventured up the road on the bike that was older than he was. The occasional hitch-hiker or walker who rambled onto the road quickly discovered that it was guarded by a huge black dog of mixed pedigree.

The black dog would slink silently out of the briars and nettles when a person following the road came within a half mile of the cottage, then skulk along behind them, gradually narrowing the distance, until the click of its claws striking stones in the road would alert that traveller that they were being followed. And when they turned, the sight of the black dog was enough to strike terror into the hardiest of travellers. It stood waist high, solid shoulders of clearly delineated muscle rippling beneath a slick coat. Its head was larger than a normal dog's, its ears laid flat against its skull, blood-red tongue lolling from its gaping mouth in which yellow-white teeth glinted. Its eyes were the colour of rust. It was its very silence that first alerted the unwary traveller that this was no ordinary dog; it neither growled nor whined, and its huge eyes never blinked. They stared, unblinkingly, at the traveller and then, its every movement precise, it would move around the traveller and block its path. And no one dared to walk past it and continue on up the road past the cottage.

In Feakle, the nearest town, the shaken traveller would buy a pint in the pub to calm shaken nerves and if they were unwise enough to mention the black dog, they would be regaled with all the local legends . . .

The dog was not a real dog, but a demoniac being known to haunt that one particular roadway and strike terror into the hearts of any who passed by. The old couple who lived there never admitted to seeing the creature, but it had been witnessed by traveller and tradesmen alike for many years.

The dog was the Devil himself . . . the spirit of a long-dead highwayman . . . the ghost of a faithful dog awaiting the return of its master . . . a portent of death . . .

And when the traveller had left the pub, the fact and fancy would have become so confused that their own encounter with the black dog would become less terrifying. If they ever thought about it again, they would remember nothing but a large black dog, perhaps larger than any other dog they had ever seen, but still a dog – nothing more.

But the black dog was much more than that.

The black dog had first appeared when the Keoghs, the couple who lived in the cottage were young, or at least younger. They had a son then, Jim, a tall, ill-tempered lout who spent his time drinking, playing the fiddle and pursuing the local girls. When Jack Keogh threatened to throw the lad out if he did not find work or even help around the small farm, Jim had towered over his father and raised his huge fists silently. The threat was unspoken at that time. But shortly after he made the threat, he punched his father. And once the first blow had been struck, others followed.

An aura of bitterness, as cold and dark as a wet winter, settled over the Keogh cottage then. Sara and Jack came to fear their son, and he, in turn, began to hate and resent them. He could have left but he had no desire to travel, not while he could intimidate his father and live rent-free without having to do any real work. Also, he knew if he left he would probably lose his inheritance – the cottage and few fields that would be his when his father died. Property prices were rising; he knew he could be sitting on a sizable fortune if he bided his time.

So he stayed.

And the bitterness stayed, deepened, fed upon itself, poisoned all three of them until one day a furious argument broke out, and Jim Keogh hit his mother with his fist for stepping between himself and his father.

In the shock of silence that followed, they all knew it would never be the same thereafter.

That night in his bed Jack Keogh could not sleep.

Although it was dark, he thought he could see his wife's bruised face, feel the throbbing heat of the bruise. And though she was silent, he imagined he could hear Sara's soft sobbing. Staring upwards, his eyes wide, his cheeks damp, he looked into the future and saw nothing but years of abuse and fear.

At last he got up and padded over to the battered wardrobe. Parting the curtains slightly to allow a little moonlight to percolate into the room, he opened the wardrobe and pulled out his fishing tackle. Reaching into the wicker box he lifted out his fishing knife, a bone-handle sliver of razor-sharp steel. He hesitated only once, turning to glance over his shoulder towards the bed where his wife lay, immobile. In the moonlight, the bruised side of her face looked black. And that decided him. Holding the knife flat against his leg, he crept out. In the adjoining room his son lay sleeping.

As he left the room, Sara's eyes snapped open. She dozed semi-conscious, unsure if she were awake or dreaming. She was aware of the gasp and a grunt, but that might have been the animals in the barn, then a muffled crackling as if someone had turned over on the straw filled mattress, but that might have been the wind blowing through the hayricks. Then silence. As she drifted back into a troubled sleep, she heard the sound of a heavy weight being dragged across the bare floorboards. The last sound she heard before the nightmares took over was the faintest of splashes, as if something large had tumbled into the well beyond the cottage.

If she remembered the sounds the following morning, she easily dismissed them as nothing more than fragments of her nightmare interspersed with the country noises that travelled far in the night.

When Jack brought her a cup of tea just after dawn, there was a note in his hand. The single sheet had been torn from a notebook, the words spelled out in pencil. 'Gone away. Will not be back.'

And that was the story they told in the village. Jack produced the note in the pub to verify his story, and the boy's disappearance was a seven-day wonder only. The boy was no loss, the locals said, and life carried on as before. Jim Keogh was one of a trinity that almost every village and town possessed: the drunk, the fool and the rogue. The first pair was harmless, but the village was usually a better place when the rogue left.

With the boy gone, things changed up at the cottage. The air of brooding menace vanished, and Jack and Sara were seen more often in town. They had a new well dug on the hillside quite a distance above the first. 'The old well's gone bad,' Jack explained.

And then the black dog appeared.

No one knew when it first appeared. About a year after Jim Keogh disappeared to seek his fortune elsewhere . . . a year and a day, others added, significantly.

Suddenly the dog was just there, shadowing the footsteps of anyone who came down the road past the cottage. Its stillness, its silence, the faintest of odours – of wetness, of dank and rot, the stink of spoiled meat – that clung to it, told their own story. Though it might look like any other scared stray there was no doubt in anyone's mind that this was a fey beast. A black dog. They were not uncommon in this part of Ireland; they walked some of the lonely roads in Scotland and Wales. Legend had it that they were the souls of the damned, condemned to walk this earth until Judgment Day.

Connections began to be drawn between Jim's

disappearance and the dog's appearance.

That was when the cottage began to be shunned and those who needed to travel that route found other, and longer, ways. Eventually, even the parish priest, a stout-hearted man, did not feel it incumbent upon him to pay many calls on the taciturn and morose couple who now rarely ventured outside their cottage. They rarely spoke to one another, as if some terrible, festering secret lay between them.

Time passed. Summer followed winter, and eventually the old couple died within a fortnight of one another; Sara first, then Jack. His body was not discovered for nearly a month after his death.

With their deaths, the locals expected that the black dog would vanish also. But the black dog remains; it continues to guard the twisting, overgrown track past the tumbled cottage.

CHAPTER TEN

A Curse on the Sea

———— ♣ ————

He was late returning; very late.

The woman who stood in the open doorway of the cottage had no need of a clock to tell the time. Moya had lived all her life on the harsh west coast of Donegal in the far north of Ireland, and she could tell the hour almost to the minute by the colour of the light on the sea, the direction of the wind, the scents of the day. Now, as she gazed out towards a storm-tossed sea with eyes as grey and turbulent as the weather, she knew that it was two hours past the time he should have docked. But the storm had blown up quickly, and she guessed that the weather had caught him far out from the land. His small boat would have found it difficult to make any headway against the offshore wind.

The same wind whipped her heavy, dark hair around her face and into her eyes, stinging them. It was only her hair in her eyes, nothing more; she brushed it aside with an impatient hand. In the moment when it had obscured her vision, a speck had appeared on the horizon. Narrowing her eyes, squinting into the gathering storm,

Moya stared at the sea as if to draw the boat in through sheer force of will.

The grey waves rose and fell, and there was no boat, just white-crested breakers pounding in to the rocky coastline.

When the light faded, first to a gritty greyness, then to full night, Moya turned away from the door and lit the lamp, returning to place it in the window where its clean light pierced the night. Then she went to bed.

She came of old stock; she knew there was nothing more that could be done that night, and she realised – deep in her core – that her strength might be needed later. Before she drifted off into a troubled sleep, she prayed that the storm would abate.

But the next morning the storm was, if anything, worse. Instead of blowing itself out, it had become a gale that threatened to tear the thatch off the roof, had it not been for the heavy ropes that held the material down, tightly secured to supports projecting from the walls below the roof. Standing in the open doorway, Moya had to grip the doorframe in both hands and lean forward into the wind. This time when the salt wind stung her eyes, she allowed the tears to come. There was no sunlight that day, but she could feel its passage behind the leaden sky, every minute an eternity.

When she finally turned from the door, it was night again. Then, broken at last, sick with the realisation of what she knew to be true, she threw herself sobbing across their bed. The wind slammed the door behind her, the sound terrible and final.

And in her womb, her unborn child kicked and kicked again.

When her husband's broken body was at last washed

ashore, the neighbours feared she would lose the child she carried, so intense was her grief. But she did not lose the baby. Instead, once her man was buried in the small local graveyard, which held so many victims of the sea, including her father and two brothers, she made preparations to leave her native Donegal forever.

'I shall go somewhere where I need never hear nor see the ocean again,' she vowed.

By selling everything she had, she was able to purchase a tiny shop in a small village in the heart of landlocked County Tipperary, as far from the ocean as she could get. Here she would begin her life afresh; the shop would provide a comfortable living for herself and her child, and she would no longer be dependent on the terrible uncertainty of wind and wave.

On the day before she left, Moya went down to the shore one last time and gazed out over the waves with bleak, sea-coloured eyes.

Ice-cold water foamed around her feet; the silibant hissing of the waves were like mocking laughter. 'I curse you, Manannan Mac Lir,' she cried aloud to the ancient sea god of her people. 'You have taken my husband and my child's father. You have taken my future. My curse be upon you forever!'

Fishermen gathered on the shore mending nets heard her wild curse and begged her to take it back. 'You must never curse the sea. For the sea is stronger than any living being; powerful and pitiless, and it is foolish to anger it.'

'I can never forgive it,' she said coldly.

'It gives us food and provides us with a living.'

'And it takes the living in return. No, my curse is upon it, now and forever.'

One of the fishermen, a man who had known her father

and husband, took her to one side and begged her to unsay her curse. He reminded her of the legend that if the sea took the father of an unborn child, it took the child too.

But Moya shook her head violently. 'The sea will have nothing more from me. I will deny it.'

'The sea will not be denied,' the old man said, turning away.

Less than two months after Moya had moved from her native Donegal, she gave birth to a healthy baby boy, the image of his late father. The boy grew to manhood in landlocked Tipperary far from the sea, and his mother told him no tales of boats or fishing or Donegal. She kept him away from lakes and ponds, and refused to allow him to learn to swim.

When he left school and was trying to find work, he never even considered following his father's old trade, even when it seemed there was no other work to be had in Ireland. Then, at last he did what so many other young people were forced to do in order to survive: he emigrated, heading west to make a new life for himself in America.

During the long weeks of his voyage across the Atlantic, his mother prayed continually for his safety, and neighbours and customers in her small shop were shocked by her haggard and drawn appearance.

When he wrote to his mother and told her that he had found a good job in a city called Cincinnati, Moya went to the local schoolteacher and had him show her the place in an atlas. She crossed herself and thanked God when she discovered that Cincinnati was a city in Ohio, in the American midlands, hundreds of miles from the sea.

As she walked down the winding country lane to her shop, she started to laugh, a gentle shaking of her shoulders that gradually convulsed her whole body, until tears streamed down her lined face. 'I have beaten you, Manannan Mac Lir,' she breathed. Then, throwing her arms wide, she cried aloud. 'I have beaten you, Manannan Mac Lir! You took the father, but you will never take the son.'

The sea is father to air and air is brother to wind, and in Tipperary the wind blows. It blew across the old woman's face, across her triumphant mouth, whipping away the proud words. The same wind blew across land, carrying the words to the sea, where they were broken and swallowed by the restless waves.

And sometimes the gods come when they are called.

When the telegram came from America, Moya was afraid. She had never received a telegram before. She looked at it for several long minutes before she finally plucked up the courage to open it with trembling fingers. Neighbours later found her sitting at the kitchen table, bolt upright, eyes wide with shock, a look of stark terror on her face. Heart attack, the doctor said, because there was no medical term for dying of fright. The single sheet of the telegram that was locked into her fingers was buried with her.

Regret to inform you. . .
Found dead on a Cincinnati street after a freak storm. . .
Autopsy revealed salt water in the lungs. Drowning. . .

CHAPTER ELEVEN

The Hungry Grass

———— ♣ ————

The doctor stepped away from the bed, closing his black leather bag with a snap. Catching hold of Henry Blackburn's arm, he led him across the room to where a fire blazed in the hearth. Robert Mortimore had been the Blackburn's family physician for thirty and more years; he had birthed the two Blackburn boys and attended at the death of poor Elizabeth, their mother, three years previously. Now, as he looked into Henry Blackburn's florid face, he knew he didn't have the heart to tell the old man the truth . . . and yet he couldn't lie to him either.

'How bad is it, Robert?' Blackburn demanded.

'I'll not lie to you, Henry,' the doctor said quietly. 'You only have to look at John to realise that he is desperately ill indeed.' Both men turned to look at the bed where John Blackburn, the youngest boy, was stretched out, the angles of bones and curve of ribs clearly visible beneath the sheet which covered his emaciated body.

The illness had come upon the young man suddenly, a shuddering bout of nausea and diarrhoea gripping him after a day's shooting. He had been well the following day, though without appetite – which was natural – but the following day and the day after that, he had no interest in food, and when he forced himself to chew and swallow, the food came up almost immediately afterwards. In fourteen days, he fell from a sturdy fourteen stone to just over seven, and now the skin hung in fleshy bags on his bones.

'Can you do anything for him?' Henry Blackburn demanded.

'I've given him some opium which will help him sleep and ease the pain,' the smaller man said. 'I've tried various combinations of tonics and herbal restoratives, but he simply cannot keep them in his stomach.'

'So you're telling me that there is nothing you can do for my son?'

'No, I'm not saying that. I'm simply telling you that I've done all I can for the moment. We'll wait a day or two to see how effective the remedy is.'

'He could be dead in a day or two! Have you given up? Tell me truthfully,' Blackburn demanded, his voice rising to a shout. The young man in the bed moaned in his fevered sleep and Blackburn lowered his voice to a whisper again.

The small, sharp-faced doctor shook his head quickly. 'I haven't given up, Henry. I will not stop trying, you know that.'

Henry Blackburn nodded. 'I know. I'm sorry.' He turned back to the bed. Leaning on the bedposts, his knuckles white, he asked desperately, 'What's wrong with him, Robert?'

The doctor turned to look at the shape in the bed. He shook his head. 'I don't know. I've never seen anything like it. No,' he said quickly, 'that's not entirely true. Many years ago, when I was serving in India, I saw a young man waste away like this. He had offended a fakir, who had cursed him. Because the young man was related to one of the ruling khans, my commanding officer volunteered me to attend to the boy, convinced that if I could save him, it would help cement relations with the tribesmen . . .' The doctor's voice trailed away as he remembered the case. Forty years ago and the details were still as fresh as if it had happened only yesterday. And the more he thought about it, the more the similarities between the two cases became even more pronounced. But that had been in the savage heart of India, while this was Ireland in the last years of the nineteenth century, the second country of the empire.

'What happened to the Indian boy?' Henry Blackburn asked. 'Could you help him?'

Robert Mortimore shook his head. 'I could do nothing for him. He wasted away to skin and bone and died in agony.'

'A curse, you say,' Henry Blackburn whispered. 'Could you not have found someone to remove this curse?'

Mortimore grinned humourlessly. 'None of the other fakirs was prepared to risk offending the fakir who had cursed the boy, lest they too were cursed in turn.' He stopped and glanced sidelong at the big, florid-faced man. 'I'm surprised you don't scoff, Henry.'

'Once I would have laughed, dismissing such nonsense as superstitious drivel. But I've lived in Ireland far too long now. I've seen things, heard things . . .' His voice trailed away.

'What is it?' Mortimore asked, trying to interpret the expression that had flitted across the big man's face. Something had flashed into his eyes – knowledge, under-standing . . . hope?

Henry Blackburn shook his head. 'Nothing. Just a

thought, a stray thought.' He turned quickly. 'Will you stay the night?'

The doctor pulled out his pocket watch and flipped open the lid. 'It's gone three in the morning, Henry. I think I'll stay.'

'I'll have Towers prepare you a room,' he said, striding out of the room, taking the stairs two at a time. As Robert Mortimore followed him out of the bedroom, Henry Blackburn was standing in the hall, pulling on his heavy coat, calling for a carriage.

'Henry . . . Henry?' The doctor leaned on the banister and looked over the rail down onto the long, marble-floored hall. 'It's the middle of the night. Where are you going?'

'To see a fakir!'

The old woman came awake in the deathly silence that precedes the dawn. Twilight was grey on the windows, but the interior of the tiny cottage was still in darkness. Red, winking embers marked the location of the fire across the room from the simple bed, but Nano Hayes didn't need a light to know the location of everything in the room. She had lived here for more than six decades and its geography was as familiar to her as her own lined flesh.

By the time the rumble and clink of the horse-drawn carriage was audible on the cold morning air, she had stirred the embers alive again, added small slivers of dried turf and well-dried sticks, and set the kettle to boil.

Moving slowly now – the damp winter mornings stiffened her joints – she trimmed the oil lamp and set it on the centre of the table, so that its light shone on the door. The jingle of harness was distinct enough for her to identify individual sounds: four horses pulling a large-wheeled carriage. And someone who knew her too, she realised, as the carriage slowed as it came through the village, taking the turning off to the right that led up to her cottage.

Nano Hayes opened the door just as the coachman reined in the carriage. A long rectangle of yellow light lanced out into the damp air, bathed the sweating horses in gold and bronze. Standing in the doorway with the light behind her, Nano Hayes looked wraithlike, insubstantial, a tiny, grey-haired woman, the delicate features that had made her such a beauty in her youth still visible beneath the fine network of wrinkles.

The coachman leaped down, but before he could reach the carriage door, it opened and Henry Blackburn climbed down onto the ground, the heels of his boots cracking the thin covering of ice and sinking into the soft earth. Pulling his coat tighter across his chest, he strode towards the old woman, wondering how she could stand the bitter morning chill with only a shawl thrown over her shoulders.

'You may remember me, madam . . .' he began.

'I remember you, Henry Blackburn,' Nano Hayes said softly, turning away, disappearing into the interior of the cottage. The big man hesitated a moment before he followed her, gently closing the door behind him, blinking in the sudden light. When he could see clearly again, he discovered Nano Hayes standing before the fire, lifting a steaming black-bottomed copper kettle off the flames. Without turning around, she said, 'Sit, Henry Blackburn. Now tell me,' she continued, pouring boiling water into a fat-bodied teapot, 'how is your son?'

'My son?' Blackburn said blankly. How did the woman know?

'Your son, Giles, how is he?' the old woman said softly, looking closely at the big man.

'Giles!' Blackburn said quickly. Giles was his first son, John's older brother. 'Giles is in good health. Married now for three years and I am to be a grandfather later this year.' The old woman nodded, but said nothing. 'And it's all thanks to you,' Henry Blackburn continued slowly. 'Four years ago, you saved Giles' life and that is a debt I can never repay. I'm only sorry that Giles didn't thank you himself,' he added.

Four years previously, Giles Blackburn had suddenly and inexplicably fallen madly in love with a local girl. Despite his father's warnings and mother's entreaties, Giles insisted that he was going to marry her. However, the Blackburns' cook discovered that an ancient Irish love spell – the catspell – had been cast over the boy. The cook brought the story to Henry Blackburn and insisted that he go to see the local wise woman, Nano Hayes. Although cynical about the woman's powers, Blackburn was desperate enough to try her remedy . . . and within a week, his son was completely cured. (See 'The Catspell', *Irish Folk & Fairy Tales Omnibus*, Warner Books.)

Nano Hayes set out two tiny china tea cups, alongside a matching milk and sugar bowl on the table before Blackburn. 'Giles thanked me,' she said with a slight smile. She held up a cup in the palm of her hand and saw him blink in surprise. 'You didn't know?' she said. 'They were a present from your son, Giles. Twelve pieces of the finest bone china.' She held the cup up to the fire for his inspection. The light turned it translucent. 'Sure, what would I do with twelve cups, saucers, plates, sideplates and whatnot? But it was a kind gesture. He has a good heart.'

'Like you, Nano Hayes,' Blackburn said quietly.

'You're troubled,' she said simply.

'It's my younger son, John,' he said, and stopped.

Nano Hayes poured tea, not breaking the silence, allowing him time to gather his thoughts. Taking her cup, she sat into the high-backed wooden chair set close to the fire. In the shadows, her eyes were bird-bright, hard and glittering.

Blackburn sipped the strong black tea, felt it sear its way down into his stomach. 'John's sick,' he said finally. 'A wasting sickness that has turned him from a strapping young man, bigger and broader than myself, to a mere shell in less than two weeks. He cannot stand, cannot even sit erect. Nothing he eats stays down. He cannot even drink water. The doctor has done all he can for him . . . but now I fear there's little enough left to do.' Realising that he'd been squeezing the delicate teacup in his big hands, he carefully replaced it on its saucer.

'Did this sickness come upon him suddenly?'

'He was out shooting on the mountains and he ventured down into the bogs. When he returned, he was complaining of feeling feverish and nauseous. I suspected that he had caught a chill on the bog and suggested he retire for the evening with a hot whiskey. He deteriorated through the night, wracked with bouts of vomiting and diarrhoea that left him ill and shaking the following morning.' He shrugged. 'He's gone downhill ever since.'

'Why have you come to me?' Nano Hayes asked from the shadows.

'Four years ago, you saved my son. I was hoping you could do it again.'

The old woman laughed gently. 'You know my reputation. The local people call me "wise woman", some call me "witch", but never to my face. I know the uses of herbs and poultices, balms and potions.' She shrugged.

'Your son's illness sounds more suited to the ministrations of a doctor. I am not a doctor. So why have you come to me?'

'The local doctor, Robert Mortimore, has attended my son every day of his illness. He is a good man and a good doctor. In the latter weeks of my late wife's life, he eased her suffering greatly.'

Nano Hayes nodded. 'I know the man. He treats gentry and peasant alike, and often forgets to charge the peasantry for his services. He is a good man.'

'Earlier this morning, he told me a tale of his days in India. He told how a young man had been cursed by a fakir – a holy man or witch, I'm not sure which – and that young man wasted away . . . much like my son is doing.'

'Do you think your son has been bewitched?' the old woman asked carefully.

'Four years ago I would have scoffed at the very idea. But that was before you proved the effectiveness of a thousand-year-old spell . . . and an equally old cure. Since then I've listened to the stories my staff tell. So many stories, of leprechauns and luricauns, cluricauns, fir dearg, banshee, merrows, peists and countless other creatures: surely they can't all be figments of someone's imagination.'

Nano Hayes laughed gently. 'I am closer to this land than you will ever be, Blackburn, and I have heard and seen creatures that you would dismiss as myth: but even I haven't encountered all of the creatures you list. Many of them,' she added, 'come out of the bottom of a glass or are found in the end of a whiskey bottle. But then again there are others,' she said quietly, 'that cannot be so easily dismissed.'

'A year ago, I heard the banshee wail for old Tom O'The Mountain,' Blackburn said quickly.

'You heard vixens yapping,' Nano Hayes said shortly.

'No banshee followed Tom's clan; the Women in White only cry for the ancient lines. I'll ask you again, do you think your son has been bewitched?'

'I don't know,' Blackburn snapped. 'I'm grasping for straws, I know that, but what else can I do? He is my son, I'll do everything in my power that might save him. I've come to you as a last resort. Is there a spell,' he continued desperately, 'something that would wreak havoc on my son, something that would eat away at his flesh, turn him into a living skeleton?'

The old woman was silent for so long that Blackburn feared that she had fallen asleep. Finally, she said, 'There is one. A terrible, terrifying spell . . .' She looked up at the big man, sweat now glistening on his bald head. 'Have you ever heard of the Hungry Grass, Mr Blackburn?'

He shook his head silently.

'It is an ancient spell . . . and yet the events of fifty years ago reactivated it, giving it a new and evil life.'

Blackburn shook his head again. 'I don't know what you mean,' he said.

'Fifty and more years ago – before you came to Ireland – the Great Famine gripped this country. No one knows how many souls fled these shores for England and the Americas, sailing in ships that were little better than floating coffins. No one knows how many died: I have heard people tell of a million, perhaps two million, but I do know that whole families, villages and towns simply ceased to be. People died on the roads and in the fields, and then rotted where they lay.'

'I don't see. . .'

'So much hunger in the land . . . so much death, so much pain . . .' Nano Hayes stood up suddenly. 'Go back to your son, Mr Blackburn. Send your coach for me at noon. I will see what I can do.'

Blackburn opened his mouth to speak, but the look in the old woman's eyes – wild and terrifying – silenced him. He finished his tea in one urgent swallow, and backed quickly from the tiny room. Pausing at the door, he looked back. Nano Hayes was silhouetted against the fire, hunched over, looking like a picture-book drawing of an ancient witch. When she raised her head to look at him, her face was in shadow. Only her eyes were visible: and they blazed with the dancing flames of the fire.

It was only when he closed the door behind him that Blackburn realised that the old woman had been looking away from the fire: her eyes should not have reflected the light.

Nano Hayes walked the almost invisible trail that wound through the forest. The early-morning fog still twisted through the trees and curled along the frozen earth. The old woman probed the ground in front of her with a long, iron-shod walking stick, testing for hidden roots or ice-covered pot-holes. She had first played in this forest when she was a very young child, she knew its every trail and track by heart. However, unlike the townsfolk, who thought that a track through the forest remained fixed and unchanging, she knew that it was constantly evolving, moving, growing. She knew enough to respect it.

She turned left at the twisted oak, taking the track that led down towards the bogland. John Blackburn would have taken this route, a tall, proud young man, son of the local squire, marching blindly and ignorantly into an ancient curse.

As she descended towards the bogland, the air grew still and silent. The chill of the mist was more biting now, damp fingers piercing through her clothing, hurting her lungs with every breath she took. The trees thinned out as she entered the marshy valley. The fog was thicker here, lying on the ground in a twisting, shifting blanket that came up to the level of her knees. Though she knew the path, she slowed, unwilling to step into icy, foul-smelling water . . . and equally unwilling to step inadvertently into the circle of the hungry grass, even though she was carrying the most effective protection of all – a simple crust of bread tucked into her belt.

Finally, she stopped and moved the walking stick through the fog in a twisting spiral, her lips shaping a language that had died out a thousand years previously. The fog hissed and burned away from the iron tip of the staff.

Planting the staff on the ground directly in front of her, she closed her eyes and drew the damp air into her lungs, allowing the events of the last few days to flow into her subconscious, drawing images from the earth and air, the emotions imprinted on the stones and trees.

She saw John Blackburn.

Tall and broad, like his father, with his father's strong, arrogant features, he strode into the clearing, his shotgun cradled under his arm, a brace of woodcocks and a rabbit in his game bag.

Sudden movement caught his attention and he whirled, the gun closing with a snap, moving fluidly to his shoulder, the sharp report made flat and distant on the foggy air. Across the clearing, a rabbit somersaulted, then lay quivering in death. The young man snapped open the gun and pulled out the smoking casing, tossing it to the ground. . .

Nano Hayes opened her eyes and looked down: she

could see the metallic glint of the casing in the dew-damp grass. She closed her eyes again.

John Blackburn strode across the soft bogland towards the trembling rabbit . . . and walked into the circle of Hungry Grass.

The first spasm hit him almost immediately, driving him to his knees, clutching at his stomach. Cold fire burned through him, eating into his flesh, sending bile into his throat, flooding his mouth with bitter saliva. John Blackburn retched, blinking tears from stinging eyes. He rolled over on the sodden ground, knees drawn up to his chest, trying to ease the agony in his stomach, the ache in the base of his lungs.

With his eyes squeezed tightly shut, he didn't see the mist curling and twisting, forming vague shapes, distorted images in the air around him, clutching at him with gaseous fingers.

Nano Hayes watched the young man drag himself to his feet, leaning on his shotgun, using it now to support himself. She saw him stagger out of the barely visible green circle on the ground and begin the long and exhausting climb up to the woods. As he moved further away from the deadly circle, the tearing pains in his stomach began to ease a little, and by the time he eventually reached the woods, he was beginning to think that it might have been nothing more than the drink from the night before. Perhaps some of the poteen, the illicit liquor brewed by the local men, had been bad.

Nano Hayes allowed the images to fade, and shook her head sadly. The moment John Blackburn stepped into the circle of Hungry Grass without the proper protection, he had been doomed.

And she wasn't sure if she, with all her lore and

wisdom, would be able to save him.

Nano Hayes stood at the foot of the young man's bed and looked at the thin, wasted figure, the angles of bones and ribs clearly visible beneath the blanket, the outline of his skull distinct and terrifying beneath a sparse covering of hair. There was no movement in his chest and although her hearing was acute, she had to strain to hear his quick and rapid breathing.

'Can you help him, Nano Hayes?' Henry Blackburn's voice was a hoarse whisper.

Clutching at the brass bedstead with frail, birdlike hands, the old woman lowered her head.

'I cannot make you any promises.' She lifted her right hand, index finger pointing upwards. 'There is not much life left in the boy, but he is his father's son and he is strong. There is a chance – a last chance, a small chance, but a chance nonetheless.' She turned to look at Blackburn and the doctor standing behind him. 'And you must trust me, trust me with the life of your son.'

'I trusted you with the life of my first-born,' the squire said simply.

The old woman turned her head. 'However, before I begin, you should know that the chances of your son surviving are slim indeed: you must prepare for that.'

Henry Blackburn nodded, not trusting himself to speak.

'Bring him to my cottage late this afternoon, before the sun sinks. Bring a stretcher and find two strong men to carry it. Use men from the village: they know my reputation, and I will ensure that they will not speak of what they hear or see at sunset tonight.'

'What are you going to do?' Robert Mortimore asked.

'Tonight, we will trade with the Devil . . . or at least

what you Christian folk would call a devil.'

A silent procession moved through the twilight forest. Nano Hayes led the way along the narrow track. Henry Blackburn followed behind her, and behind him two strong stablehands carried a light wooden stretcher bearing the still and almost weightless body of John Blackburn. Robert Mortimore took up the rear.

The light had almost faded by the time they reached the boglands, and mist was curling up from the damp ground, making footholds treacherous in the fading light. Blackburn and Mortimore lit oil lamps and held them aloft, but the old woman moved confidently without benefit of the light, her earlier visit having imprinted the path in her mind's eye.

Nano Hayes stopped and raised her left hand. Without turning around, she said, 'Now, you must do as I say – without demur, without question. Is that understood?'

Blackburn and Mortimore spoke together. 'Yes.' The two stablehands said nothing; they were both terrified of the old woman, they would obey her without question . . . and they were being handsomely paid for their time.

'You two, stand here and here,' she said, turning to point at the two Englishmen. 'You must not move from this spot. It is vitally important that I know where you are at all times. Now, you two come forward and carry the stretcher into the centre of that clearing.' She pointed with her stick. As the first man came abreast of her, she stretched out her left arm, stopping him. 'Have you the bread?'

'Yes, ma'am. In both pockets.'

Nano Hayes nodded.

John Blackburn was carried into the clearing and laid on

the ground in the centre of a circle of brightly coloured, yellow-green grass. The stretcher was slid from beneath his body and the blanket pulled off him. He was naked, the length of his bones, the curve of ribs and collarbone, the jut of ribs clearly visible beneath the pallid flesh. The young man's eyes flickered wildly beneath closed lids, then opened briefly, pupils huge and dilated, darting around the clearing. He opened his mouth and attempted to cry aloud, but it came out as a hoarse whispered, 'No!'

Their part in the bizarre ceremony completed, the two stablehands hurried from the circle and disappeared down the path without a backwards glance.

Planting the staff point first in the soft earth on the very edge of the circle of grass, Nano Hayes closed her eyes – and waited.

'Nano . . .?' Henry Blackburn said later, much later, when the night had completely claimed the forest and the first of the night stars were beginning to glitter in the purple sky. 'Nano?' he said again, when the old woman didn't move.

'Patience,' Nano Hayes said suddenly.

'My son will die of exposure,' Blackburn snapped.

The old woman turned her head, her face a pale oval in the night. 'Your son passed beyond this world the moment he stepped into the circle of the Hungry Grass. For the past days he has lived in the Otherworld; it has snared his soul, and by doing so claimed his body.'

'What is the Hungry Grass, Nano Hayes?' Dr Mortimore asked softly.

Swivelling around to look at him, the old woman shook her head. 'No one knows for sure; its origin is lost in the mists of Irish folklore. They are usually, though not always, circular, and not always on grass either. I have come across areas associated with the Hungry Grass on stony soil. To anyone with a trace of Sight or any drop of the old blood in their veins, they will appear as cold, inhospitable, forbidding places, places to be avoided. But to the unwary, they are deadly indeed.' The old woman pointed across the clearing to where John Blackburn lay, looking pale and insubstantial in the wan light. Smoke-grey mist was curling up from the ground, wrapping the young man's body in a shifting, twisting blanket.

'Within this circle lies an area of the Hungry Grass. All the local people know it, and are aware of its reputation. Most avoid it, but if they are forced to cross it, then they will take the precaution of carrying a piece of bread with them.' She reached into the folds of her dress and held out a battered crust of bread. Stretching her arm out over the circle, she closed her hands, crushing the bread to crumbs. As the breadcrumbs touched the grass, they twisted and shuddered into mould-ridden specks. 'No animal will venture into the circle, and neither bird nor insect will fly across it.'

'What is it, Nano?' Dr Mortimore asked. 'It cannot be natural. . .'

'There speaks the man of science. Fifty years ago, your science would have been called magic. The humankind have forgotten so much, so much. Science is only now rediscovering a fragment of what was once known.' Pointing out across the circle, the woman said, 'This place is one of the gateways between this world and the next, and between this time and the past.' Throwing her head back, she closed her eyes, breathing in the cool, sour night air. 'Once a proud people came to this land of Erin, though this was before it was known by that name. They were the followers of Partholon, the King-Slayer. They were not the first to take the land, there had been others before them: the followers of Banba, who named the land, and the Fomor, who stole it from them, but the Partholonians made the isle grow. They used the Wild Magic to shape and twist and make the land, and they waged war on the Fomor, the beast-folk.

'They fought the last battle with the Fomor on the Plain of Ith, on the day sacred to Bile, the god of death. Many died that day, including Cichal Onefoot, Lord of the Fomor host, and Partholon, the leader of the humankind. But the humans were triumphant and broke the power of the demonkind. Many years were to pass before they rose again, and then their reign was brief and they were defeated by the Shining Folk, the Tuatha De Danann.

'But, although the Partholonians defeated the Fomor, the beast-folk had the final revenge. Partholon was poisoned by Cichal's blood, and as his body lay in the ground, a festering illness spread from it, claiming first the beasts of the fields and the birds of the air, then the humans. The sickness took the form of a terrible hunger that ate away flesh and bones from the inside, reducing a man to a skeleton in days.

'All that the Partholonians had worked so hard to establish was wiped away in less than three moons. The first dead bodies were buried, then as the people began to understand a little of the disease, corpses were burnt. However, as more and more died, there were fewer and fewer people to bury the corpses, and huge mounds of decaying flesh rose everywhere.' Nano Hayes took a deep shuddering breath. 'Just outside Dublin is a place known as Tallagh, but the old name for the place is Tamlecht Muintre Partholain, the plague grave of Partholon's people.' The old woman crouched down on the edge of the circle, her head tilted to one side, as if she were listening.

'The places known as Hungry Grass have grown where the Partholonian bodies were piled up. As the diseased flesh decayed, the foulness flowed into the ground, marking it forever, and the spirits of those who had died in agony were trapped around the place also. And as the disease claimed their bodies, so too did it rob them of their minds, making them bitter and evil. So the curse is twofold: a malevolent spirit standing guard over a patch of diseased ground. They claim the unwary, rob them of life and energy, and then, when they have died in agony, their soul is added to those who fester in the ground.'

Henry Blackburn coughed into the silence. 'And now?' he asked. 'What happens now?'

'Now they come!'

The stench came first – a cloying foulness that pervaded the night, overlaying the damp odours of earth and bog. Blackburn and Mortimore recoiled from the stench, pulling handkerchiefs from their pockets, pressing them to their mouths. Only Nano Hayes seemed unaffected by the odour.

The mist, which had been steadily rising as the sun disappeared, suddenly flowed into the centre of the circle, washing over the naked young man, completely blanketing him. Then the mist gathered higher about the body. It was tinged yellow and green now, the colours pale and fungal, twisting, shifting, curling, shapes appearing only to vanish immediately.

Nano Hayes called aloud, her voice harsh and cawing, like the cry of a wild bird, startling both men . . . and the twisting mist froze.

Henry Blackburn squinted into the mist: he thought he could see dozens of shapes, figures, twisted creatures that were neither man nor beast. One of the creatures, clearer than the rest, was bent over the body of his son, arms that ended in nothingness poised over his chest.

Nano Hayes spoke again, her voice calm, demanding.

The mists danced briefly, then sped into the single creature, abruptly giving it shape and form and definition.

Blackburn and Mortimore shrank back in horror.

Perhaps the creature had once been human, but no longer. It was completely hairless, its flesh faintly green, its eyes huge and protuberant, lips pulled back from savage teeth. Scraps of mouldering cloth still clung to its emaciated body, but the curve of its ribs, the bones of thigh and forearm were clearly visible beneath the taut flesh. Long black nails tipped skeletal fingers.

'Stop!' Nano Hayes commanded.

The creature hissed at the woman, black tongue protruding through thin lips. Coils of yellow saliva dribbled onto its hairless chest. 'He is ours, old woman. He walked willingly into our domain.'

'He is not yours,' Nano Hayes said firmly.

'He is ours under law,' the creature hissed. 'Ours to keep, ours to eat.'

'You made the law.'

'It is a natural law.'

Nano Hayes shook her head firmly. 'To eat the flesh of another human being has always been against the natural law. You justify your cannibalism because you broke the natural law and fed off your own kind, the humankind. And what did it make you? What are you now, you remnants of a once-proud race? You are creatures of darkness, neither man nor beast, not fully of this world, nor part of the Otherworld. With every soul you take in this manner you condemn yourselves to wander on the borderlands between the worlds.'

The creature straightened and moved away from the human body. Walking up to the edge of the grass circle it stared out at Nano Hayes, its eyes black and fathomless. 'You have knowledge, old woman. Knowledge enough to call us forth, to give us a physical existence in this world. But you have not the knowledge to control us, to tame us . . . you cannot make us give up this morsel.'

'There is no need for you to do this. You do not have the capacity to feel hunger. Why do you persist in taking human souls?'

The creature laughed, a terrifying bearing of its teeth. 'For all your knowledge, you are ignorant.'

'Then enlighten me.'

The creature jabbed at the woman, the very tip of its black fingernail brushing the edge of the circle. A tendril of grey smoke curled up into the night air, and the creature jerked its finger back. 'We are the last of the Partholonians. When the plague took this land, it destroyed all the food, not only the livestock, but also the fruits and grains. When we had eaten our stores there was nothing left. But we were a proud people, a defiant race and determined to survive. We piled up the bodies of the dead . . . and we ate their flesh to survive. We still eat the flesh to survive, only now it is our spirits which we keep alive. We need these unwary humans; their flesh and blood, their souls, their essence give us another chance to exist for a little while.'

Nano Hayes leaned on her stick and looked into the creature's huge eyes. 'The Partholonians are no more. Even their name is almost forgotten now. The races which followed yours to this land, the Nemedians, the Tuatha De

Danann, the Fir Bolg, and the Milesians have replaced you. It is time to let go.'

'Never,' the Partholonian hissed. He turned his back on the woman. 'We will consume this creature and live again for a little while.'

'You said you were a proud people,' the woman said softly.

'We were. We are.'

'You do your race no honour by this practice. I have always thought the Partholonians the proudest of the peoples who came to Erin. But what image do you leave me: foul cannibals stealing flesh and souls from the humankind so that they can snatch a few moments of shadow-life.' She shook her head quickly. 'It is time to let go, to move on, to leave this plain of existence.'

The creature shook its head, but the movement was uncertain.

'A man said once, that a single deed can make a great nation. . .'

' . . . and a foul deed undo it,' the creature finished. 'That was Partholon, Lord of the Partholonians.'

'Then do the single great deed. Relinquish the boy, destroy forever the last of the Hungry Grass. Make the Partholonian name great again.'

'We were great once,' the creature said wistfully.

'You can be great again.' Nano Hayes gestured right and left. 'Let these men leave here with the knowledge that the Partholonian people were proud and honourable, give this man back his son. Let them tell others of the greatness of your people, and by their very telling, return your race to their former glory.'

The creature shuffled forward and hunched over the body of the naked young man. Then it glanced up at Nano

Hayes, huge eyes flicking left and right at Blackburn and Mortimore. 'They would do this?'

'They would,' she said firmly.

'Then so be it. I will instruct my people to lift the curse off the Hungry Grass.' The creature was suddenly insubstantial, losing definition and detail as it spoke.

'Wait,' Nano Hayes called. 'Give me your name so that I may tell others about the last of the Partholonians.'

'Once I was Brechan, the son of Partholon of Scythia,' the creature said and vanished.

Nano Hayes slumped and would have fallen had Dr Mortimore not caught her. She looked at Henry Blackburn and waved her hand forward. 'Go, get your son.'

As the big man ran across the marshy ground, the doctor eased Nano Hayes back to a flat stone. 'What have we just seen?' he asked quietly.

'The death of a curse, the end of a legend.'

CHAPTER TWELVE

The Standing Stone

♣

Standing in the centre of a field no farmer ever attempted to plough, the stone thrust upward from the earth like a grey and pitted finger pointing accusingly at the sky. The field was bordered by a great, gnarled hedge of twisted hawthorn, normally the preferred nesting site of countless birds, but no birds nested in the hedge surrounding the standing stone, no streaks of spattered white stained the ancient granite. The soft earth surrounding the stone was smooth, unmarked by spoor or marks of animals or insects.

When Jacinta Farrell first saw the stone, she was startled by the almost palpably grim aura that flowed from it; how could a simple shaft of rock project such an intensity of feeling, she wondered.

That night she mentioned it to her brother, Gerry. 'It gave me the strangest feeling,' she tried to explain, as she laid out the cups and saucers on the chequered cloth. 'I actually wanted to turn and run away, and I don't even know why.'

'I do,' Gerry Farrell snapped. He was becoming

increasingly tired of his sister's constant emotional outbursts. 'You never wanted to move to Louth in the first place and you're looking for things to dislike about the place.'

Jacinta's thin lips whitened. The accusation stung, because there was more than a grain of truth in it. 'That isn't true! You know I appreciate all that you've done for me, all you've sacrificed . . . including the move here.'

'Would you rather have stayed in Cork and let everyone know you were going to have a baby – and you with no husband?'

Jacinta's face flamed red. 'Of course not. I wouldn't have been able to live with the shame of it. The move was the best thing to do, I know that. At least we're strangers here and if I say I'm widowed, people will believe me.'

'I hope so,' her brother told her. He tugged his pocket watch and flipped open the top, squinting in the dim lamplight to read the time. Jacinta took the hint and disappeared back into the tiny kitchen.

Gerry relaxed when she left the room. In truth, he was glad to leave Cork himself. The shop had been fading fast, it had maybe a month or six weeks left in it before it collapsed beneath the weight of debts. This wasn't the first time he had lost a business, but he'd always been able to use the money their late father had left Jacinta and himself to pay off the debts. But that money was gone now. He owed far too many people money, and some of them weren't too particular about how they collected it. This move across Ireland to a new county and a new life with a new surname would mean a fresh start for them both.

Unfortunately, as he knew all too well, Ireland was a small country and everyone knew everyone, or knew someone who did. There was always a chance that their past might catch up with them, but people would be looking for a bankrupt shopkeeper and his spinster sister. By that time he hoped they'd have established themselves as a successful small shopkeeper who was supporting his widowed sister and her child. Although they had talked about adoption and she had tentatively agreed, he knew that once Jacinta held the babe in her arms she would never give it up for adoption. There were times when Gerry found it very easy to dislike his sister, times when he actively hated her. She was two years younger than him, with broad, peasant features, framed by coarse, greying hair. Jacinta looked like a spinster . . . or a widow. She certainly didn't look like the type of woman who would become pregnant by a total stranger at thirty-three. But she had always been foolish and wilful.

Now here she was with this story about a stone in a field that frightened her! A pregnant woman's fears. 'Stay away from the field,' he shouted back into the kitchen. 'Don't go near it again. Are you listening to me?'

'I'm listening,' Jacinta sighed.

Jacinta meant to follow his advice. But when Gerry set off each morning to walk the three miles into the village to open the tiny shop he'd purchased with the last of their money, she found herself alone in an empty cottage with the day stretching before her. Walking was a relief and the doctor had told her that she needed plenty of exercise. And on the winding country roads of County Louth, it seemed that her feet brought her, again and again, to that one particular field where the standing stone waited.

'Drawing me,' she told herself on one occasion, her voice sounded flat on the morning air . . . and that sparked an idea at the back of her mind. Drawing.

Since she could not avoid the stone, she finally got up enough courage to enter the field by way of a sagging iron gate in the hedge. Although most such farm gates were fastened in some way, a hook of wire or length of looped rope, this one had nothing, and its hinges squealed, rust flaking away, as if it hadn't been opened in a long time.

Jacinta walked cautiously across the uneven ground. She was six-months pregnant now, becoming heavy and clumsy. It had not yet begun to move in her, and she occasionally woke from terrified dreams in which she believed it was dead. And sometimes, late at night, lying alone and cold in her bed, she wished it were . . . only immediately to feel guilty, and then she would pray for the child to be born healthy, a strong, dark-haired, dark-eyed boy, the image of his father. No, not a male then, a lying, cheating, conniving male, who preyed on lonely women and then abandoned them. Maybe the child would be a girl.

Jacinta stopped in front of the stone. From a distance, its surface seemed smooth, almost polished, but now she was close, she saw it was pitted and scored. It was deeply gouged for most of its length, as if it had been savagely hacked by a blade or struck with an iron bar. Hairline cracks radiated from these gouges, creating the merest suggestion of countless tiny images on the stone's surface. As she was walking around the stone, she realised what she was seeing. Faces. Eyes and foreheads, noses and mouths, open, gaping mouths. And as the clouds crawled across the sun, shadows moving, flickering, she watched the faces take on an expression of extreme malevolence.

She stepped backwards . . . and then, for a single instant, she thought she heard a sound like a baby's soft cooing.

Jacinta turned, looking around the field. Doves? But no, the sound was definitely that of a child, a new-born baby's gentle gurgling.

'What did you do today?' Gerry asked, when he returned late in the evening, a hint of whiskey on his breath.

'Walked,' she said shortly. His dinner had congealed to a greasy mess hours ago. She was tempted to dish it up to him, but she knew he was capable of violence when he had a few drinks in him. When she first told him she was pregnant, he had beaten her so badly she hadn't been able to leave the house for a week.

'Where did you go?'

'Nowhere in particular,' she snapped, and then she added, 'I'm tired, I'm going to bed.'

'Must be all that walking,' he grinned drunkenly.

Next day, it rained, a cold, slanting rain that kept her indoors. Jacinta stood at the windows watching rain twist and sneak down the heavy glass, and was surprised when she realised that she was seriously thinking about heading out for a walk. Shaking her head at her own foolishness, she went into her bedroom and spent the next fifteen minutes looking for her sketchpad, abandoned since she left art class, when she realised that her young lover, who also attended the classes, had forsaken her.

Her thin, white fingers lifted a stub of charcoal and traced the outline of the standing stone on the thick, creamy paper. Then, as if with a will of their own, her hands moved, sketching a few dim figures hovering around the stone, amorphous shapes without any clear definition.

Jacinta looked down at what she had drawn, curious,

slightly frightened – the stone had been sketched in surprising detail, a talent she never realised she possessed. Somehow, she was not surprised she had chosen that image.

Next day it was cloudy, but there was no rain. Jacinta waited impatiently until her brother had left for the shop, then immediately set out for her walk. Wrapped in her shawl, she hurried along the winding country road as if she had somewhere important to go. There was now a briskness in her step that had not been there before, a sense of purpose she had lost when she discovered she was pregnant.

When she reached the field she pushed open the rusting gate without hesitation and strode across the rough ground to the stone. Once there, however, she was suddenly uncertain, confused as to why she had come. Twice she reached out as if to touch the stone with her fingers, but drew back before her flesh brushed the cold granite.

The third time she allowed her fingers to rest on the roughened rock. At once she heard the sound again, the small, infantile cooing, distant, but distinct.

For a long time the woman stood beside the standing stone, just touched it lightly with her fingers, her eyes closed, head tilted to one side, listening . . . listening . . . listening.

Thereafter, every day for the remaining three months of her pregnancy, Jacinta visited the stone, no matter what the weather. She never told her brother.

With the passage of days, she heard more voices at the stone. The soft cooing was joined by fretful whimpers, little moans, small gurgles, all the sounds of infancy. It was like being in a room full of babies. Resting her hands on her bloated stomach she listened and imagined that there were hundreds of lonely ghost babies somehow trapped in the stone, waiting to get out as her baby was trapped in her, waiting for its freedom.

As she focused on the stone, she stopped thinking altogether of the young man in her art class. His image faded completely from her mind, to be replaced by the grim, grey figure of the standing stone.

The stone began to occupy her every waking moment and when she slept it was there in her dreams. The dreams were always the same. She was naked, both hands locked beneath her heavy belly as she stood before the stone. And the stone was now smooth, the faces and images in the rock had vanished. In her dreams she saw herself reaching out to brush the stone, and it felt smooth and silky to her touch . . . like flesh. The childish giggling and gurgling would swell, and then small shadowy childlike forms would be gathered around her, spilling out from behind the rock. Their tiny hands were soft on her skin as they stroked her legs, arms and belly. Once – twice – she thought she caught the glimpse of white teeth, but when she looked closely, they had vanished and, try as she might, she couldn't make out the children's faces. Because they were children, she knew that instinctively, long-dead children who had never known a mother.

Until now.

Gerry Farrell was unaware of the change in his sister's behaviour, her long silences, her dreamy state, although he did remark that she seemed happy and content. Obviously pregnancy agreed with her, and he was happy for her . . . happy, too, that business in the shop began to improve noticeably.

Every day Jacinta visited the stone, touched its rough

surface with her fingers, listened to the sounds she heard, dreamt increasingly vivid dreams where the line between fantasy and reality blurred until she was occasionally unsure which was the dream: this world, this petty life or her role as mother to the shadow-children. Every day, before she left the stone, she embraced it, wrapping her arms around it, hugging it close.

And every day brought more and more people into her brother's shop.

The pain, the sudden, clutching spasms shattered her dreams and brought her awake. They caught her again, deep in the pit of her stomach, lancing down into her thigh. The agony clamped an iron band around her chest, forcing the air from her lungs, so that she couldn't even call out to her brother in the next room. When the pain passed and she could breath again, she opened her mouth to call out ... and then stopped. Maybe it was just indigestion – too much bacon with the chicken, and Gerry had said the potatoes hadn't been properly cooked.

'If it happens again, I'll call him,' she said aloud into the darkened room. Five minutes later she was asleep.

In the morning she felt fine. She waved her brother goodbye, and stood in the doorway and waited until he had disappeared from sight around the bend in the road. She forced herself to wait another few moments until she was sure he had gone, then pulled the door closed behind her and set off down the road.

She was in her ninth month now and her swollen belly meant she could move only slowly. As she made her way to the field she felt the suggestion of pain again in the pit of her stomach. She stopped twice to catch her breath, but she never thought about turning back. She had to get to the stone . . . to the children.

As she pushed open the rusty gate, sudden pain lanced through her body, doubling her over, and for an instant her mind was clear. She was frightened. What was she doing here, in the middle of nowhere? The pain caught her again. 'Is it the baby?' she said aloud, her voice flat on the morning air. 'Is it the baby?' She turned to look back at the gate. She was going to turn back, she didn't want to be caught so far from home if it was the child coming . . .

Then she heard the sounds from the stone. No soft cooing this time, but loud wails, the crying of a multitude of infants, lost and frightened, crying for their mother. . .

Jacinta straightened and hurried across the field towards the stone. She wasn't dreaming now . . . but she could actually see amorphous shapes flowing from the stone, moving to meet her, swirling around her. Tiny, cool hands touched her body, moved smoothly across her flesh, plucked at her dress, while others pushed her from behind, propelling her forward. She stumbled, tried to stop, but the pressure from behind was too great. A dim thread of panic laced through her brain. . .

'Hello? Hello?' Gerry pushed open the door and stopped when he realised it was empty. 'Jacinta?'

Digging in his waistcoat pocket he pulled out his pocket watch and checked the time. Ten minutes to eight. Where was she? Maybe she'd gone down into the town to look for him. He had intended closing up for lunch and coming back to check on his sister, but today had been the busiest so far – he'd even sold out of some items – and he hadn't had the opportunity.

He grew alarmed when he moved into the kitchen and discovered that there was nothing cooking on the stove and the breakfast dishes remained on the kitchen table.

The baby. The baby must have arrived.

Well, they'd planned for this day. As soon as she even suspected that the baby was coming, she was going to head for the O'Reillys, their nearest neighbour. He was smiling as he walked the quarter-mile down the road to the farm house. She'd probably had the baby hours ago.

But Jacinta wasn't at the O'Reillys and they hadn't seen her all day.

Nor had she been to the doctors, or the local midwife.

When the police arrived, they conducted a thorough search of the fields and farms surrounding the cottage. She'd probably gone out for a walk and was simply too exhausted to return, the sergeant consoled Gerry.

'I've had seven. I know the sort of peculiar things pregnant women do. You should rest now, try and get some sleep, we'll continue looking until we find her. And don't worry, she'll be fine,' he added with a confidence he did not feel.

But Gerry refused to rest and continued searching through the night, bullseye lamp bobbing over the fields, his voice becoming hoarse and ragged as he called aloud her name.

At dawn, exhausted, almost asleep on his feet, though still determined, he was leading a small group of neighbours down a narrow country lane, when he noticed that a rusty gate leading into a field was standing ajar. He had been long enough in the country to know that all gates should be locked and was just reaching over to pull it closed when he noticed the stone, rising out of the morning mist.

The standing stone.

Hadn't Jacinta spoken about a standing stone. . .?

As he stepped into the field, he noticed the figure lying at its foot like a pile of discarded clothing.

He was screaming as he ran across the field, a mixture of triumph and fear.

Jacinta Farrell was alive; that is, her body was alive. Her mind was gone. For the rest of her days, there would only be one image in her brain and she would never be able to communicate it to anyone, though she tried in a constant, maddening, incomprehensible babble.

And no one ever discovered what had happened to the child in her womb. It was gone as if it had never existed.

And the terrified local people never gave Gerry Farrell any believable explanation as to why the fissures of the standing stone were running red with blood.

CHAPTER THIRTEEN

The Bog Road

♣

In the far wilds of Connemara, close to the sea where the peaks of the Twelve Bens dominate the skyline, there is a lonely bog.

Time rests heavily upon the ancient boglands, and all bogs seem lonely, but this one is exceptionally so. Yet it is a lovely place, a watercolourist's dream. Wildflowers bloom in profusion, yellow and blue and delicate pink. In its season, bog-cotton covers the surface of the bog with fluffy white balls like the high puffy clouds reflected in the still water of bog-pools. A heron cries; a lark sings.

All is peace and tranquillity.

Or so it seems.

A single narrow road winds its way through the bog. Once it was used by the local turf cutters, but the roadway is sinking and derelict now, for no one ventures into the bog for their fuel any more. Though it costs money – which is scarce in these parts – the local people would rather buy bags of coal in the town than take their share of the traditional fuel provided in the bog. If pressed, they will say that the bog has a reputation. If pushed, they will admit that something exists in the heart of the dark boglands, something that too many have seen.

The White Spectres of the Bog Road.

The story took hold in the last years of the last century, but its roots went deeper, back into a distant, pagan past.

Thomsie Duggan was the first to admit that he had actually seen something on the road. The broad-shouldered young man was neither fool nor braggart, so when he spoke in the local pub, a silence fell, until his was the only voice in the gloom.

'There's a white creature on the bog road.' The big man shivered, though the room was hot and still. 'I've seen it. Tall and thin, so thin it would have had to stand twice to make a shadow. But it cast no shadow, in spite of the setting sun behind it. No shadow at all.' He finished his drink in one long swallow. 'I was coming back from the north bog with Mick and Donal when we saw it . . . didn't we, lads?' He looked at his two companions.

Big Mick hitched his belt higher. 'Aye, well, I reckon we did see something, but it was no tall wraith I saw, but a twisting ball of shivering lights.'

Donal brushed his hair out of his eyes with quick, nervous gestures. 'I saw neither,' he said quietly. 'But I did see a tall dark figure that beckoned me with evil, obscene gestures. I heard it too,' he added in a whisper, 'and it was crackling.'

Three spectres. At the same time, on the same road, appearing to three different men who were walking together.

There was no explanation. The old people of the region had never heard of ghosts on the bog road before. There were not even stories of people who had wandered into the bog and disappeared, though such tales were very common with most bogs. This one had always seemed unusually innocent.

But that innocence was over.

Within a month, Tom Bawn, the carter, travelling the bog road with a load for delivery to the nearest village, was almost killed when his horse shied violently. It flung itself sideways against the shafts of the cart, then bolted off the road, dragging the unbalanced cart after it. Not ten paces from the road the horse sank up to its shoulders in a bog-pool. Within minutes it was drowned, and the cart dragged down with it. The terrified driver barely escaped with his life.

'I've never seen a horse so frightened in all my days,' Tom Bawn reported afterwards to the silent bar-room. 'This mare wasn't just frightened – she was terrified. The eyes had rolled clear back in the poor brute's head until only the whites were showing. And screaming! Screaming like a woman in bad childbirth. But there was nothing at all to see,' he added, totally mystified. 'The day was clear and cloudless, and it was two in the afternoon.'

From that day on stories began to circulate about the bog road. No two tales were the same. Every traveller had a different experience. This only added to the superstitious fear which soon kept folk from the bog.

Each new sighting added fuel to the fires of fear. A man searching for a stray cow reported a tumbling black cloud that came rolling down the bog road straight towards him, in the middle of a sunny day.

' 'Twas not more than a couple of feet above ground,' Rory claimed, 'and there was a roaring coming from it such as I never heard. Turned my back and ran, I did. I heard the animal screaming behind me.' Rory shuddered. He would never forget the animal's wailing as long as he lived.

There was no explanation for the black cloud, and it was never seen again.

Each apparition appeared once, to one person, and never again.

In time the bog was universally shunned. Cottagers living along its borders put heavy shutters over the windows on the bogside of their house, and the few who could afford to do so, moved away to live with relatives at a distance from the place.

The others who could not move resented the intrusion of the apparitions into the homeland their people had occupied for generations. But there was nothing anyone could do. The ghosts – if ghosts they were – were such random and unconnected visitations they could not even be given a name. 'The bog road' came to be a term applying not only to the setting, but to the hauntings.

At some stage an exasperated parent threatened to take a naughty child out 'to the bog road', and from then on it was used to control children, its notoriety spreading beyond Connemara to become a part of Connaught folklore.

Priests of either denomination walked the road and prayed upon it, attempting to exorcise whatever demons now possessed it. But they all failed. Some were even driven from the road by their own personal spectres.

Years passed, and the bog road was left to whatever haunted it. Inevitably, from time to time some stranger who did not know the legends found himself, or herself, on its muddy surface, and would arrive some time later at the nearest house or village with a white face and staring eyes.

The legends grew: a shower of blood falling from a cloudless sky, a headless figure in a flowing robe, the sound of a woman sobbing as if her heart would break, a herd of stampeding horses, insubstantial as cobwebs but terrifying in their hysteria.

The list of spectres went on and on.

A few months after the Easter Rising in 1916, a traveller who wandered on to the Bog Road by mistake even claimed to have seen the ghost of the martyred leaders of the rising, Pearse and Connolly and Clarke and MacDermott, all walking together side by side down the road.

Seen once, never again.

The bog road remains in Connemara, cutting through the rich, brown peatland where still pools reflect the sky. No one travels it now.

No one living.

CHAPTER FOURTEEN

Summer Solstice

♣

In all the years that Maura Malone had loved Patrick Hanrahan, she had never known how he felt about her. Their eyes sometimes met at Mass, and once or twice he smiled at her on the high street and wished her a good morning . . . but so did everyone else in the small town. His life went one way and hers another, or so it seemed.

Society and pride would not allow Maura to make the first move, so she was forced to watch him from afar, and listen greedily to the few scraps of gossip that came her way.

'He's trying to make a go of the farm since his father died. He's on his own now.'

'Did you hear – he went up to Dublin, and spent a whole weekend there? Probably a woman.'

'I hear tell he's been walking out with one of the Deering sisters. The eldest one. You know her. The spinster: she'd be twenty-five now.'

The last piece of gossip hurt Maura Malone deeply, though she knew she had no right to be hurt, she had no claim on Patrick. She found herself watching him intently, looking for any sign that he had changed and assumed the air of a man about to be wed. She was barely civil to Sheila Deering, but Maura was such a private person that no one noticed.

Like most small town gossip, however, it went the round for a few weeks, then died away when another, even juicier piece of scandal came around.

Maura breathed a sigh of relief. There was still a chance.

And then the day came when their eyes met as they passed in the street. Something sparked between them, tangible, palpable, and this time neither looked away.

That evening Patrick Hanrahan called at her cottage with a sackful of vegetables. Maura invited him in for supper. If he noticed that she had prepared enough for two, he said nothing.

The weeks and months that followed were like a glorious dream. Patrick was everything Maura had imagined, tender and ardent, and when he asked her to marry him, on bended knee with cap twisting nervously in hand, she said yes so quickly he hardly had time to complete his proposal.

'Before you say yes,' the big man said slowly, choosing his words carefully, 'you should know that the farm is not doing well. I'm not the farmer my father was, I haven't the gift for knowing the exact moment when to sow and when to reap. I've lost some animals to disease and a few more to predators.'

Maura leaned forward on the straight-backed kitchen chair. 'So what are you saying?' she asked gently.

'I'm telling you that it's not grand living I'm offering you. You shan't want for love,' he promised, 'but you may have to turn your hems and mend my coats.' He touched her tiny feet in their high-buttoned boots. 'You may not see another pair of these for a long time.'

'But I'll see you every day. I'll be there by your side every hour of every day. That's enough for me. Now, you must say no more of it. In six months time we shall be wed, and you will make me the happiest woman in all Ireland.'

However, Patrick desperately wanted Maura to have everything. He began driving himself harder, desperate to make a success of the farm before he met Maura on their wedding day. He worked from before dawn until long after dark; pushing himself to exhaustion, scrimping and saving every penny. When a repair was needed to the cottage he undertook to do it himself rather than bringing in one of the village tradesmen.

On the day before their wedding, he climbed up onto the roof of the cottage to replace a couple of the slate tiles that had shifted out of position and were allowing water into the bedroom. It had never bothered him before, but as he lay in bed the previous night, he had suddenly realised that he would be sharing it from now on.

But the tiles were wet and the rafters rotten, eaten through by moisture. When Patrick put his weight on them, he felt them shift and give. Scrabbling desperately, he failed to find a handhold on the damp tiles and slid off the roof. It was only a single-storey cottage and he should have broken an arm or a leg, or maybe cracked a few ribs. But Patrick Hanrahan snapped his neck when he hit the ground, and died instantly.

The accident almost destroyed Maura. She wore her wedding dress continuously for a month until it was nothing more than a filthy rag, and then one morning she rose from her bed, stripped off the soiled dress and burned it on a blazing bonfire outside her cottage.

Then she started to put her life back together.

They had made so many plans together, it was hard to believe they had all ended in an untimely grave.

Maura tortured herself thinking of the cottage he had promised to build for her, and the furnishings she had planned for it. She dreamed of her unborn children, whose very names she knew. Her life as a married woman spread out before her like a promise and she could not give it up. She would not give it up. It had become too real to her.

She *would* have a husband.

Maura had loved Patrick since childhood, and the habit was very deep in her. It would not be easy, she knew, to transfer her affections to some other man, and he would never, ever, replace Patrick. Those few months with Patrick, however, had taught her the comfort of real love, taught her the depths of her loneliness.

The date they had set for their wedding had been the summer solstice.

'Midsummer. The best time for a farmer,' Patrick had explained. So, when a year of mourning had passed, after the next solstice, Maura forced herself to return to the land of the living and began going to dances, meeting people, returning smiles in the high street. They were not Patrick's, but she returned them.

Yet she could not shake off the feeling of somehow being unfaithful to him each time she did.

He still seemed very close to her. Each morning when she awoke, she automatically spoke his name into the silent bedroom; 'Patrick.'

But the seasons were kind. As they passed, they gradually softened the intensity of her feeling, so that the spoken name became more of a habit than a ritual.

Around the time of her twenty-eighth birthday, Maura Malone began longing in earnest for the wedding she never had and the future she felt was her due. The years were passing; if she was to have a family, she must soon begin. She smiled more often in the high street. She danced more frantically at the dances.

She had never been a pretty girl, and she became plainer as she matured. When she watched the younger, prettier women vying for the attention of the men in the dance halls, she realised that few of them asked her to dance, and that those who did were the rejects, those who were either too old or too foul to catch the attentions of the younger women.

A certain frenzy seized her then. When she said 'Patrick' every morning it was no longer a fond salutation, it was rather a desperate screech, a curse, a plea for help.

When the tinkers came through the town, Maura was one of a number of women who visited the withered old woman who sat apart from the others and whispered fortunes and gave advice in return for a coin.

Maura Malone's question was simple. 'How do I find a husband?'

The tinker woman wheezed delightedly. She had spent her entire life on the roads of Ireland . . . and this was the question lonely women, and sometimes men, always asked.

'What month is this?' she whispered.

Maura frowned. 'June.'

'This is solstice month. You know what the solstice is, child?' the old woman asked quickly.

'I know. Midsummer.'

The old woman grinned toothlessly. 'More than that. It is a magic time, a time when the year hangs in the balance. If you wish to see the face of your husband, you must read a mirror.'

Maura shook her head. 'I don't know what. . .'

'It's simple, child. On midsummer's eve, place a lighted candle before a mirror in your bedroom. Then turn your back on the mirror and quickly look over your left shoulder. If you see a face in the mirror other than your own, then you will lie in that man's marital embrace on the following midsummer's eve.'

Maura pressed the coin into the woman's hand. 'And it never fails?'

'Never.'

Waiting the four days until midsummer was an agony of suspense. The days lengthened with the approach of the solstice, until the twilight lasted most of the night.

On midsummer eve, Maura tidied the bedroom and spread a new coverlet on the bed. Lighting a new beeswax candle she placed it before the sparkling mirror, then took a deep breath and turned her back on the mirror. She was facing the bedroom, empty, so lonely. The great white bed so chaste, so cold.

'Not another year,' she said in a soft, despairing voice. 'Not another year like this. Please.'

It was almost a prayer.

Then slowly, deliberately, she looked over her left shoulder.

And saw nothing but her own reflection.

Then, in the misty depths of the mirror, a figure seemed to form. Maura's heart started to pound. Her eyes widened. The figure drew closer, resolved itself into a recognisable human form. Broad shoulders. A shock of unruly hair. Bright green eyes. Someone familiar. Someone she knew. . .

The face became clear.

It was the face of Patrick Hanrahan.

Maura's screams rang through the house again and again.

By the time the alarmed neighbours reached the bedroom, it was too late. Maura Malone lay dead on the carpet in front of her mirror.

The doctor who signed the death certificate attested that Maura Malone had died of heart failure, the result of a previously undiagnosed heart condition.

He dated the certificate 21 June. The summer solstice.

CHAPTER FIFTEEN

The Priest

♣

The young priest stood at the open window, gazing out across the green fields of Tipperary. The golden sunlight of late summer slanted across his face, highlighting its sharp planes and turning his colourless eyes into yellow mirrors. People often commented on Father Michael's strange eyes, which were more like alabaster than human irises, giving him the appearance of one who was blind, but his eyesight was excellent.

As he stood by the window, he was looking at the distant spire of a church in a village miles away. The village itself was hidden in a deep valley and only the spire, rising like an accusatory finger to the early morning sky, indicated the location of the house of God below. The bishop's voice rose querulously, bringing the young priest's attention back to the present.

'And so, my son, we have regretfully decided you are not yet ready for a parish of your own. I know your hopes had been raised, but they must be deferred for a time. One of the many lessons we all learn in this life is patience.'

The young man continued to stare at the faraway

steeple for a few moments, then turned and faced his bishop. 'Why?' he asked bluntly.

Bishop McCabe sighed. Such a question, spoken almost challengingly, was proof enough that Father Michael Casside did not yet possess the qualities of humility and obedience necessary for a parish priest. Folding his hands together, he began to explain the reasons why the young priest had been passed over – again.

'How long before I can have my own parish?' the young man interrupted. 'I'm strong, I have commitment and energy. . .'

'That, I fear, is part of the problem,' Bishop McCabe told him. 'You have almost too much strength and energy. If I may speak frankly, you are like a caged tiger. Look at you now: pacing up and down the room, glancing out the window, your thoughts undoubtedly leaping here and there. My fellow bishops and I sense a hunger in you that is far too great to settle for the quiet life of a rural parish priest.' He stopped and added softly. 'I fear the inactivity would destroy you . . . or lead you into unfortunate habits.'

Father Michael's nostrils flared. 'Then what do you propose to do with me? You must admit I excelled in my theological studies. I was not driven into the priesthood by my family, nor chose it as a soft option because I could find no other employment. I *wanted* to be a priest; I have a true vocation.'

'I agree, you do,' the bishop nodded. 'But we have yet to discover just how God intends to make use of your, ah, special qualities. We will all pray for God to guide you.'

'And how long will that take?' the young priest snapped.

Bishop McCabe's voice hardened. 'As long as it takes.'

'And what do I do until then?'

'You will stay here under my guidance and tutelage. You will take the position of my librarian. I need someone working full time right now to catalogue the vast theological collection bequeathed to the church by the Browne family.'

'Catalogue books?' Father Michael's mouth twisted sourly. 'Is that all I'm good for?'

'I did not say that, my son. I merely said it was best if you satisfy yourself with the work for now. Perhaps it will give you an opportunity to curb your impulsive nature and achieve the inner serenity you still lack. Only then can you be of use to some parish.' The bishop stood, effectively ending the interview. He extended his hand and the young priest knelt to kiss the ornate ring of office.

Father Michael Casside strode down the long echoing corridor, hands clasped behind his back. Through the leaded windows to his left, he could see flashes of the distant spire of the town. He knew that town had a need for a new parish priest. And he was ready, more than ready to serve the community. It was painful to be denied his opportunity to prove himself. And now he was forced to remain here – under the bishop's eye – cataloguing books. A clerk's duties. The young priest breathed deeply, his broad chest swelling, as he attempted to control his temper.

So. He was to be the bishop's librarian. It was a minor position, certainly, but at least the Browne collection contained a great amount of material on local history and folklore, culled by three generations of the Brownes. The priest smiled tightly: Bishop McCabe was no fool, he knew Michael Casside's interest in history and lore, knew he would become so interested in reading and researching through the books and manuscripts that he would soon forget his anger.

But he wanted to be more than just a clerk. A lot more. He just didn't know what.

What am I to do with my life? As he turned into his small room, he slammed the door hard enough to rock it on its hinges, and then drove his fist into the solid wall. Plaster crackled and crumbled to dust.

Strength pulsed through his body; a terrible surging energy that demanded an outlet. ... before it destroyed him.

Standing before the window, resting his hot forehead against the cool glass, he remembered the precise moment almost superhuman power had come to him. It had flooded his body, surging through his heart and soul when the witch-woman called Sorcha had sacrificed his twin brother, Peter. Using a spell that was almost older than mankind, the witch had intended to redirect Peter's energies into his twin brother, then take control of Michael herself. Had her plan succeeded, she would have created a man containing the life-force of two within the body of one . . . and then she would have used his body and elemental strength to work very powerful magic. (See 'The Lovers' Reward', *Irish Folk & Fairy Tales Omnibus*, Warner Books.)

But Michael had escaped her. Horrified by what she had done to Peter, he had fled as far as he could from the arms of the beautiful witch-woman. The church had provided a refuge . . . and the means for him to preach against the dangers of the old witchcraft.

He had never told any of this to his confessors, his teachers, or his bishop. The omission was a sin on his conscience, but he was afraid it might in some way discredit him. If his superiors thought him mad, he would be sent to one of the distant enclosed orders and spend the rest of his days doing menial work. Besides, this was the modern, enlightened nineteenth century . . . and Ireland had never been caught up in the witchcraft mania that had convulsed Europe; there had never been witches in Ireland.

But there were witches in Ireland. They were called wise-women and herb doctors, and a dozen other quaint names, but he knew them for what they were: witches and warlocks, intent on destroying the church and corrupting the faithful . . . as his brother had been corrupted and destroyed by Sorcha.

He wondered where the witch was now. He was certain she was still plying her wicked trade somewhere in the land . . . but they would meet again one day. He swore it.

But until then, he was destined to spend his time as a librarian.

Sitting at the small oak desk, piled high with red leather-bound cataloguing ledgers, Michael Casside looked around the room at the dozens of boxes. This was going to take years.

'The Brownes were the foremost antiquarians of this century,' the bishop was saying, moving slowly from box to box, picking up a book, glancing at the title and putting it down again. 'For over three generations, they pioneered work into the ancient monuments that litter this land. Do you know,' he said with a cynical smile, 'they have speculated that some of these grassy mounds were once imposing constructions of wood and stone? Ridiculous, isn't it?'

The priest nodded obediently.

The bishop squinted at a sheaf of vellum inscribed in

crabbed Latin. 'The old man and I were quite close,' he continued, 'and often took port together. He theorised that many modern churches are built on the ruins of ancient sites, and that many of our modern holy days are merely pagan feasts renamed.' The bishop dusted off his fingers. 'I will leave you to it, Father Michael.' He paused with his hand on the doorhandle. 'Oh, and if you should come across material which you consider . . . unsuitable, do not catalogue it. Bring it to my rooms, and I will arrange for its disposal later.'

The young priest waited until the bishop's footsteps faded down the long hall and, with a sigh, settled himself to his work. Unsuitable? What did the bishop mean by unsuitable . . . or was he simply warning him that some books did not suit the collection?

Father Michael suddenly grinned. He knew now why he had been assigned to catalogue the collection. An 'unsuitable' book might very well cause the aged cleric who acted as librarian to keel over. The man refused to allow anatomy texts into the library because they showed naked flesh. Rumour had it that he had once removed every picture and engraving of the crucifixion from the bibles because they showed images of Christ's naked body.

Still smiling, he reached deep into the first box and pulled out a book – and then he laughed aloud. The title alone would have given the old librarian apoplexy. It was a detailed and lurid account of witchlore and legend in fifteenth-century Italy, complete with woodcuts of witches at their sabbaths. Initially, he thought it strange that such material had been bequeathed to the Church, but, on reflection, he knew there was no better place than the Church to house the secrets of evil. The Church was committed to rooting out evil, and if it were to succeed, it needed to know the adversary.

'I wonder if this is unsuitable,' Michael murmured, poring over the pages of the tome. Within five minutes he decided that it definitely was. Written by a Franciscan, the book contained detailed accounts of incubi and succubi, foul demons who haunted the sleeping hours of men and women, enticing them with erotic dreams, riveting images of sexual practices beyond his innocent imaginings. He was both fascinated and repulsed. He thought of the witch-woman, Sorcha, again. It was through her sexual attraction that she had enslaved his brother Peter and prepared him for sacrifice. In spite of himself, he felt his own sexuality responding to some of the sensuous images portrayed in the book he was reading.

'God in heaven!' The priest slammed the book down on the desk. 'Get thee behind me, Satan,' he muttered, acutely aware of his heart thumping in his breast, his rapid breathing. He rose and began pacing the floor, his hands behind his back, his colourless eyes troubled. When he had regained control, he returned to his desk and selected another book from the dusty pile. He picked what looked like a theological text. 'Something safe,' he muttered. As his fingers closed on its leather cover, something sparked from the cover, tingling into his fingertips.

The priest dropped the book and stared at it. His fingertips were throbbing, the pads red and swollen. So it hadn't been his imagination.

He moved the book with a pen, pushing it around the desk. It seemed quite ordinary, a slim volume bound in rather brittle leather, with faded gilding on the spine. Stretching out tentatively, he touched the cover with his index finger. Nothing happened. 'Imagination,' he said shakily, sucking his throbbing fingers.

Lifting up the book, he turned it to the light, to read the lettering on the spine. Much of it was rubbed away.

A Full Account of . . . Sight . . . and . . . paritions

Opening the book, he discovered that it was a handwritten notebook in three distinct hands, a journal of local ghostly appearances and other supernatural events begun by William Browne, continued by his son, also called William, with additions by his son, Samuel. Father Michael realised that the complete title had been *A Full Account of Local Sightings and Apparitions*.

'This should be safe enough,' the priest murmured.

Most of the stories in the book were the usual collection: headless horsemen and headless horses, which the priest found rather ludicrous, undead corpses, wailing banshee, werehares and pookas, the sort of stories used to entertain guests at country-house parties of the Anglo-Irish gentry. There were some other, less obvious tales, involving hidden fairy gold, the leprechaun's pot of gold, a reappearance of some of the figures out of ancient legend, Fionn MacCumhal and Cuchulain. They were wry and amusing, and the priest found himself wondering if there were even a grain of truth in them. There was usually the basis of truth in most legends and most folklore had its roots in the real world.

He found the story in the latter half of the book, between an account of a cure for headaches, and a scratchy line drawing of a local high cross. It was written in the hand of William the son, but towards the end of his life when his handwriting had faded almost to illegibility. The word 'warlock' initially caught the priest's attention. Carrying the book to the window, tilting it to the brilliant morning sunlight, he read through it slowly, deciphering the cramped spellings and tortured syntax. When he had read through the brief paragraph twice, he closed the book and turned to look at the church spire of the distant parish across the valley.

William Browne claimed that beneath the church in the local parish was a veritable warren of ancient vaults dating as far back, perhaps, as the coming of the Normans. These vaults were reputed to contain the tomb of the most fully attested male witch, or warlock, ever to stalk the Irish countryside.

Father Michael Casside turned the book to read the name . . . and felt ice settle on the back of his neck and curl down into his spine. The name of that warlock was Ronan Cleirigh – the same surname as Sorcha, the witch who had taken his brother. The priest quickly calculated the dates: Ronan Cleirigh might well have been her grandfather!

Father Michael thought he knew the area and its legends well, yet he had never heard of the warlock in the crypt. Was it possible that the only known mention of the legend was, by some strange coincidence, in the book he held in his hands.

But the priest did not believe in coincidence. Things happened because they were supposed to happen as part of a grand design, God's will. This was one of the tenets of Michael's personal belief. During the long period of grieving for his brother, he had taken comfort from the knowledge that Peter's death must have some meaning that would be revealed to him in time. And he had always had an absolute, unshakable confidence that he would confront the witch again.

'Thou shalt not suffer a witch to live. . .'

Now this clue to Sorcha had been delivered into his hands.

Michael nodded to himself, half smiling, but the smile was cold, cruel. The flickering light of the paraffin oil lamp awoke strange shadows in his colourless eyes. His powerful fingers closed on the cover of the book, the pressure cracking the leather.

Vengeance is mine, sayeth the Lord. . .

Vengeance.

The word snaked through his soul.

'Justice,' he said aloud, but he knew that in this case, justice was just another word for vengeance. He determined to follow this unexpected clue wherever it might lead. The moment the decision was made he felt strength gathering in him, waiting to be used.

The first mystery to be solved was the question of why an unholy warlock had been entombed in the cellars of a Christian church, which was undoubtedly consecrated ground. By custom and all known tradition, such creatures were usually burnt to death or buried at a crossroads with a stake driven through their bodies.

Michael reopened the book . . . and discovered the answer staring up at him. Squinting, he deciphered the crabbed hand. 'So great was the evil power of this man that on the occasion of his death it was believed no grave could hold him. And so his body was secretly entombed in the dead of night, beneath the church itself, so that the full weight of God's house would sit upon him and force him to lie still.'

Added in the margin, in tiny, spidery writing was a single line: 'God grant it had been so. But alas.'

Michael felt the hackles rise on his spine.

'I am delighted, indeed, gratified, to find you have taken to this task with such enthusiasm,' Bishop McCabe said carefully. 'Take as long as you like. You are certain the church records are important?'

'Indeed, I am. Some books in the Browne collection have led me to believe there is information there which is necessary for a full understanding of the collection,' the young priest explained. It was an evasion, but not totally dishonest.

'Go with my blessing.'

The day was one of leaden skies and a pervasive drizzle as the young priest drove towards the village in a creaking, broken-backed cart drawn by the bishop's ancient horse. He had a letter of introduction from the bishop to the aged parish priest, requesting permission for Father Michael to 'examine the vaults with an eye to historical researches'. He also carried with him a leather bag not unlike a doctor's bag, containing a variety of objects which he considered might be of more practical use than a letter of introduction.

His reception by Father O'Brien, the parish priest was frosty, and Michael guessed that the old priest knew that Michael Casside had requested the parish.

After a few minutes polite conversation, Michael passed over the letter and explained. 'I need to examine the records in the vaults.'

The rheumy-eyed parish priest stiffened. 'You want to visit the vaults of St Drostan's? But no one ever goes down there.'

'I have the bishop's permission,' Michael assured him.

'Well, I can't take you,' Father O'Brien snapped.

'The bishop . . .' the young priest started to protest, when the parish priest continued with a cold smile.

'I'm too old and the air is too damp. However, Martin, my sacristan, will help you.' He rang a small bell on the table and the aged sacristan appeared. 'Assist Father

Michael,' Father O'Brien said curtly and opened his bible, concluding the interview.

As they left Father O'Brien's bare chamber, Father Michael explained to the sacristan that he wanted to be taken to the vaults.

The old man was horrified. 'I've taken no one to the vaults in many years.' He shook his head firmly. 'I cannot take you there. It's not safe.'

The young priest drew himself up to his full height, towering over the sacristan. Taking a deep breath he swallowed the anger bubbling within him and when he spoke to the old man again, his voice was barely above a whisper. 'You will take me there. Now!' he said calmly.

Martin looked into the priest's implacable eyes, and all but fled down the corridor and out into the early-morning sunlight. A small graveyard separated the priest's house from the church, generations of local families buried beneath the poor soil. The sacristan made his way through the listing gravestones, along a well-worn path. However, instead of following the track around to the front of the church, he turned off to the right and stopped outside a narrow wooden door set into the west wall. His hand trembled as he searched for the key amongst the bundle on his ring. Cold, damp air wafted out as he pulled the door open.

'This leads down to the vaults,' he said, making no move to step onto the deeply grooved stone steps that led into the darkness.

Father Michael reached into his bag and pulled out a thick candle. While he was lighting it, Martin continued.

'The vaults are ancient, the floor is uncertain and in places the ceiling is bowed. Some of the local men tried to shore them up with timbers many years ago, but a section of the ceiling caved in and three were badly injured. I'm not sure how safe it is now. There are rats and mice aplenty . . . and the rats are fearless,' he added.

'Anything else I should know?' Father Michael asked, stepping into the narrow passage. Standing on the top step, he watched as the candle flame leaned backwards, blown by a breeze he could not feel.

The old man looked uncomfortable. 'The bishop would not thank me for saying this, nor would Father O'Brien, but you should know that the vaults have an evil reputation.'

'I'm not surprised,' Father Michael muttered.

'People have reported seeing things down there . . . hearing noises.'

'What type of things, what sort of noises?'

'Shapes, shadows, sighs, moans,' the old man said, lowering his voice to a whisper.

'The same could be said of every vault in Ireland.' Father Michael took a step down into the darkness, candlelight puddling around him. 'You can go now. When I finish, I can find my own way out.' Without a backward glance the priest descended into the darkness.

Martin watched until the wavering light had disappeared and the priest's echoing footfalls had faded, then he quickly crossed himself and turned away.

Alone in the vaults below St Drostan's, Michael Casside raised the candle high above his head and slowly turned around, surveying the space. It was low-ceilinged and heavily cobwebbed, with massive stone vaulting that belonged to the earlier construction that had occupied the ground before the church had been built on it. Whatever edifice the vaults had once supported was gone without trace. He passed the section where the ceiling had given way, raising the candle to examine the fingerlike roots of a tree – the ancient oak that grew at the back of the church, he realised – that hung suspended in the air. His strong teeth flashed in a quick grin. No supernatural agency had injured the local men as they worked to repair the roof, simply the relentless pressure of nature.

Wandering deeper into the vaults he was surprised to find that they did not contain, as most such places did, the costly tombs of important local families or clerics. There appeared to be only one tomb under St Drostan's – a stark rectangle of roughly dressed stone thrust far back into the darkest recesses. There was no carved inscription to identify what lay within.

Placing the candle on the floor, the priest approached the tomb. As he neared it, he could feel the chill biting deep into his bones, settling in the pit of his stomach, raising the hairs along the back of his hands.

There was power here, old power, ancient energy. Even before he scraped off the accumulated grime of bat and rodent droppings that coated the tomb, and read the incised inscription of crabbed letters, he knew he was looking at the tomb of the warlock, Ronan Cleirigh.

He paused to open his leather bag. He had spent the previous night consulting some of the books of magic he had found in the Browne collection. By the time the candle had burned down to a pool of tallow and dawn had turned the library windows milk white, he had found what he was looking for: the ritual of exorcism.

The young priest carefully removed the contents of the black bag and arranged them on the ground before him in their prescribed order.

With a piece of chalk, he carefully drew a protective circle on the dusty floor in front of the tomb. He set twelve small, white candles around the perimeter, lit them, then sprinkled the flame of each with a few crumbs from an assortment of tiny bags of herbs.

Grey-white tendrils of bitter-sweet smoke wafted up to the ceiling.

Before he stepped into the protective circle, the priest removed his garments and folded them neatly inside the black bag. Then he used a bottle of holy water to scrub the grime from his face and hands. He had already bathed before he had set out on the journey, but he knew he must carry no dirt into the circle. Naked, he knelt in the centre of it and faced the tomb of the warlock. Raising his hands, he began chanting.

Without a priest's black cassock and Roman collar to identify him, the young priest became simply a naked, well-built young man, anonymous, unremarkable ... except for the power that rippled through him as the chant built in volume, the same power that danced static sparks through his thick, black hair made his muscles twitch beneath his taut flesh.

Michael Casside had never fully surrendered to the power before, never reached out and opened himself to the occult forces the witch Sorcha had awakened in him. Part of him had always been afraid.

And he was afraid now.

But part of him was wildly excited by the sudden leaping of his heart, the racing of blood in his veins, the breathtaking intensity of emotion that caught him in its vortex and swirled him around until his head spun with lights and sounds, his body tingled with sensation.

Was this magic?

Unconsciously his head nodded. This was what people from time immemorial had called magic. Black, white, good, evil ... whatever this feeling was, it was terribly seductive.

Michael Casside tried desperately to hold on to some stable, rational part of himself, to use the forces he had roused rather than letting them use him. Too late he realised the danger and knew that this was a temptation he might not be able to resist. This was *glamour*, in all its strange beauty and infinite mystery. He felt he was standing on the edge of an abyss, in which was contained all the knowledge of the world, and the wind blowing up from the pit was warm and sweet and tempting. All he had to do was to step off.

Was this what Sorcha the witch had felt when she killed his brother?

The thought of Peter dragged Michael shudderingly back from the abyss. The sweet wind turned sour and foul, the pit now threatening rather than inviting. He had to remember why he was here, what he wanted. Squinting his eyes against the smoke that now seemed to be filling the underground vaults, he began making mystic signs with his hands, using symbolism that had been ancient before Christ walked the earth.

'Ronan Cleirigh, I conjure thee! Arise from thy unclean sleep and answer the questions I put to thee!' His voice seemed high and almost childlike in the vaults. Taking a deep breath, he repeated the conjuration.

Nothing happened.

In the long silence that followed the echoes of his voice, Michael experienced agonising doubt. Was he, after all, nothing more than a foolish and deluded man? Was he mad? Had he lost his reason? He knew he had gone mad for a while when the witch had slain his brother. Surely only a madman would be here, naked in a deserted cellar calling upon a long-dead warlock? The very act of trying had probably imperilled his immortal soul. A shiver ran across his shoulders.

Then another. Ice settled like a blanket across his shoulders and chest. He realised they were not natural shudders, but something else, his flesh recoiling from . . .? Throwing back his head, he breathed deeply: the texture and odours of the air had changed, there was a smell of something like salt, like ice, like rotting hay, beginning to override the sweet herbs . . .

The priest's teeth flashed in a quick grin, and all his doubt faded.

Bending his head, he summoned his strength and concentrated, repeating the summoning for the third time. Power surged through him, flooding up from the core of his being. He felt it reach out, heart and mind, body and soul becoming one, felt a thunderclap of joining that shook him violently. He almost lost his balance and tumbled out of the protective circle, but at the last moment he caught himself.

He squeezed his eyes shut as tiny spots of colour danced on his retina.

In that briefest of moments while his eyes were closed, a figure had appeared. When he opened his eyes it was already there, dimly seen in front of the tomb, watching him. A dark, shadowy, almost translucent figure whose insubstantial form pulsed with a dull malignance.

The sight of the creature sickened Michael. Its face was old beyond imagining, the eyes deep sunk into its skull, the mouth collapsed inward, the skin shrivelled and shrunken, stretched taut like paper, allowing the bare bone to show through. It had all the appearance of the long dead . . . except for its eyes, and they had fixed hungrily upon the priest.

Michael Casside's mouth went dry. 'I conjure thee . . .' he whispered hoarsely.

The figure interrupted him with a shocking laugh, the sound of phlegm gurgling in a long-disused throat. 'You need not conjure me, foolish man. I am already here. I have watched you since you came down those stairs. Did you think to take by surprise a man who has not closed his eyes in sleep for a century?'

'Man,' Michael repeated slowly, 'are you a man?'

The figure wavered. For a moment its shimmering outline threatened to collapse. Then it gathered its energies and its form solidified. 'I was. Once. Man . . . and warlock. I was, I am Ronan Cleirigh.'

'And now?' Michael could not help asking.

Again the figure wavered. And the priest got the impression that the creature was in pain. 'Trapped!' it groaned.

Michael was baffled. 'What do you mean?'

'I died unshriven and unmourned. Hated. You see how they have entombed me.' The shape gestured towards the tomb with one skeletal arm. 'Inside that stone lies my rotting body, with a silver cross upon its chest. My soul is unwelcome in heaven and unfree to seek hell. I am just . . . here. A ghost, if you will, but without the freedom of those shades.' There was another burst of sickening laughter. 'And you think to conjure me, as if with your limited power you can bring pressure upon me? With what would you threaten me, human? What could be worse than this?'

He had been prepared to hate this creature, to loathe it as a servant of the evil one, but he couldn't help but feel sorry for it. 'I did not intend to threaten you, merely to force you to help me.'

The shadow form shook its head, its features blurring.

'You can force me to do nothing.' The voice wavered. 'Though you are powerful. I confess I am surprised that you have been able to do this much, clothing me in material form so you can see me.'

'Do you not sometimes appear thus?' Michael hazarded. 'The priest and sacristan appear to be nervous of whatever is in this vault.'

'They feel me, nothing more. Few have been able to see me since I died. It is not my power, but yours, that puts shape on my spirit and makes it visible.'

'My power?'

'Yes priest, your power. Surely you are aware of it. You would not have tried even that simplistic ritual had you not possessed some knowledge of your own magical potential. How come you by it?'

Michael Casside breathed deeply. Much depended upon how he would answer. He finally decided on the truth. 'Your descendant, Sorcha Ni Cleirigh, is responsible. She killed my brother, my twin brother, and directed his life-force into me.'

Cleirigh laughed, his skull-like features twisting into a rictus of delight. 'Aaah, the blood runs true. My descendant, my granddaughter, my daughter's daughter. Sorcha. And is she a powerful spellcaster?'

'She is a witch,' Michael said coldly. 'A witch who enticed and then murdered my brother, then directed his life-force into me. She intended to use me, to direct and channel the power in me.'

'She would have bred you,' Cleirigh hissed. 'She would have born a child – a daughter probably – who would have been powerful indeed. Continue,' the spirit said lightly.

'There is little enough to tell. Because of her I have sworn to fight such evil, to dedicate my life to it. I mean to find and destroy her. That is why I conjured you, to make you tell me how to find her.'

Ronan Cleirigh showed his few rotted teeth in what might have been a smile. 'I already explained you can make me do nothing. But tell me this, priest.' He said the last word with contempt, his empty eyes flicking to the circle around Michael's feet. 'Though revenge is a tasty dish – best served cold – why devote your life to it? Surely a man with your enhanced abilities could have the world at his feet if he chose.

'Do you not know that a great crimson-and-gold aura pulses around you with every breath you draw? With only a little tutoring – from myself, perhaps – you could become the most powerful witch ever to walk Erin's fields. And beyond Erin, there is an entire world waiting for you. Nothing could be denied you.'

The ghost lifted its hands and swept them through the air in a gesture not unlike the one Michael had employed for his summoning. This time, however, the result was a panoramic vision that burst across Michael's mind with dazzling clarity. He saw himself ensconced in a grand house close to the sea, with mountains, purple and green in the distance, luxurious gardens surrounding him. The house was alive with people: servants running to do his bidding, beautiful women hung on his every word, golden-haired children clustered around his knees, patting him lovingly with their little hands. Carriages drove up the long, tree-lined driveway to his grand home, and the doors of the carriages bore the crests of the gentry of Britain and Ireland.

Michael Casside had been born poor. He had been born . . . nobody. But this – this vision – had always been his mother's dream for her sons.

Ronan Cleirigh crackled. 'Yours for the taking,' he said. 'With my help.'

'And what would you want in return?' the priest asked, his voice heavy, the words reluctant.

The ghost made a deprecatory gesture. 'Nothing you could not give. If I teach you how to enhance the abilities you already have, you could free me from this monstrous captivity I suffer. Nothing I did in my life merits this for all eternity. Surely you, a priest of the cloth, preaching forgiveness, can find in your heart some pity for a sinner?'

Michael was not certain he understood. 'What are you asking?'

'I am offering you the opportunity of saving my soul. The soul of Ronan Cleirigh. Would that not be a star for your crown in heaven? The redemption of a great warlock?'

Temptation glittered; shimmered. Michael struggled to hold onto his reasoning mind. 'But are you not proposing to teach me to be a warlock like yourself? If I became one, would not heaven be denied me?'

The unstable shape of the ghost darkened with anger. 'You think to manipulate me with sophistry. But I am too clever for that. I have offered you a straightforward proposition. Accept me as your teacher, let me fulfil myself through you, and then I will surrender my soul to your God while you continue to enjoy all the bounties this life can provide. Who ever had a better offer?'

Was the offer genuine? The ghost's voice was eerie and inhuman, it was impossible to judge its sincerity.

'Pity for a sinner,' whispered the ghost. 'Christian pity.'

A flare of rage burned through Michael Casside, searing through his confused thoughts. 'Where was Christian pity when your granddaughter murdered my brother?' he cried. 'She did it to attain what you are offering me – power, dark, occult power.'

'And does that not tempt you?' the ghost inquired insidiously, as if it could see into his soul. 'Does that not tempt you, just a little?'

Michael felt the gnawing self-doubt. He was honest enough to admit that he was indeed tempted. The vision he had seen would have tempted a saint, and he was no saint. It had been cleverly designed to appeal to his specific ambitions and desires, like the thin edge of a stonemason's wedge driven into a fissure to crack the stone apart.

And it had almost worked. The fissures in his soul were clearly revealed to him. There was no mistaking the arrogance and ambition inherent in his vision of himself heroically waging war against the Forces of Evil. It had been empty posturing, a child's play acting. Who did he think he was? The age of heroes was long dead.

Filled with disgust at himself, the young priest looked away. He found he was staring at the white strip of his collar protruding from the bag where he had stored his clothing.

He did not deserve to wear the cassock, he thought. He was too easily tempted. There was too much of the adversary in his own soul. Even the bishop realised that he was not good enough to serve as a parish priest and offer guidance to others. That was why he had been given the lowly task of cataloguing books in the bishop's library.

The ghost of Ronan Cleirigh emitted a cackle of pleasure, watching the young man writhe in self-inflicted pain. How delicious. 'Aaah yes, the torture of doubt,' the warlock cried delightedly. 'You must learn never to doubt yourself. You must always believe that you are right, and that others are wrong. There is only one law, and that is to do what you will.'

The creature started laughing, ghostly cackles echoing and re-echoing off the old stones, stripping away the nuances of pity from his words, revealing the naked cruelty, the delight in the priest's pain, that lurked beneath them. Disgust cut like a knife through Michael's self-absorption. Cold anger flared in its place, freeing his mind and body.

Reaching down, he picked up the tiny silver snuff-box he had carried into the circle with him. It contained his most precious possession: a lock of his dead brother's hair.

Clutching the circular silver box in a white-knuckled grip until it grew warm in his flesh, he flung it at Cleirigh's ghost.

The small, shining silver object passed right through the incorporeal body and bounced with a hollow ring off the stone tomb behind it, spinning on its edge like a top until it clattered to a stop.

For a heartbeat, nothing happened. The ghost stared at the box, then turned to look at Michael with its horrible, empty eyes. It opened its mouth, and the priest thought it would laugh again.

But there was no more laughter.

Michael's keen ears detected the faintest hissing sound, like a tiny flame burning the smallest scrap of paper. Then, as he watched, a pinhead, red glow appeared in the upper part of the ghost's figure, where the box had passed through. The glow enlarged, flickering red and black and white, became a circle of fire eating away the apparition from the inside, searing the incorporeal flesh, like a hot coal dropped in the centre of a sheet of paper.

Flame crackled. The circle widened, burning more

furiously. The vaults filled with the burning stench of something like old leather and damp cloth, and then this was replaced by a scent more noisome still, that of the grave.

The spirit of Ronan Cleirigh shrieked as if his flesh actually burned.

'You wanted to be free,' Michael cried savagely, his pale eyes blazing. 'So – be free!'

Instinct made him raise his hands, slowly, slowly, palm upward, as if lifting a suffering soul from its burning body. The dark shape of the warlock's ghost rose upwards, twisting and gasping, clawing at the air, mouth wide and howling, but soundlessly now. Then all at once it burst into one single, scarlet flame that scorched the entire front of the tomb, then died away, leaving pulsing after-images on the young priest's eyes. The air was filled with spiralling grey ash which curled to the ground. When the priest stepped out of the mound, his naked foot left a perfect impression in the dust.

Trembling, he bent to retrieve the silver box. Its gleaming surface was marred and streaked with soot. When he opened it with nerveless fingers he saw that the lock of his twin's dark hair had shrivelled and melted to a couple of coiled strands.

Michael was shaken by a spasm of grief as fresh as if his brother had died the day before. He felt the power flow into him then, and he accepted it, welcomed it, felt it flood his body, his soul, heightening his senses. He closed his fingers on the snuff-box and his fingers left distinct impressions in the metal. Opening his hand again, he marvelled at his newfound strength.

Then, slowly, moving like an old man, he gathered up his clothing and began to dress. He took one last long look around the now silent vaults, and wearily climbed the steps.

The sacristan was sitting on a canted tombstone, aromatic white smoke from his pipe wafting up into the afternoon sky. Michael was surprised to discover how much time he had spent underground. 'Did you find what you wanted?' the older man asked anxiously. 'Did you have any . . . trouble?'

'Trouble?' Michael's eyes were opaque, hiding his thoughts. 'I had no trouble. Thank you for your kindness.'

The old man looked distinctly relieved.

But when Michael went to get into the trap to drive the pony home, the little animal rolled its eyes and snorted, trying to sidle away from him. He reached for it, but its eyes widened and it began champing on the bit. It had never been nervous of him before, he thought, bemused.

But perhaps he was not the man he had been before.

The young priest spent the night in long hours of earnest prayer. Some time before dawn he returned to the Browne collection, searching for something he dimly remembered. He discovered what he was looking for in a badly translated collection of ancient myths. Michael read the names aloud, the sounds flat on the dry library air, until he reached the one he wanted.

'Morand,' he said finally. 'One of the judges of Banba, whose judgments were always fair. Perhaps,' he remarked aloud to the silent room, 'that is enough for a man to aspire to. Neither to be right or wrong, but simple, fair and honest in all things. Especially if he must be judge and jury and sometimes . . . executioner.' Then, pulling the library door closed behind him he went to see the bishop.

*

'I cannot understand what's brought this on,' Bishop McCabe said in dismay. 'You have so much to offer, yet you propose to walk off and throw it away. Are you doing this out of petulance, Father, because I would not give you a parish?'

'I assure you there is no petulance involved. You were right to deny me a parish, I would have made a poor sort of parish priest at best. And perhaps not even an adequate librarian, though that is a task I might have enjoyed very much.

'But fate has decreed otherwise. I realise now that I have been brought, step by step, to this crossroads in my life. I have prayed for guidance and I believe I see the way I am meant to go. And not as Father Casside. That man no longer exists, if he ever did.'

The bishop was dismayed. 'Surely you cannot be thinking of giving up the priesthood?'

Michael smiled gently. 'Not at all. I just mean to serve Mother Church in a different . . . capacity. One for which I have been singularly well equipped.'

'I cannot be responsible . . .' the bishop began, but the young priest shocked him by interrupting.

'I shall be responsible for myself,' he said. 'Father Casside is no more. Now I am Morand, the Judge. From this day forward, I intend to devote my life to seeking out those troubled souls and offering relief, to exorcising demons and driving off witches.'

'There are no witches in Ireland,' the bishop said shakily.

'But there is evil – by whatever name you may call it.'

'I urge you to reconsider. . .'

'Why? Is this not why I joined the church?' he demanded. 'Do you doubt my abilities?'

The bishop started to shake his head, then suddenly he became aware of the force radiating from the younger man, cold energy that flowed from him, bringing the silver cross on his breast to blazing light.

'I do not doubt your abilities,' Bishop McCabe said softly. 'God go with you, my son.'

'He does,' Michael Morand said sincerely.

But for the rest of his life, as stories filtered back to the good bishop about the strange career of Father Michael Morand, known throughout Ireland as the Witchfinder, he would sometimes find himself wondering whether it was God or the Devil who rode with the priest.

CHAPTER SIXTEEN

Red Aoife and the Kilkenny Cow

———— ♣ ————

'The tide is turning. Bring me my armour!' The woman spun away from the window, her heavy hair swinging around her like a shimmering, crimson cloak. While the servants scurried to fetch armour that had been specially adapted to her female form, Red Aoife MacMurrough prepared to go to battle.

Red Aoife was no dainty woman. She stood an inch over six feet, making her a veritable giantess in eleventh-century Ireland. Her big-boned frame was in perfect proportion, but her most striking feature was her mane of flaming red hair which gave her her nickname. Flowing in a wave to the backs of her knees, it had never been cut and even her husband, the most powerful man in Ireland, knew better than to suggest it.

Red Aoife was the wife of Richard Fitzgilbert de Clare, Earl of Pembroke, more commonly known as Strongbow, the leader of the Norman invasion to Ireland. The name had become synonymous with fear and death, but there were some who said Strongbow's Irish wife was even more to be feared than her husband.

'Hurry, damn you!' Red Aoife leaned close to the arrow slit in the castle wall, peering down toward the foot of the keep. Strongbow's banner was in danger of being taken. The cries of the O'Rourke clan, her husband's relentless enemies, grew louder.

The big woman held out her arms and one servant buckled her spiked cuirass around her chest while another braided her hair and wove thick metal rings through the plaits. The rings served two functions: they could prevent a blade from reaching her skull . . . and they also turned Red Aoife's hair into a devastating weapon. With her hair spinning around her in a red blur as she fought, the deadly ornaments could send an unwary enemy reeling, blinded, or with shattered nose or fractured skull from a blow of the iron rings. Those who survived the perils of her hair might be less lucky in avoiding the woman's embrace. She was even stronger than she looked. In the heat of battle, Red Aoife would seize an opponent and crush him to her chest – impaling her victim on the iron spikes that studded her armoured cuirass.

And lately a new rumour had been added to the legend of Red Aoife: those who had seen her fight swore that while her enemies shuddered their last spasms in her arms, she tore out their throats with her teeth.

Strongbow's battle cry went up from below the window, echoing and re-echoing from the stones of Kilkenny Castle. Turning her head to one side, twisting her thick hair off her ear, she listened for the response from Strongbow's warriors.

But the sounds, when they came, were surprisingly few, and weak.

'Enough!' she cried. Pushing away the hovering servants, she snatched up her sword and ran from the room into a narrow passage letting on to the battlements. She squeezed through a window-sized aperture that led out onto the roof. Almost directly below, she saw less than a dozen of her husband's men gathered protectively around their leader. They had held off a vastly superior fighting force for the best part of the day, but now Tiernan O'Rourke had brought in mercenaries from neighbouring tribes. None of them had any love for Strongbow, the foreigner, the alien, even if he had married an Irish king's daughter.

As Red Aoife watched, her husband rose to his full height, his sword whirling around his head in a deadly blur of steel.

The woman's face was impassive, though she felt her husband's pain. His armour was battered and bloody, pieces missing, and she guessed that at the very least ribs were broken. Raising his great sword one last time, he prepared to meet the final charge of the O'Rourke forces.

Leaning out over the battlements, the woman measured the distance from the main gate. Her husband and his few surviving warriors were less than ten feet from safety, but his enemies were too close, and the distance could easily have measured miles.

The mercenaries rushed towards him, howling their triumph, sensing victory and unimaginable triumph, the death of Strongbow. What had started as a minor skirmish would end as a great victory. Tonight Tiernan O'Rourke would keep an old promise and dine, as victor, in the captured hall of Kilkenny Castle, beneath the severed head of Strongbow.

Strongbow's surviving twelve men, all of them

wounded, moved into position around him, prepared to defend him to the last. They were facing three times their number, and though they knew they had no chance, none even considered turning and running. They were Strongbow's men – to the last.

O'Rourke's men charged.

And Red Aoife leaped.

With a scream like an eagle stooping on its hapless prey, the big woman in armour launched herself into the sky. Leaping upwards and outwards from the battlements of the castle, she hurled herself onto the unsuspecting heads of the enemy below.

The fall should have killed her.

But her fall was cushioned, as she intended, by the bodies of her enemies. Her full weight came down on three of them at once as they stood clustered together. Two men died instantly of broken necks and a third snapped a spine beneath the crushing blow.

The charge faltered. To O'Rourke's men, it seemed as if she had fallen from the heavens, like some monstrous, avenging angel.

She scrambled to her feet while they were still paralysed with shock. The breath was knocked out of her and she knew that at least two of her ribs and possibly her wrist were broken, but that could not stop her. Nothing had ever been known to stop Red Aoife in full spate. Twirling her deadly braids into the astonished faces of her enemies, she grabbed the nearest man and pulled him to her, impaling him on her spiked breast.

Her husband, grinning hugely in spite of his weakness and injuries, rallied himself to fight beside her.

It was over in a few minutes. O'Rourke's men were totally demoralised. Red Aoife's rage and courage in defence of her husband were more than they could face, and they took to their heels. They did not fear Tiernan O'Rourke half as much as they feared Strongbow's wife.

Her father, the infamous Dermot MacMurrough, King of Leinster, was hated in his lifetime and reviled after his death for having brought the Normans into Ireland. Her husband Strongbow was despised for centuries as the Armed Invader.

But though Red Aoife was feared, she was neither hated nor despised. Her devotion and loyalty to her husband were legendary; a man could not help admiring her and envying him.

But no man could conquer her. She had given herself once and forever to Richard de Clare, in the smouldering ruins of the city of Waterford after the Norman invasion, and she was a woman who never went back on her word.

Men desired her. One of Strongbow's bitterest enemies, Desmond Quinn, was determined to have the woman. He considered her a challenge to his manhood. And when he railed against Strongbow again and again, all knew that his real goal was to have Red Aoife MacMurrough for himself.

Only he was unable to see that he did not stand a chance.

But he never stopped trying.

Even after Strongbow was dead and lying in his crypt in Christchurch Cathedral, Quinn was still marching warriors up to the gates of Kilkenny Castle and demanding that Red Aoife surrender to him.

From the battlements, she laughed at him.

Her taunts enraged him. Skirmishes between his followers and hers became a frequent occurrence, keeping the countryside in upheaval. When a delegation called upon Red Aoife, pleading with her for a means to put an end to the constant fighting, she sent word that she would meet Desmond Quinn personally and settle the matter in the traditional manner: a trial of strength, hand-to-hand combat, with the spoils to the victor.

At first Quinn was astonished. Then he replied that he would not lower himself by fighting a woman. Those who knew him, however, refrained from suggesting that he was afraid of the woman.

Red Aoife had rarely been so angry. In a fury, she summoned the chieftain of the Quinns to Kilkenny Castle, and told him to his face before the assembled warriors and chieftains that he must either fight her, or she would brand him a coward throughout Ireland.

The two stood toe to toe in the great hall of the castle, shouting at each other. Both were into their middle years, grey-haired and red-faced with emotion, their roaring voices echoing from the timbered ceiling above them.

'Accuse me of cowardice, you wretched *Norman woman*,' Quinn spat, calling Aoife by the lowest name he could think of, 'and I'll slaughter you like the cow you are and hang you to drain, slitted from crotch to gullet, from one of your own oak trees!'

Red Aoife's laughter mocked him. 'Harm me and I'll come back to haunt you and yours until Ireland is a desert of sand!'

'If the ghost of you was within a day's walk of me I would know it,' Quinn replied, 'and have a priest to exorcise you.'

She drew herself up to her full height, looking like the Red Aoife of old before the years put streaks of grey into her flaming hair and etched lines into her face. 'But first you will have to recognise me, Desmond Quinn. A cow you call me and a cow I will be. My ghost will take the shape of a cow and haunt you, and the children of your children. I will drive them insane, and take pleasure in their insanity.' The big woman bared her teeth. 'And are there not hundreds – no, thousands – of cows in Kilkenny? How will you know which is Aoife?'

They continued to scream threats and taunts at one another until both were exhausted. At last Desmond Quinn retired to his own stronghold, finally forced to accept that there was no future for Red Aoife and himself . . . at least not together. And like many men, who must destroy what they cannot have, he began a concerted campaign to slay Strongbow's widow.

But the end, when it came, happened by accident. A year to the day later, one of his men loosed an arrow in the direction of the castle. By a fluke, it took Red Aoife through the throat and she troubled Quinn no more.

Not in life.

The man who trudged along the road from Jerpoint Abbey toward Kilkenny town was tall and thin, dark-haired, with strange, colourless eyes. The barefooted boys tending their herds of cattle in the grassy meadows bordering the River Nore glanced curiously at him as he passed by, and then quickly crossed themselves and looked away. No one wished to draw the Witchfinder's attention to themselves.

On the road, Father Michael Morand was invariably greeted with a nervous courtesy bordering on obsequiousness. He was polite in turn, but reserved, distant, some would have said cold.

But his reserve lacked the arrogance of authority, making him seem all the more human. He was merely . . . *different*. Special. A priest who seemed to function outside the normal channels of the Church, undertaking a job no one else would, or could, do. For reasons known only to himself, the man now known as Father Morand had dedicated his life to seeking out souls lost to the Dark One and attempting to reclaim them, to exorcising demons and dismissing the traces of the Old Race who clung to their shadowy existence.

His search took him to some strange places.

Most recently, it had led him to the bleak, rotting shell of a once great house on the Kilkenny border, wherein dwelt the surviving members of an ancient, noble family. Once, the descendants of Desmond Quinn held all the surrounding land as far as the eye could see – before the coming of the Normans almost eight centuries earlier. Now, while they still possessed a grand house, it was dilapidated, the family fortune was gone, and they were left with little more than their ancient name and their history.

Yet curiously, they did not attribute the fall in their fortunes to current politics or the passage of time. Instead, they blamed the natural misfortunes of a decayed family upon a haunting.

'Or,' as Phelim Quinn explained to Father Michael Morand as they sat together in Quinn's library, surrounded by rotting tapestries and the pervasive smell of mildew, 'nothing has gone right for Clan Quinn since Red Aoife died. She haunts us, you know. Her evil is in the cows.'

'In the cows?' Father Morand had schooled his face to impassivity and raised his eyebrows. Though still a young man, he had seen enough to keep him from disbelieving anything. Still, a malign cow seemed unusual. 'A cursed cow?' he enquired mildly.

'A cow, Father. It is a cow, always a cow. Generation

after generation. And we never know *which cow*. It could be one of our own herds, it could be a beast belonging to a neighbour, it could be an animal miles away. Yet I tell you, Father, as long as one person is still alive who has the blood of Desmond Quinn in his or her veins, somewhere in Kilkenny there is a cow whose spirit is tainted by the curse of Red Aoife. And Red Aoife cursed the Quinns.'

Father Morand did not laugh. He felt a surge of pity for the wizened little man sitting facing him, almost lost in the depths of a tattered armchair. Phelim Quinn was no more than forty years old, but he looked seventy. Like all his clan, he aged fast and would die early. The Quinns withered on the vine without ever ripening, some said.

The Quinns themselves said it was the doing of the Kilkenny cow and Red Aoife's curse. And after almost eight hundred years, they had had enough. They were using what little money they had left to hire the famous witchfinder to locate the cow currently containing the spirit of Red Aoife MacMurrough. 'And send her to the darkest corner of Hell!' Phelim cried, shaking his palsied fist.

The priest with the colourless eyes replied, 'Do you not think she has suffered enough if she has been forced to exist in the body of one cow after another over so many centuries? What more punishment could hell offer her? Surely you would show her some mercy.'

'Mercy?' Phelim spat a gob of phlegm onto the ruins of the carpet, which was in such bad repair that no further maltreatment could make it worse. 'I want her shown no mercy. Since her death she had blighted my family, whittled our holdings away from us, caused our sons to be born simple and our daughters born ugly. Find her and make her pay, Witchfinder!'

'I shall find her,' Father Morand promised, 'but what I do with her is my own concern.'

And the glare from the priest's colourless eyes silenced the older man.

Now Father Michael Morand walked the roads of Kilkenny, his eyes raking the meadows as he passed, trusting his heightened senses to spot the creature. The witch-aura was unique, and one to which he was finely attuned. Carrying his usual black leather bag, almost like a doctor making his calls, he went on his way, crisscrossing the county, searching, searching. He saw many cows: short, black Kerry cattle, larger, creamy-coloured animals newly imported from England, glossy, red Kilkenny cows with coats like a red setter's. But none of them was more than a cow, gazing back at the priest with placid, bovine eyes.

But he was patient. If there were a bewitched cow anywhere in county Kilkenny, he would find her. If the curse held true. After eight hundred years, the curse could easily have withered and faded, and the Quinn's ill fortune might be just that: ill fortune.

It was beside the Nore he found her, in a watery meadow where the yellow flag bloomed. He had paused at midday for prayers and to eat a bite of the food he carried with him. Arranging a tiny campsite for himself close by the singing river, he prepared to bathe his face and hands before eating.

As he knelt by the water, he became aware of someone watching him. It was the sense of eyes on the back of his neck, the faintest of odours in the air, the merest whisper of a chill, quite unmistakable for a man of his perceptions, that made him stiffen, straighten, and turn around slowly.

The red cow stood behind him, watching him.

She could hardly have looked more harmless and commonplace, a big, red cow, hornless, heavy-uddered, as natural in that scene as the green grass in which she stood.

But there was something not quite natural about her. Her eyes were not placid and bovine; they bore the gleam of an acute intelligence and focused intently on the priest. Concentrating hard, the priest saw that the air around her shimmered very faintly with a dull light, a human aura, quite unlike a beast's.

The Kilkenny cow was one of the most unlikely beings Father Michael Morand had ever confronted. Yet he knew, the moment her eyes met his, that he was seeing the living embodiment of the spirit that had once been Red Aoife MacMurrough. Pride and power and an undying will flamed in those eyes. She had devoted centuries to the vendetta against the Clan Quinn. If she was indeed the author of their misfortunes, through some form of witchcraft, she would not be easily dissuaded.

'Is it yourself, Aoife MacMurrough?' Father Morand asked softly in the oldest spoken Irish he knew. How much it might resemble the language she remembered he could only guess.

The creature stared at him unresponsively.

The priest cleared his throat and tried again. 'I know you for who you are,' he told the cow.

She chewed solemnly on her cud, her jaws moving from left to right.

Just for a moment, Father Morand doubted his own instincts. 'Desmond Quinn!' he said aloud in a harsh voice.

The fire that leaped into her eyes eliminated all his doubts. This creature could understand him well enough.

A strange sensation swept over the priest. He was in the

presence – albeit peculiarly disguised – of a figure from Ireland's ancient history, a woman who had been witness to the turning point in the long saga of her land and its people. More than a witness, Red Aoife had played a part in the coming of the Normans. She had been one of the prizes offered to lure Strongbow and his army to Ireland in the first place.

She had been the link between the Irish and the invader, their marriage and subsequent unexpected devotion to one another a metaphor for the absorption of the Normans into Irish culture.

And her spirit remained alive.

It animated the body of the cow, standing knee-deep in a Kilkenny meadow, swishing a tail like a lashing of red hair, chewing a cud, staring at Father Morand with an intensity that would have unnerved a lesser man.

He drew a deep breath. 'The survivors of Clan Quinn have sent me to free themselves from your spell,' he said deliberately. Aoife had always been a straightforward woman, if the legends surrounding her were to be believed. And it was Father Morand's experience that in Ireland all legends contained a seed of truth.

The cow stopped chewing. The fire in her eyes became a murderous spark. Lowering her head like a bull about to charge, she pawed the ground with one cloven hoof.

Even without horns, an enraged, fully grown cow can be dangerous. The priest was well aware that if she knocked him down, she could trample him. But he dared not run from her. If she had power enough to damage the Quinns at a distance, she had power enough to outrun him. She glanced up once, judging the distance.

He fixed his eyes firmly on hers, drilling her with his singularly penetrating gaze. The priest's eyes were like ice, but with a maelstrom of emotions swirling in their depths. They looked at the creature and fixed her to the spot.

The cow hesitated.

And then, in the summer sun, the red cow shivered.

Moving slowly so as not to provoke a charge, Father Morand bent and opened his leather bag. From it he drew a crucifix and a phial of holy water recently blessed by the Abbot of Jerpoint.

Against ordinary apparitions, these were sufficient protections. But he knew the red cow was no ordinary apparition. She had been a Christian in life, however. Surely some remnant of her faith lingered within Aoife's beast body.

When Father Morand lifted the crucifix, the cow's eyes followed it. Some of the fire died in them.

But only some.

Father Morand addressed the cow again, his tongue struggling with the difficulties of early Irish. 'Where there is evil, there is also good,' he told her. 'One cannot exist without the other. It is to the goodness in you I speak, Aoife MacMurrough. The dark side of your spirit has been attracted to the arts of evil, but the bright side still exists, waiting to throw off the shackles that have bound you all these centuries.

'Let go your hatred and your ancient bitterness and be free, Aoife MacMurrough. Then your soul will likewise be free and able to move on.'

The cow watched him fixedly.

She comes from an older time, the priest reminded himself. Simple reasoning will not do for her. Only rituals that would have been credible in the eleventh century will be enough to convince her, to win her belief.

He had come prepared.

He reached into his bag a second time and drew out a wreath he had woven from the wild plants of Ireland. Hemlock and hemp were twisted together with Devil's bit, bindweed, and mullein, the most powerful herb against enchantments. In her time Red Aoife would have recognised all of these and perhaps used them, for as châtelaine of Strongbow's castles, she would have kept his keys and brewed his medicaments when necessary.

Holding the crucifix aloft in his right hand, Father Morand took the wreath in his left and began to swing it back and forth, hypnotically. At the same time he chanted, 'I abjure thee in the Name of the Living God and of the True One, of the Three that are One and the One that is All. I command thee in the Name of the Most High God to relinquish thy quest for vengeance and cease doing harm to those who have not personally harmed thee or thine. I. . .'

Before he could finish, the red cow lowered her head again and charged.

And in that moment Father Morand flung the wreath with an expert twist of the wrist that sent it flying to land around her neck.

'And in the names of the ancient ones whose spirits walked the lands in your day!' he cried aloud in a still stronger voice. 'In the names of Lugh of the Long Hand and Nuada of the Silver Arm, in the names of Angus Og and of the three great queens of the Tuatha De Danann, Banba, Fodla, and Eriu!'

As he shouted this earlier trinity, these names that predated Christianity but had continued to coexist beside it in Ireland until well after the coming of the Normans, Father Morand realised that he had taken yet another step away from his Catholic teaching.

But he was convinced that this was not blasphemy, though he could never explain that to the bishop. He was simply calling upon all the faces of God, the old and the new, drawing upon the intermingling of beliefs – pagan and Christian – that lay at the heart of Ireland. Present-day churches had been built upon ancient sites, modern-day feast and holy days had replaced the original pagan festivals. In Aoife's time, such customs would have been more vivid, closer to the source.

So the priest called upon the ancient deities of Ireland while continuing to hold up the crucifix. And as the herbal wreath settled around the cow's neck, speaking for the land itself, a startling transformation took place.

The big red cow dropped to her knees, her hind end still standing. She moved her head back and forth, dazedly. Lifting her eyes, she met Father Michael Morand's colourless eyes one more time. At first, her expression was angry. Then it became almost . . . beseeching.

As he watched in wonder, the massive bovine frame shuddered, shimmered, losing form and definition. He felt fire course along his fingertips, springing in forks of jagged, blue light from his body to hers, encircling her in a dazzling aura. Within that glowing circle the Kilkenny Cow writhed as her bovine shape melted away.

And for one brief moment, Father Morand looked upon a figure no one had seen in eight centuries.

Lying on the green grass, almost at his feet, stretched the body of Red Aoife MacMurrough. She was as big as the legends had claimed. Her strong-featured face was handsome, her green eyes piercing, but most memorable of all was her flaming red hair, spread over her like a great crimson cloak as she lay there, looking up at Father Morand.

Her lips shaped silent words. Leaning forward, he thought they said 'Richard.'

'Go to him now!' exhorted the priest. 'Go and find Richard de Clare and torment your old enemies no longer!'

A spasm swept the massive frame. And then, all at once, like the extinguishing of a candle, she winked out of existence.

Father Morand staggered with sudden weakness. He felt as if every particle of strength had been drained from his body. He slumped onto the grass and sat there, breathing heavily, shivering as if with fever.

It was later, much later, before he had the strength to raise his head and look at the meadowgrass beside him. There was no woman there, and no red Kilkenny cow.

Only trampled grass. And a small packet of damp grass stems that might have been the cud of a cow, dropped and no longer needed.

And a wreath of ancient herbs, now withered to dry husks. As he watched, they dissolved in the breeze.

CHAPTER SEVENTEEN

May Day

— ♣ —

The boy drew one deep breath into his lungs and ran as fast as he could through the dew-wet grass, bare feet sliding and squeaking through the blades, water droplets splashing his knees and thighs. He cursed last night's heavy dew, though he knew his sisters would be pleased. Back at their cottage, they would be washing their faces in the dawn dew, for everyone knew that the dew on May Morning had special properties and could make a plain girl pretty and a pretty girl beautiful. None doubted this; this was more than superstition, more than lore; it was proven fact. This was May Day, the ancient Celtic festival of Beltane, a time of magic and mystery.

But Ciaran was interested in none of this. This was the morning to prove his courage. A dozen other lads of about his own age, on the brink of puberty, had gathered beside Lough Gur to see if he was brave enough to be one of their own. If he failed the test he would be relegated to childhood again, doomed to seek companions among little boys rather than those who thought themselves almost men.

The day was grey and overcast, the air so moist it clogged the lungs and clung to the skin, slicking Ciaran's raven hair to his skull. There was a decided chill in the air, belying the promise of summer to come.

The boy's foot turned on the grass, and he felt one of the razor-sharp blades nick his heel. Blood! What would happen if he spilt blood here? Would the Wizard Fitzgerald rise and feast off it? He didn't know, but the very thought was terrifying.

The boy's dark eyes ranged over the uneven ground, deliberately concentrating on it, trying not to think about anything else as he ran towards the lake. He did not dare think. If he thought too long about what he was about to do – he simply wouldn't do it. He must throw himself into the water before his mind could sensibly prevent him.

His bare feet touched the muddy verge of the lake. It was a heartbeat away. His staring eyes were fixed on the silvery surface of Lough Gur. The water was quite opaque beneath the sunless sky, looking like a sheet of lightly polished metal.

The lads who had gathered to observe this rite of passage grinned wickedly and elbowed one another. They had all done this and knew what Ciaran was about to experience: the heart-stopping chill of the water, the aching muscles, then the long, shivering walk back home and the beating by mother with a wooden spoon or father with a leather belt. And, if you were particularly unlucky, you caught a cold afterwards and spent the best part of a week coughing and sneezing in bed.

But the boys of the village had been jumping into Lough Gur on May Morning for as long as anyone could remember. No one knew who had started it, though they all knew the story behind it. Everyone knew the story . . .

or a version of the story.

The mighty Earl of Desmond was notorious in the sixteenth century for his practice of the black arts. He brought shame to his illustrious name of Fitzgerald, and struck terror in the heart of his countess, a pious woman. He was reputedly able to change into a bird or animal at will, spying on his tenants and horrifying his enemies.

When the man known to many as Wizard Fitzgerald finally died, there were those who said it was a hoax, that he could not die, that he had made an unholy pact with the Devil to preserve his foul life forever. Some of his family tried to claim he was more sinned against than sinning, but the common folk would not listen. Tales of his spectral form were soon being told throughout the south and west of Ireland.

Once every seven years it was said that on May Morning he emerged from beneath the waters of Lough Gur in full armour to gallop across the surface of the lake on a mighty charger shod in magical, silver shoes. And the only evidence of the spirits passing would be the splashes etched into the still waters of the lake. Legend had it that the wizard would be forced to repeat this performance time and again until the horseshoes wore so thin that they fell off. And it was claimed that his fury at being so bound made him more dangerous in death than he had been in life.

Lough Gur was a place to be avoided, once every seven years. But at some time in the past, the young lads of County Limerick had devised a scheme to put their burgeoning manhood to the test. In the intervening years, the run was accompanied by shouts and cries and echoing laughter, but on the seventh year, the run was conducted in silence.

And this year Ciaran O'Carroll was running to prove he was a man.

He would have preferred to forego the honour, but he could not bear to be branded a coward. So he must run at full speed towards the lake and throw himself in just as Wizard Fitzgerald was expected to rise from the waters.

And just because the wizard hadn't risen from the water in the past, that didn't mean that this couldn't be the very morning. . .

Ciaran measured his steps to the water's edge. Six . . . seven at the most.

Beyond the lake stood a remarkable, and ancient, stonework. In a time beyond the known history of Ireland, an earlier race had erected numerous stone circles around the country, testifying to rituals lost in the mists of antiquity. The largest of these stood beside Lough Gur. Aligned with the stars and the seasons, it might once have served as a calendar. According to the local old women, however, who relished a bloodier tale, its purpose had been human sacrifice, and it was the aura of these dark deeds that still lurked in the stones and held the wicked Earl of Desmond in the waters of Lough Gur.

Four steps. . .

It was a good story. The boys gathered on the lakeshore believed it, as much as they believed in anything in their youth and bravado.

Two. . .

At the very last moment, Ciaran thought he saw movement just below the surface of the lake in front of him. He tried to stop, but by then his momentum was too great.

One. . .

With a despairing wail quite unlike the courageous yell he meant to give, he plunged into water.

Although Lough Gur was deep at its centre, a shallow shelf extended from the lakeshore, which meant that the boy didn't immediately plunge beneath the surface. The shock of the cold water drove the breath from his body and he floundered momentarily. If he had been able to get a good purchase with his toes in the mud, he might have turned back then and scrambled ashore. He was a good swimmer and didn't fear the water. But the mud was old, slick ooze. Trying to walk in it was the surest way to lose one's balance. He lurched sideways, flailed his arms wildly, then suddenly sat down, disappearing beneath the surface.

The watching boys laughed and shouted and yelled encouragement.

Ciaran came spluttering to the surface. He spat out a stream of lake water. A sense of elation flooded through him. He was in the lake, he was alive, he had actually gone under and come up again. No wizard had appeared, no hand had snatched him down.

An idea occurred to him.

Watching the lads gathered on the bank as he did so, he flung up his arms again and screamed convincingly. 'A hand grips my ankle!' he cried, his voice rising. He ducked beneath the surface, waited a moment, then came up again. 'Something's holding onto me,' he screamed.

He ducked under again, bending over double in the cold water.

The boys on the shore exchanged startled glances, suddenly unsure. It wouldn't be the first time a trick like this had been played . . . and everyone thought they were unique. But this time the screams sounded so convincing . . . was Ciaran really in danger?

What would happen to them if they left him there to die?

Who would dare go in after him?

While they struggled with their consciences, Ciaran, still below the surface so they did not see him, made his way laterally along the shore, holding his breath. If they came in for him he would not be where they thought. And he would have the last laugh, sitting on the shore, watching them getting their good clothes wet, whereas he had been careful to wear his oldest, shabbiest clothing.

In a group, the boys raced down into the shallows, calling Ciaran's name. The bitter chill of the water stopped their rush and they waded cautiously in, staying very close together, and began feeling around under the water, its surface now cloudy with mud and silt, trying to catch hold of their friend's arm or shoulder.

They were not far from the shore.

When he was certain he was clear of them and above them, Ciaran surfaced and looked back. He was only a step from the bank. The others were in to their waists and shoulders, white-faced with panic, calling his name and taking great gulps of air before they ducked down to try to find him on the lake bottom.

None of them was in any real danger, however.

He was raising his arm to call them, when it began.

Ciaran was the only one who saw it. The others were too busy looking for him. They did not even realise he stood a dozen or so yards away from them.

Staring.

Staring in horror as the waters roiled at the exact centre of the lake, and a gleaming metal helm broke the surface.

The Great Wizard rose up from the dark depths in one tremendous thrust, holding a sword above his head as if he had used it to cleave the water. Lakewater streamed off him like quicksilver, weed from the bottom of the lough festooned his shoulders and hung across his armoured chest in great slimy swags.

His horse was a chestnut stallion almost the colour of blood. Caparisoned in the fashion of the sixteenth century, with the earl's faded and rotted colours, the animal leaped upward from the lake and drew air into its nostrils with a tremendous snort.

Ciaran screamed.

The other boys turned, startled, and looked towards him. But their reactions were too slow. All their surprise was focused on seeing him alive and well. They did not comprehend the meaning of his outstretched arm and wildly pointing finger.

They did not see the Great Wizard galloping silently, terribly, towards them across the surface of the lake, the horse striking watery sparks from the water.

The earl rose in his stirrups and swung his sword.

With an earsplitting scream, Ciaran threw himself the last few feet to shore and ran off across the dewy meadow much faster than he had come. He did not look back until he was several hundred yards away.

By the time he could force himself to stop and turn around, there was nothing to be seen. The surface of Lough Gur was disturbed only by the wind, ruffling it into tiny wavelets . . . and by the spreading pool of crimson that floated intact for a little time before it was dispersed by the waves.

Ciaran O'Carroll never regained his senses and although he lived on into the middle of the twentieth century, he was never able to speak of what he saw that day.

The other boys were never found.

And the wizard still rides the lake once every seven years.

CHAPTER EIGHTEEN

A Certain Small Hotel

———— ♣ ————

On a narrow street in Dublin, in a part of the city that has never been fashionable, stood a certain small hotel. Built of rose-red brick, it blended so well with its surroundings that one could pass by and never notice it, unless one had a specific reason for mounting the granite steps and entering beneath the stained-glass portico.

The lobby was pleasant but unpretentious. Chairs were arranged for easy conversation. Small tables holding boxes of good cigars stood close to the larger armchairs, while those seats that might lure a lady were placed at an angle to the lace-curtained windows, so the light falling across the woman's face would be kind.

It was an hotel left over from an earlier age, and its clientele were regulars.

On a rainy day in April, a young woman passed beneath the portico and entered the lobby. As she did so, a middle-aged gentleman on his way out, carrying a suitcase, stood back and doffed his hat with casual, practised ease and smiled at her.

But she did not notice. She paused uncertainly in the

lobby, holding a travelling case by the handle with one hand and brushing ash-blonde hair out of her large, grey eyes with the other. She might have been pretty once, but her face was thin and drawn, and her beautiful eyes were shadowed with grief.

A liveried porter hurried forward and gently extracted the bag from her hand. 'Does milady have more luggage outside?'

The young woman managed a wan smile at the old-fashioned phrase. 'This is all I have with me,' she said, indicating the case in the porter's grey-gloved hand.

A desk clerk leaned forward, smiling a welcome. He was silver-haired and clean-shaven, his suit immaculate.

'Nora Robertson,' she said softly.

'You have a suite booked, I believe,' the clerk said, running a manicured finger down the register.

Once again the young woman smiled, this time at what she assumed was a mistake.

'Not a suite,' Nora said softly, a trace of the country in her accent, 'just a room, a small room. Someplace quiet,' she added.

The clerk's smile never wavered. 'All our accommodations are suites,' he said, 'and they are all quiet. It is one of the particular attractions of this hotel. Our guests have come to insist on that particularly.'

'Oh,' she breathed. 'But I'm not sure I can afford a. . .'

'It is out of season. Suites are no more expensive than single rooms would be,' the clerk hastened to reassure her. 'And we keep our prices very low. Very low.' He held out a pasteboard square, elegantly printed in copperplate lettering, indicating the hotel's charges.

The young woman gazed at it in disbelief, her eyes scanning the sums not once but twice. 'Is this all?' she said at last. 'Are there no hidden charges?'

'None, milady, I assure you. As you see, we are very competitive. In fact, if I may say so,' he lowered his eyes, 'we like to think that we have no competition.'

'I should think not!' Nora said quietly. A quick laugh took some of the shadows from her eyes for just a moment. 'Very well, then; I shall take whatever suite you have available. And thank you.'

'It is our pleasure, milady,' the clerk replied formally, the corners of his eyes crinkling in the merest suggestion of a smile. The heavy, leather-bound register was turned for her signature, a handsome pen pressed into her hand. She signed, noting that her blocky, angular script seemed crude against the elegant writing of the other guests.

She was shown to a suite overlooking the back of the building by an aged clerk, who deposited her bag and then disappeared while she was fumbling in her purse.

Crossing to the windows, she pushed them open and looked out across the many-layered rooftops of the city. In the distance she could see the spire of Christchurch. Directly beneath the window was a tiny scrap of grassy lawn bordered by tree-roses grown in tubs. It took her a few moments before her grief-numbed mind registered the astonishing fact that the roses were blooming profusely. In April.

Turning away from the window, Nora looked around the suite. The sitting room, though small, was tastefully furnished. Nothing excessive, nothing garish; all in the best of modest, old-fashioned good taste. A panelled door opened onto a bedroom of almost equal size, with a large, canopied bed. One corner of the bed was already turned down invitingly, revealing snowy linen and plump pillows.

It was all Nora Robertson could do not to fling herself face down across the bed and give way to the tears that had been choking her for days.

But she had not cried at the funeral. She would not cry now. Her father had always called her, 'My brave girl', and he would not want her to cry. When they had known he was dying, he had insisted she was not to waste her youth and beauty mourning him, but get on with her life.

'It is my deepest shame that I leave you with so little,' Dennis Robertson told his only child as he lay on his deathbed. 'But I have made what arrangements I could, and I hope they will be sufficient.' He gave her one last, tender look, squeezed her fingers and then closed his eyes forever.

After the funeral, the family solicitor gave Nora the necessary bank books so she could draw on a minuscule income that would keep her a step above genteel poverty, and the few trinkets that had been her late mother's 'jewellery', none of it very good.

'One last item,' the solicitor told Nora as she was preparing to leave his offices. 'Here.' He held out an envelope on which was written a name and address. 'It was your father's express instruction that you should stay in this hotel in Dublin for the fortnight following his death.'

Nora looked at the envelope, but made no move to take it. 'Why am I to stay in Dublin? Can I not go home now?' Even as she said the words, however, she felt a tiny wash of relief. Home was now a very empty house in Kildare, and facing it with her father gone was almost more than she could bear.

'This is your father's last wish,' the solicitor replied, pointing to the envelope. 'I trust you will honour it.'

She had.

Now she found herself in the hotel he had designated, with no idea why she had been sent there. Perhaps it was no more than the eccentric fancy of a terminally ill man who had begun wandering in his mind.

But Nora could not quite believe this. Her father had seemed lucid to the end, always in control of what had been a fine brain. A dedicated reader, even though he could never afford to collect the library he longed for, he had known something about everything. On his deathbed he had been able to discuss his condition knowledgeably with his doctors, and use the most esoteric medical terms correctly. His friends and neighbours considered him an 'antiquarian', someone with knowledge in the lore and folklore of the locality. It was a title he delighted in.

Nora, who had always trusted her father implicitly, now had to trust that he knew what he was doing in sending her to this obscure little hotel for a fortnight.

He had a reason. He had always had a reason for everything he did.

Nora just wondered what the reason was this time. Sitting down in one of the comfortable chairs that furnished her new sitting room, fingers unconsciously stroking its padded arms, savouring the soothing sensation of silky fabric, she looked blankly around the room.

'Do not waste your youth and beauty mourning me. Get on with your life.'

How could he have given her those instructions when he knew she would mourn him? Her mother died in childbirth and her father had reared her. They had grown beyond the relationship of father and daughter into friends, their minds so alike, so attuned to one another.

Once, he laughingly told her he would have to find a young man for her, since she inevitably compared her suitors to her father and always found them lacking. 'I shall find you a younger version of myself,' he offered. And he meant it. His generous heart did not want to keep her trapped with an old man.

She blinked at tears she dare not shed, feeling her eyes burn beneath her lids.

'How can I let you go?' she whispered into the quiet room. 'It's too hard, too final.' Bending forward, she buried her face in her hands. There was a solution to her pain, an ending, which flittered at the back of her mind. A cold and final solution that would allow her to join her father . . . or would it? Not according to her beliefs.

Then she heard the singing. An Irish tenor rose from behind the bathroom door of her suite, in a not-quite-on-key rendition of 'I Hear You Calling Me'.

It had been her father's favourite song. And the voice singing was his voice.

Nora's spine turned to ice.

She sat paralysed on her chair, staring at the closed door.

It had long been her father's habit to sing in the bathroom as he shaved. The same song, morning after morning. Her earliest memory. One of her last.

The singing she heard now was so normal, so healthy, that for a moment she could believe she was back in their own house with the clock rolled back a year. All that pain and grief had never happened. All that loss was but a bad dream.

Nora drew a deep, shaky breath.

She heard the tap running; water splashing. He was in there, alive and well. She had not lost him.

But the walls that surrounded her were the papered walls of a Dublin hotel, the gentle sprigs of blue flowers on the design were far different from the faded, red stripe of the sitting room at home.

Yet her dead father was in the bathroom, singing.

Nora's head swam. Blood thundered in her ears. Suddenly faint, she bent forward and put her head between her knees, and breathed deeply until the dizziness passed.

When she straightened up there was silence in the suite.

Freed from her paralysis now, she stood up and walked to the bathroom door. But she hesitated with her hand on the knob.

He would not be in there, of course. It was simply an hallucination brought on by grief and stress.

But as long as she did not actually open the door and confirm his absence, some small part of her mind did not have to give him up. Not yet. Because she knew that when she opened the door and discovered that he was not there, she would be finally forced to accept that he was gone.

Nora Robertson took a slow, careful step back from the closed bathroom door.

She needed a cup of tea. She very, very badly needed a cup of tea.

Habit made her turn to her case and snap open the locks. She took out her nightdress and one fresh blouse and skirt, and went to hang them in the wardrobe.

And stopped.

Her father's second best suit was already hanging there, with the folded corners of a white linen handkerchief neatly peeping from the breast pocket, as always. The scent of his aftershave floated into the room.

Heart thundering, Nora stumbled backwards, passing

her hand over her eyes. She had the overwhelming conviction that if she turned around, she would see him emerging from the bathroom.

The young woman ran out into the hall and down the stairs, desperately seeking the tiny restaurant she had glimpsed off the hotel foyer. A cup of tea, she thought, her mind stuttering on the words. A cup of tea, a cup of tea to calm her nerves. Breakfast had been a cup of tea and a single slice of overburnt bread and she had missed lunch. Hunger was making her feel faint. . .

The dining room was deserted. The waiter smiled at her as at an old friend. Bowing with the exact degree of pleasant formality, he showed her to a small table set in the embrace of a bow window.

The table, Nora saw with widening eyes, was set for tea for two. 'The gentleman will be delayed,' the waiter said, 'but he asked that you go ahead without him.'

Numbly, Nora sat down and watched as tea was poured from a silver pot. The delicious fragrance told her the tea was her father's favourite, Lapsang Souchong, smoky and exotic.

Somehow – she would never know how – Nora forced herself to sit there and drink the tea, and managed to choke down one of the dainty biscuits served with it. All the time she was aware of her father as a presence just beyond her range of vision; he was going to enter the room in a moment . . . he was just across the lobby . . . he had just popped out to buy a newspaper, or an ounce of Top Mill Number One snuff. He was *here*, alive and vital and supportive, as always.

She was not alone. He was not gone, not completely.

She was not alone.

Deep in her core, a rational part of her mind knew she

should be frightened. Either she was being haunted by her dead father's ghost or she was losing her mind. But she felt no fear.

She was . . . curiously comforted.

She sipped the tea slowly, feeling its warmth revive her. From time to time she glanced out the window beside the table, watching people going up and down the street in a most ordinary manner, doing mundane things.

When another hotel guest entered the dining room Nora gave the newcomer a swift, discreet glance, then politely looked away. But not before she had seen that the middle-aged woman was wearing black, and had red-rimmed eyes, radiating pain and loss like a perfume. A recent widow. Nora felt a rush of sympathy.

She returned to her suite. Her father's suit was missing from the wardrobe. But his pipe lay on the washstand. The bowl was still faintly warm, the stem moist.

For a fortnight, Nora Robertson was a guest of the small hotel. During the first few days she never left the building, afraid that if she did, she would return to find no trace of her father's presence. But as the days passed she began to feel a longing for open sky over her head and pavement under her feet, and gradually she found the courage to venture out.

When she returned he was in the bathroom. She could hear water running in the tub. 'I bought some magazines at a newsagent's,' she called out. 'And your newspaper.'

Before going down for tea she left his folded copy of the *Irish Times* on the table in the sitting room.

When she returned it was lying spread across the floor, damp finger marks on the edges of the pages.

It was strange, sharing a hotel suite with someone she

never saw. But then she realised that there had been whole days at home when they never saw one another. They had moved through the large house, occupying different rooms at different times, each comfortably aware of the other's presence and needing no more than that; living separate, compatible lives.

Nora suddenly began to see how she could go on without him.

And as the realisation came to her, he began to fade. Not all at once, but little by little over the fortnight. The tenor voice emanating from the bathroom began to sound just a little distant, as if the singer were not in that bathroom, but in one beside it giving onto the next suite.

The man's suit was gone from the wardrobe for longer periods.

The table in the dining room was more and more frequently set for one.

The bowl of the pipe on the washstand was cold to the touch.

Nora felt him leaving, withdrawing from her discreetly in this most discreet of hotels. It was not the painful wrenching away of death, but a sense that they were both . . . growing . . . in different directions. He was not lost to her; she was not alone. Life was just taking a new course.

And death was not the end. She knew that now.

On the morning which was to be the last of her stay in the hotel, she awoke aware that the suite was empty.

Nothing of her father remained there, not even that faint disturbance in the air that lingers behind in a room after someone has just left it.

Nora was the only person occupying the suite.

When she went down to settle her immoderately small bill, the desk clerk wore a waiting expression, as if he quite expected her question.

'What sort of *hotel* is this?'

The man behind the counter smiled. 'Less a hotel than a way station, milady. At least, that's how we like to think of it. We offer a certain service, when needed, to people who are in transit, like yourself.'

'My father. . .'

'Indeed, a lovely man,' the clerk agreed. 'He booked accommodations for you some months ago, and assured us you would be coming.'

'He knew of this place?'

'Obviously.'

'How many others know about it?'

The clerk responded with a noncommittal shrug. 'Not very many. All we can handle. We are small, you know. But we do our best.'

As Nora left the hotel she met a couple coming up the steps. They were young, and both bore the lined and haggard faces of recent, terrible grief. A child, perhaps. . .

She smiled at them, gently, as she stepped out into the brilliant morning sunshine.

On a narrow street in Dublin, in a part of the city that has never been fashionable, stands a certain small hotel.

CHAPTER NINETEEN

The Most Haunted House in Ireland

♣

From the verge of the road the land slopes sharply downward, covered by a forbidding tangle of briars. At the bottom of this hill is a damp and narrow valley permanently shaded by massive oaks, an occasional pine, beech and sycamore. There is a narrow lane winding through this valley, but it is barely discernible; its overgrown, unpaved surface is edged with unpruned hollies.

At the head of the valley, lost among the trees, stands a magnificent period house of cut stone with a symmetrical façade and well-designed roofline. Broad steps sweep upward to a welcoming doorway, but few ever venture through it. The pretty house is shunned . . . and with good reason.

It was built toward the end of the seventeenth century by Captain John Larrimore for his bride, Phoebe. Captain John, as he insisted on being called by everyone, had been granted a parcel of land in return for services to his sovereign, in addition to a small allowance. Just what he had done for the King of England none of his new neighbours in Ireland knew. Speculation, however, was rife. Many remarked upon his dark, heavily tanned skin and guessed that he had seen service in the tropics. He was known to be fluent in several barbarous tongues and there was the suggestion that his military service had been discreet, if not downright secret. Captain John, however, neither confirmed nor denied the rumours. He was a close-mouthed man and the only hint to his background was the faintest trace of a Sussex accent.

The Irish workmen paid to construct his house were insulted to discover he had imported foreign supervisors to oversee the work, and foreign craftsmen were called in to install such niceties as the stairway and interior plasterwork. There was a certain amount of grumbling among the local men, who felt they could do as fine a job as any foreigners. When the foreigners stopped off at the local pubs, they found themselves the object of derision and when drink was taken, threats were passed, and in time the French, Italian and Egyptian craftsmen grew nervous and handed in their notice, leaving their work unfinished.

Having quietly observed the craftsmen at work, the local men completed the job themselves and pocketed the larger wages that had been going to the foreign specialists. And when the work was complete, no one was ever able to tell which portion of stairway or plasterwork was shaped by Irish hands.

When Captain John arrived to take possession of his new house, he was pleased with what he saw. When Phoebe subsequently took up residence there he made a great point of showing her the expensive Continental craftsmanship built into the house for her sake. He was especially pleased with the broad sweep of the oak-banistered staircase that took up much of the hallway.

Phoebe, who had recently completed a tour of Europe, recognised the Italian styling, and was flattered that Captain John should have thought so much of her to go to all this trouble. Perhaps he really did love her. She didn't love him, but the marriage was a good one – what more could a woman ask for? In time, when she had given him a child or two, she would take a lover, someone dark and handsome . . . and young. Captain John was three years younger than her father.

But within a year Phoebe was dead, from a fall down the elegant staircase, her unborn child dead with her.

No one was to blame. She had tripped at the top and grabbed the banister. But her soft flesh had slid off the highly polished wood and she had tumbled down step after step. She had stopped shrieking long before she hit the bottom. When the servants reached her, it was too late.

Captain John took his wife's death very hard. He began drinking more port than was good for him, and eating less than he should. The fine holding he had been granted lost its charms; he stayed away from home more and more frequently. Sometimes he went to Dublin or even back to England and was gone for months, leaving the servants to run the house in his absence.

They were decent, conscientious folk and did their best, but as time passed they became aware of a certain inherent melancholy in the house. It could be attributed to no one factor; some said it was rising damp, some said the trees were beginning to shade the property too darkly. The fanciful said it was Phoebe's ghost, but no ghost had actually manifested itself. There was just a pervasive sadness that thickened the atmosphere like gathering clouds.

One by one, the servants sickened and had to be replaced. Arriving strong and healthy, they invariably declined, though of no one particular ailment. Some came down with consumption, others with tumours, one fell ill with brain fever, another lost his sight. There were two related suicides: a housemaid, wronged by the under-gardener, drank rat poison and died in agony. The young man hanged himself in remorse.

And not only were the humans susceptible to the climate: the roses in the garden and the fruit in the orchard were subtly blighted. Household pets had unnaturally short lifespans. The water from the well was, ever so slightly, bitter.

In time, word came from Captain John that he was returning to his ancestral home in Sussex, and he ordered the house to be sold. It was still a pretty house in a desirable location, and the estate agents placed their advertisements in the fashionable Dublin and London papers. Within six weeks a new purchaser was found, and four weeks later, Edward Caldecott, together with his wife and six children, took up residence in the house.

The first of the children fell ill after six months. He was dead within the year, and his sister was diagnosed as consumptive.

Five years later Edward Caldecott was a widower with but one surviving child, and that a sickly boy – he was not expected to last the winter.

Local people began to whisper that there was a curse on the house, though no one could say why. Perhaps, some speculated, the foreign craftsmen had been jealous of those who had driven them out and cursed the building.

But it was a far-fetched assumption, and few believed it. The real reason for the house's misfortunes must be closer to home and more powerful.

Yet no one could name it.

Edward Caldecott buried his wife and children in the small, private graveyard beyond the house, which had been started by Captain John. Phoebe Larrimore rested there, her unborn child within her. Now she was joined by Emily Caldecott, then by Francis and Alice and Eleanor and William.

When little Percy was added to the list, Edward Caldecott took his one surviving child and fled the house forever.

For a time it stood empty. If any ghosts walked its halls, they gave no sign. The graveyard was quiet, ferns growing up to caress the faces of the gravestones. No more peaceful scene could be imagined.

Eventually the apparent tranquillity of the place lured a new owner. This time a sturdy widow from Glasgow took possession of the house and whatever it held. She had heard whispered stories and laughed at them. 'Such tales just lower the price,' she told her friends. 'It is the very sort of house I have been seeking, and I shall purchase it for half its true value!'

So events proved. Annie MacDonald was delighted with her success, and promptly moved her dark, heavy furniture into the beautifully proportioned rooms. She appraised the sweep of the staircase with a knowing eye, and wrote back to Scotland that she had obtained 'a little gem that only cost me buttons'.

That same winter a blood vessel burst in her brain as she climbed the stairs, and after lingering a few weeks, paralysed, she died in her bed. No sooner was she laid out by the local women – who exchanged knowing looks as they did so – than the staff she had hired fled the place.

The widow MacDonald's relatives back in Scotland were as practical as she was, and saw no sense in paying to have her body shipped home, not when there was a graveyard on the Irish property. They ordered her to be buried there, and the house and grounds let.

It took their agent, however, a long time before he found a tenant.

Eventually, Padraic Fahey, a cattle dealer, was convinced by his wife – who had ambitions above her station – to take a lease on the house. The Faheys moved in with their two teenage sons, but not before the cattle dealer had taken the prudent step of having his local priest bless the house thoroughly, and celebrate Mass in the sitting room.

The first weeks the Faheys spent in residence were nervous ones, but nothing untoward happened. There were no steps on the stair, no groans in the attic, no chill presences in the halls. The family began to relax. Padraic even paid a visit to the small, sadly neglected graveyard to read the lichened tombstones and remark, with a shake of his head, 'Extraordinary. All a sad coincidence, nothing more.'

The rattling branches of the winter bare trees mocked him.

Michael, the elder of his sons, was killed by lightning the next week, while felling a tree in the woods. Before the family even learned of his death, both Padraic and Liam, the younger son, were gored and trampled by a mad bull at the local sale.

The sole survivor, Maura Fahey, spent the remainder of her days in a 'home'. Locked in her own private world, she was unaware that her husband and two sons were added to the number in the graveyard.

The atmosphere in the house thickened, darkened, intensified. As if eaten by its own rotten heart, the structure began to decay. Mortar crumbled, shutters sagged from their hinges and fell into the rooms, floorboards warped and buckled, plaster peeled from the walls, revealing the blotched stonework beneath.

The estate agents didn't even bother advertising the house, so even they were surprised when two middle-aged brothers and their spinster sister offered to buy it. They had recently received a small endowment from their mother's will and sought to invest it in a 'property'.

For the first few months, all seemed well. The new owners seemed happy enough, and sank the remainder of their fortune into repairs.

Then, in the middle of an October night, one of the brothers stabbed the other, decapitated his sister, and finally hanged himself from a tree in the woodland beyond the house.

No one would ever know why.

His victims were buried in the small graveyard and their murderer laid beside them, the family reunited in death.

In the years that followed, the tale was told again in the surrounding towns and villages. Occasionally details were added, but at the heart of the story was the mystery. Why had he done it? Why had three lives ended so tragically that night? And were they – *surely they had to be* – connected to the mysterious deaths of previous years?

Yet no one ever saw frightening apparitions. No one heard shouts and screams drifting down the narrow damp valley, no supernatural manifestations ever appeared. If they were troubled spirits, they never revealed themselves.

But now everyone said it was haunted. Had to be. How else could its unrelentingly tragic history be explained? Ghosts, or a curse, or malignant fairies. . .

Something was terribly wrong with the house.

The latest owner, a distant nephew of the last three victims, never actually visited the place. And no local person would have anything at all to do with the property. It could not be sold, let, or given away, not to an Irishman. Its management passed from the hands of one firm to another, and occasionally tenants were found in Edinburgh or York or Bristol . . . and those who remained alive never stayed long. Those who remained were inevitably buried in its graveyard.

Yet no ghosts walked – not that anyone saw.

In the nearby village there were many theories. That most favoured concerned a great battle that had been fought on the land now occupied by the house, a battle fought in ancient times between the Tuatha De Danann and the Fir Bolg, before the coming of the Gaels to Ireland.

'I can tell you solemnly,' the local storyteller insisted, 'that the ground itself is haunted by the dead spirits that lie under it, their blood is in the soil, their bones in the earth, and nothing will ever thrive above that patch of earth.'

His listeners believed him, filling their pipes and nodding with narrowed eyes through the smoke. But the tale was never repeated within the hearing of the increasingly rare new tenants – not until after they had suffered a death, that is.

Years passed.

Generations passed, and were buried. The house was no longer pretty, but shabby and neglected, constantly on the verge of collapsing altogether but never quite doing so.

And every once in a great while, someone ignorant of its history would be persuaded to take it.

For a time.

A brief time.

Just long enough to add another name or names to the stones in the graveyard.

When many fine houses were burnt to the ground in Ireland during the Troubles, the house escaped the torch. Local people felt a disinclination to go there, although no living person would have stopped them.

The house still stands today. It is not difficult to find. From the verge of the road the land slopes sharply downward, but a sharp eye can discern the laneway in the damp valley below. Follow the lane to the head of the valley, where a symmetrical structure of cut stones appears, at a distance, to be an ideal period home just waiting for some lucky family. There is a faded sign tacked to a gnarled oak tree.

'To Let.'

CHAPTER TWENTY

First Communion

♣

Little Marie was named for her grandmother. The first grandchild, she was a great favourite with the family, petted, spoiled and indulged, her tantrums and petulance quickly forgiven.

It was hard not to love her. No little girl ever had more silky golden curls, or bigger blue eyes, which she could use to devastating effort.

To her parents' distress, it eventually became apparent she was also going to be an only child. The sons they longed for were never conceived. Doctors were consulted who pronounced both Tom and Kate McVey quite capable of having children, but it just did not happen.

So the love, not only of her parents, but of her two sets of grandparents and an innumerable number of aunts and uncles and cousins focused on Little Marie like a burning-glass. She was the *pet*, the *baby*, the *sweetheart*.

Every tender care was given her, and every tradition employed on her behalf, every event in her life was specially marked and celebrated, as if to make up for the fact that she had no brothers or sisters to play with. Little

Marie didn't seem overly concerned and revelled in the spotlight.

So, when the day of her first communion approached, the entire family flung itself into preparations that would have been more suited to a wedding.

Grandmother Marie, who had been a prizewinning seamstress in her youth, announced that she would make the child's first communion dress herself. She would be completely responsible for its every detail – silk-covered buttons, trimmings of lace from Little Marie's mother's wedding veil. Grandmother Marie made a number of trips to the McVey house, half-way across town, in order to measure Little Marie.

'It must be perfect,' the iron-haired woman reminded her small and wriggling subject. 'And are we not dressing you for the most important day of your life? Stand still now, love, do. We would not want to stick a pin in you.'

And day by day, stitch by stitch, the costume grew, until at last it was ready, on the very eve of the long-anticipated first communion. Grandmother Marie brought it to her daughter's house in a pasteboard box lined with tissue paper and held together by a swath of ivory ribbon, where the entire family had gathered for supper, commemorating the eve of the event. Because Little Marie was the only small child among so many adults and grown children, every occasion in her life had become 'an event'.

But first communion was a special event, marking a child's official entry into the Church, able to receive the host.

By family tradition, girls were not allowed to see the completed communion dress until the next morning, when the girl dressed for Mass. Little Marie, bored with adult society but well-mannered, sat perched on the edge of a chair with her hands folded and pretended to listen, although her gaze was turned towards the window and the beckoning summer evening beyond. She didn't care that it was her communion in the morning, nor did she care that a small fortune had been spent on the material, gloves, the shoes, handbag, rosary beads and prayerbook, and the meal that would follow. Little Marie didn't see what all the fuss was about.

When supper was almost ready, Grandmother Marie went upstairs to freshen up. As she emerged from the bathroom she heard a giggle.

'Little Marie, is that you?' she called softly.

Another giggle.

The grandmother tiptoed down the passage and peeped around the door into her daughter's bedroom. There was no one in the room. The old woman was turning away when she stopped and looked towards the big mahogany wardrobe on the far side of the room. Little Marie's communion dress had been stored in the wardrobe. She had seen her daughter turn the key in the lock . . . when she realised that the door was open . . . and a bright little face was peering around the corner of the wardrobe. Grandmother Marie caught a glimpse of white lace. Her lips twitched, suppressing a smile. 'What have you done, child?' she asked. 'Come out and let me see you.'

With another small chuckle, the bright face vanished, and the door swung to.

Grandmother Marie took a step into the room. Now she could see, in the dim, shadowy corner beyond the wardrobe, the figure of her beloved granddaughter, fully attired in her first communion costume, from white shoes to lacy veil.

The child was so lovely Grandmother Marie did not

have the heart to scold her, but turned away with tears in her eyes and made her way downstairs to join the others. Half-way down, she had to stop and take a handkerchief out of her pocket and blow her nose. The child was a vision, a beauty; in ten years time she'd still be breaking hearts.

When she entered the dining room she saw that the table was set for the meal. She stood aside as her daughter appeared carrying a platter heaped with bacon. 'Not too much for Little Marie. We want her to sleep tonight. I just saw her upstairs in her first communion dress. I suppose she could not wait for tomorrow, and I hadn't the heart to. . .'

Kate McVey let out a shriek and dropped the platter of bacon. It fell to the floor with a thud, scattering the thick slices of hot, pink meat in all directions.

'My baby!' the terrified mother cried.

Grandmother Marie stared at her, as the room filled with family. 'Whatever do you mean?'

The woman couldn't speak, could only point to the window, with a trembling finger.

Puzzled, Grandmother Marie crossed to the window and looked out. And stopped. There, in the gathering twilight, was Little Marie, dressed not in the bridal white of first communion, but in the same pink dress she had been wearing all afternoon, playing contentedly.

'She went outside when you went upstairs,' Kate told her mother. 'She's been there ever since. You couldn't *possibly* have seen her upstairs in her new dress.'

Grandmother Marie felt a cold hand clutch her heart. 'But I did. As clearly as I see you now,' she whispered hoarsely. She turned back to the window, already realising the significance of the image, desperately trying to keep her face impassive.

But Kate was watching her mother closely. With a strangled sob, she threw her arms over her mother's shoulders. 'It's Marie, isn't it? It's an omen. My baby's going to die!' she moaned. Her family tried to comfort her, but she would not be consoled. Holding tightly to her mother and husband, she kept repeating over and over, 'My baby's going to die.'

The festive supper was forgotten. The little girl was hastily brought inside where she was quite astonished at all the excitement.

'Maybe you crept in to try on the dress,' Grandmother Marie suggested, desperately praying that the child would nod and smile and agree.

The girl shook her head firmly. 'I've been in the garden the whole time. I did not come in. I did not try on my dress. Honest, Grandma, I didn't.'

It was the truth.

Yet Grandmother Marie had seen her.

Some of the uncles tried to laugh it off as a trick of light brought on by overwrought nerves, and the strain on hurrying to finish the dress, working long hours into the night in poor light. They insisted things should go on as before.

But Little Marie had a restless night, and by morning her forehead was hot and flushed, her cheeks bright red.

The doctor said she had caught a chill and that she would be up and about in a day or two.

The fever took her in three days.

And two days later, a week from the day Grandmother Marie had seen her image in the bedroom, Little Marie was laid to rest in a snow-white coffin. She was buried in her first-communion dress.

CHAPTER TWENTY-ONE

After the Ball

─────── ♣ ───────

The house stood a few miles beyond Belturbet. It had been in the same family for many years, and enjoyed a fine reputation for hospitality. Hardly a day passed that some carriage did not draw up under the broad portico to dislodge guests. More often than not they included a bevy of pretty young ladies, for the family had been blessed with three eligible sons who were fond of parties, and gave as many as they attended.

A lively house party was underway on the last weekend of the summer when Isabella Clifton visited the house for the first time. She was chaperoned by her aunt, a formidable lady who rejoiced in the equally formidable name of Griselda Lake Clifton-Morris, and had made it her personal duty to see her niece betrothed before the year was out. She set about achieving this aim with the same determination that had seen her wed – and widowed – three times. So she had arranged for invitations to be issued to herself and Isabella to attend the party of the season, at the home of the widower Penrose Lewis and his boys. And no doubt Griselda had wondered if a lonely widower might be looking for a wife. Although she had been particularly unlucky with her husbands, she was willing to have another chance.

The three Lewis sons were very much in evidence as the ball began. They stood beside their father in the grand entrance hall, greeting the guests with manners polished in Dublin society and, it was rumoured, at court in London. While their practised smiles concealed their utter boredom, they grew genuinely attentive when Miss Clifton appeared alongside her aunt. The young woman glided smoothly up the wide steps toward them, tilting her parasol skilfully so it shielded her face from the sun without hiding any of her charms. She had wide-set eyes and a dimple in her chin, and the three young men came forward as one to welcome her.

At the ball that night, Isabella Clifton was the unquestioned belle. Other young ladies from the vicinity stood around the edges of the ballroom and gossiped spitefully behind their hands and flickering fans as Isabella danced tirelessly with one partner after another, beguiling them all with a mixture of charm and innocence.

From the sidelines, Griselda's razor-sharp face was expressionless as she watched the proceedings, before she turned her attentions to Lewis Senior, terrifying him with a smile.

Young Gordon Lewis, eldest son of the family and the heir to considerable property both in Ireland and the family mining interests in South Africa, was Isabella's most frequent partner. In fact, he could not leave her alone, but repeatedly claimed her from the arms of other men, in a shocking breach of manners. He was quite obviously smitten.

The buzz of gossip rose in volume.

'Who is she?'

'An heiress from Dublin, I believe. She's on the Viceregal guest list.'

'Why have we never heard of her before? And why is she monopolising the best young men in a provincial country?'

'Let her return to Dublin and spread her charms in Dublin Castle and Merrion Square.'

However, the gossips fell silent when they realised they were under the implacable stare of Griselda Lake Clifton-Morris, whose humour was not helped by the extremely uncomfortable, gilded chair she was perched on.

So far so good. She was pleased that Isabella was an obvious success. And relieved that her niece's reputation obviously had not extended as far as Belturbet and environs.

The house party arranged around the ball was to last three days. The dancing itself lasted until a sumptuous breakfast was spread in the dining room the next morning, so that none of the young people put head to pillow. During the following day, many of the young ladies retired to their rooms to drowse away the afternoon and restore their beauty. But the vivacious Isabella Clifton was not among them. She appeared to possess an inexhaustible store of energy, and took advantage of her opportunity to gather the young men for a picnic on the riverbank.

Sounds of laughter and song drifted up to the house from time to time. The young ladies who had chosen to retire for the afternoon fretted on their beds, regretting their decision. But Griselda Lake Clifton-Morris, sitting in a bathchair with a blanket around her legs, smiled to herself, hoping that the day would end favourably. And, despite Lewis Senior's seeming oblivious to her own considerable charms, she still had hopes.

No proposal being forthcoming – at least on such short acquaintance – the indefatigable Isabella was at last forced to return to her own room and prepare for the evening.

There was a supper party, whist and charades, and more dancing. Once more Isabella was the centre of all eyes and in the heart of every male in the group. If anything, Isabella seemed even more energetic, and left partner after partner sitting sweat-soaked and slumped in exhaustion after each dance.

Griselda began to worry. Her sharp scrutiny detected a certain rising flush to her niece's cheeks and an increasingly feverish tempo to her speech.

The young people sought their beds considerably earlier than the night before. Isabella's aunt had the room adjoining hers, and insisted on leaving the connecting door open. She then tried to stay awake, one ear attuned to the slightest movement on the part of her niece. When she heard Isabella's breathing settling into a gentle rhythm she allowed herself to relax.

She awoke in the silence before the dawn and immediately checked on her niece, and was relieved to discover that she hadn't left her bed. The old woman crossed herself. Maybe it was over. Maybe nothing would happen.

But something had happened.

It began shortly after midnight with a rattling of pots and saucepans in the kitchen belowstairs, almost as if a train had rumbled along a track close to the house. But there was no train. There were no tracks within miles.

The rattling pans were soon joined by the clinking of crystal and the pinging of pottery. Wooden mixing spoons trembled in their pitcher on the kitchen work table, the cutlery quivered in the drawers. The rising clamour alerted both Cook and her skivvy . . . whose screams, when they discovered the place in noisy turmoil, roused everyone belowstairs.

But the most terrifying aspect of the phenomenon was its duration. It continued for more than three hours and grew in intensity as the night progressed. Metal cutlery twisted into arcane shapes, heavy copper pots and saucepans flew across the room to shatter against the stone walls, every razor-edged knife in the kitchen was dulled, the tines on the forks bent double. An underbutler was almost killed when an iron skillet sliced across the room and buried itself quivering in the wall by his head. Finally, the servants bolted in panic and closed the kitchen door, and then spent the rest of the night listening to the noise within.

Silence fell before dawn, but it was only when the sun came up that the door was opened. And when the butler and Mr Lewis toured the room, they discovered everything was in order.

Under the butler's savage interrogation, most of the staff began distancing themselves from what they had seen and heard, and only the cook and her skivvy kept to their stories. But it was well known that the cook was fond of her gin and the skivvy was a half-witted local girl.

The story caused considerable mirth among the weekend houseguests when it got out. Only Griselda Lake Clifton-Morris made no comment. She did, though, cast stern eyes on her lovely niece and shake her head as if in warning.

Isabella stared blankly back at her, refusing to be intimidated.

The day passed uneventfully, punctuated with croquet and lawn tennis, and a boat trip up the river. That night after the young people retired to their rooms, worn out with fresh air and flirtation, Griselda prudently turned the key in her niece's lock to make certain Isabella did not leave her bedroom before morning.

But no sooner had the house grown quiet than the silence

was shattered by the brandy decanter in the library hurtling itself across the room to smash against the marble mantelpiece. The alcohol fuelled the dying embers bringing the fire to blazing life. Silver-framed photographs danced and spun on tables before shattering on the floor. The antique Parisian mirror fell from the wall and exploded across the Sheraton sideboard, gouging chunks of wood from its beautifully worked surface. Prisms dropped off chandeliers in tiny tinkling pops.

Lewis Senior and his sons attempted to gain entry to the room, but the door was warped shut and they were forced to stand in the gardens and stare in through the windows, watching as the flickering firelight illuminated the macabre scene. Their houseguests joined them, silent and terrified – except for Isabella, who was securely locked in her room, and her aunt, who was on her knees by her bed, head bent in prayer.

As the nightmare of destruction continued – which was all the more terrifying because it was confined to one room – the distraught houseguests began leaving.

Yet no source for the trouble could be identified.

The first grey light of morning revealed a room that had been completely destroyed. Everything was broken, all the smooth surfaces were scored and scratched, the plaster-work hung in shredded strips from the ceiling, the velvet curtains were now little more than rags.

In company with the other guests, Isabella Clifton and her aunt were preparing to leave. A mutual embarrassment had seized hosts and guests alike. No one knew what to say. Transparent excuses for leaving were offered, to be met by red-faced apologies.

Soon a procession of carriages and carts began arriving under the portico to take the shocked guests away. Isabella

Clifton was among the last to leave. Young Gordon Lewis remained standing in the hall, white-faced, the scored remains of an oil painting of his late mother clutched in his hands, too distracted to bid Isabella a suitably flattering farewell. She hesitated on the steps, casting languorous glances in his direction, but to no avail.

At last her aunt gave her sleeve an imperious tweak and made her get into their carriage. 'It's no good, it's too late,' Griselda hissed to her niece. 'That weekend is ruined . . . just like so many others,' she added ominously. 'How can you expect a man to have courting on his mind in such circumstances? Oh, why can you not control. . .?'

She did not finish the sentence, but sank back in her seat and rolled her eyes heavenwards. Where would they go next? At this rate, they would soon exhaust the possibilities in Ireland and she would have to take her ward elsewhere, to the Continent, perhaps, to find a husband. Her thin lips twisted at the thought of Isabella marrying a foreigner.

They were not welcome in Dublin any more. Dublin society began to suspect, after several incidents like this most recent one, that it was not wise to have Isabella Clifton in one's house. If she received any more invitations around Belturbet, in time the same conclusion would be reached.

No, it was best to move on, to try and find a rather more obscure hunting ground.

But how, poor Griselda wondered, feeling an old depression beginning to creep back over her, how does one marry off a niece who is permanently afflicted by . . .? She dug in her purse and pulled out the scrap of paper upon which she'd written the strange word, the word she had only recently discovered to describe her niece's affliction. She pronounced the word slowly.

'*Poltergeist.*'

CHAPTER TWENTY-TWO

The Brothers

———— ♣ ————

Off the coast of Donegal, the Atlantic Ocean boils and rages. The storms it blows onto the land are fierce, but no fiercer than the passions that can rage in human hearts.

The O'Donnell brothers, who lived in a long, thatched cottage above a tiny cove, had loved and hated one another all their lives. Aidan and Aonghus looked enough alike to be twins, though they were not; Aidan was two years older. But both were tall and broad and sturdy, with burning, blue eyes and wild, copper-red hair and beards. Whatever one did, the other had to do better, whatever one said the other had to disagree with. There was no end to the rivalry between them.

Nor to the love, either. In the nearby fishing village it was said, with some truth, that 'They might beat each other to death one day, but they would join together to beat to death any man fool enough to attack one of them singly.'

The O'Donnell brothers were seal-killers, at a time before mankind developed a conscience about such things. They made a living from selling hides and seal oil, and lived as richly – or as poorly – as everyone else in the area, their livelihoods inextricably linked to nature and, despite their constant bickering, they thought themselves content.

Until Honora Ryan appeared.

She was from Belfast, a woman widowed in her early twenties when her husband had died in an accident in the shipyards. To escape the city and its memories, she had gradually moved west, earning her living on farms and in small shops. She was a large, buxom woman, with tangled dark hair and wanton eyes. She found work serving behind the bar in the village and from the moment the O'Donnell brothers saw her, they were instantly smitten. For herself, she saw nothing to choose between them and so flirted with both equally, teasing one, ignoring the other, then favouring one with a touch, a smile, a soft word. She had been less than two weeks in the village and the brothers were close to killing one another.

Soon Aonghus had dragged his bed to the far end of their cottage so he might put as much distance between himself and Aidan as possible. They no longer wished one another a grudging 'morning' or 'good-night', and they no longer spoke to one another at meals. But as neither Aonghus nor Aidan was willing to leave his brother alone for fear the other would use the time to court Honora, they watched each other like hawks.

They had always been close. Now they were never out of each other's sight.

The air between them grew as electric and acrid as the air before a storm.

Honora was delighted to be the cause of such passion, and not above provoking it to greater heights for pure devilment. When local folk gathered in someone's cottage on Sunday nights for a bit of music and a jar of local poteen was passed around, Honora would always insist on seating herself between Aidan and Aonghus, and putting a hand on each arm. She dispensed intimate squeezes in equal measure, spiced with sidelong glances and slight twitches of her body that gave the brothers equal opportunity to peer into her low-necked bodice.

'Hussy . . . shameless wanton,' was the consensus of the older women. But none of the local men had a bad word to say for Honora. 'She's young and high-spirited,' was their defence, 'and she's had it hard up to now. Widowed at nineteen. Sure, life will wear her down soon enough. Let her have her fun.'

However, because she was not cruel at heart, she took pity on the pair. She called by their cottage on her way home when the pub had closed for the night, and while they both scrambled to make room for her at the table, she said simply, 'I've reached a decision.' Both brothers swallowed hard and glanced sharply at one another. 'I am only too aware that both of you want me to walk out with you.' She smiled her quick, flashing smile. 'And it's a walk that will end at the altar, I've no doubt!'

The silence in the cottage was deep enough to hear the distant hissing of the sand on the beach as the brothers waited for Honora to continue.

'I will walk out with the one who brings me four of the finest seal pelts. I've a mind to make myself a cape,' she added, 'such as the women in the cities wear. The pelts must be of the finest quality,' she reminded them, and walked away.

The next day Aidan and Aonghus were up before dawn, embarked upon the most important seal hunt of their lives.

The profession which they had inherited from their father was not ordinarily a hazardous one. It involved selecting a beach frequented by seals, preferably one encircled by cliffs, and then placing oneself between the animals and their only avenue of escape, the sea. In the water the seals were more graceful than birds, but on land they were clumsy. A strong man with a club could do great damage in a short period of time to a seal herd.

But not just any seal was suitable for harvest, as the brothers knew. If the pelt was the prize, the seal must be young and healthy, and furred for the winter. It must also be as free from scars as possible. In any herd of seals, only a very few might have skins of the quality Honora desired for her cape.

The brothers knew the basking-ground of the finest seals in the area, a crescent-shaped beach a few miles north of their cottage. By silent mutual consent, they launched their boat together and rowed up the coast, each thinking his own thoughts. It would take both of them for the hunt; they must work together until their quarry was found and slain.

But then. . .

What then?

The brothers rowed in silence as heavy as the sea.

They found the beach they sought, and on it a large herd of seals. As the boat rowed in to shore, the animals raised their heads and regarded the humans with gentle, liquid eyes. Then a big bull seal sounded a cry of warning and suddenly they were all floundering towards the water.

The hunters swiftly beached their boat and ran to head off the seals. There was no time to be selective; they would kill every seal they could, then pick out the best skins afterwards.

The clubs fell clean and rose bloody.

At almost the same moment, Aidan and Aonghus spied the group of young animals clustered together as if for protection at the far end of the beach, four or five of them, all very pale, their new fur shimmering like pale ivory. White seals were a great rarity and very valuable. Neither man had ever seen more than one at a time before, and here in one herd were enough to make a cape no woman could resist!

With a shout of triumph, the brothers ran toward the white seals.

A few minutes' bloody work and the prize was taken. The men stopped, panting, and gazed down at their kill.

Aidan squared his shoulders. 'You'll help me skin them,' he ordered.

'I'll help you? And why should I be doing that? They are not yours but mine. You can help me skin them, I'll pay you.'

Aidan glared at Aonghus. 'I'll pay *you*. I am the oldest, these are mine by right.'

Never before had either suggested such an arrangement. They had always hunted together, split the work and the profit too. But this was different.

They quarrelled, furiously and inevitably, while the dead seals lay wallowing in blood at their feet and the rest of the herd made its frantic escape. Bitter words turned to blows. And when one brother at last raised his club to strike a fatal blow to the other, nothing living was a witness.

Later – much, much later – Aonghus brought his white sealskins back to the village. People ran forward to gaze in wonder at the rarity and Honora preened like a queen, knowing they were for her.

Then someone asked the question. 'And where is Aidan. . .? Surely half of these are his.'

Aonghus's face turned pale and he hung his head. Tears were seen to drip from his blue eyes into his flaming beard as he said, 'We caught these creatures at the edge of a cliff, and Aidan overreached himself trying to strike one, and lost his balance. His body fell into the sea. I searched and searched but could not find it. The sea has him now,' he added in a voice low with misery.

The silent villagers retreated to their cottages and small shops. Such tragedies were not unknown. There was hardly a family in the village who had not lost someone to the sea. But later, as the story was told and retold about the village, questions began to be asked, especially by men who had hunted and fished all their lives, and the question asked again and again was; 'Whoever heard of seals taken on top of a cliff? How did they climb? Are they not usually down on the beaches?'

And in time, little by little, people began to shun Aonghus.

The white sealskins were made into a wondrous cape for Honora to wear as she walked proudly by his side on Sundays, but even the splendour of her garment was not enough to distract her from the suspicious glances and rumours that began circulating about Aonghus. She began to feel uncomfortable with him herself. Once he had been a jovial man, given to laughter and singing, but he was increasingly morose. She could not break through his brooding silences.

So one bright spring morning – six weeks before her wedding – Honora Ryan ran off with a raven-haired traveller. And, if that weren't insult enough, she took the sealskin cape with her.

For a time, the local folk thought Aonghus would lose his mind. He strode along the clifftops and he prowled the beaches, sometimes weeping, sometimes shouting aloud his anger at the perfidy of women, sometimes cursing the creature who had stolen his white sealskins.

Sometimes, in silence, he brooded over the terrible price he had paid for them.

No one attempted to comfort him. The proud Donegal people had a strongly developed sense of right and wrong, and most thought he was getting what he deserved. So they left him alone in his grief and anger, and no storm off the Atlantic was more.turbulent than the soul of Aonghus the seal-killer.

Leaving the cottage that had been his family home for four generations, he wandered up and down the coast, looking for peace. He killed a few seals, enough to support himself, but there was no pleasure in it now, no thrill in the smack of wood off flesh, the splintering of bone, the hot spurt of blood. Now, other – darker – images came to him. And in the liquid eyes of every seal he killed he could see his brother's expression.

He never wandered far from the sea, which drew him again and again to wander along the shores, head down, shoulders slumped, only occasionally rousing himself enough to stare out to sea. But when he did stop, he would stand for hours, with his eyes fixed on the long Atlantic rollers as they came crashing in to the shore.

Sometimes the round head of a seal would appear briefly in the shallows, gaze unblinkingly at Aonghus, then disappear beneath the surface of the water. It was a thing seals often did, being inquisitive creatures. Once he would have given it no thought. But now when a seal looked at him like that, his heart seemed to stand still.

A seal's head looked almost like a human head. Wreathed in a nimbus of sea mist, it might be his brother Aidan out there, watching him.

'Have mercy on me!' he cried aloud when it happened once too often and his nerve broke. 'Forgive me! She was not worth it!'

The watching seal remained a moment longer, then

dived beneath the surface and was gone.

Almost every day thereafter something similar happened. Wherever Aonghus went along the coast, a seal would surface to watch him. Then he would shout out the pains of his tormented soul. He confessed his jealousy of his brother, his misguided love for Honora, the moment of madness that had led him to murder, and most of all the terrible regret that was eating him alive.

'I am the most accursed of men!' Aonghus wept aloud, standing on the shore and beating his red head with his great fists. 'She was not worth it all, not worth it at all . . . Love makes men mad . . .' Sinking to his knees in the gritty sands, he bent his head sobbing bitterly.

And from the shallows the seals, gentlest of creatures, observed his pain.

Lying curled up in agony on the beach, Aonghus was at first unaware that he was no longer alone. Then he felt a gentle nudge. He opened his eyes.

A large seal lay on the beach beside him, regarding him soulfully. Its coat was the same lustrous ivory as those he had slain for Honora. And its eyes were the same burning blue as his dead brother's.

Recoiling, Aonghus tried on hands and knees to scramble away from the seal. But it followed him insistently, repeating the gentle nudges with its head. At last the man stopped trying to escape and sat on the sand, holding out a timid hand.

The seal pushed its round head under his hand.

Aonghus remained sitting on the beach for a long time, with his hand lightly resting on the seal's head. The creature made no move to leave him. The man wept again, cried away in pain and hate and fear, and when he was done, he felt a sense of peace as deep and serene as the depths of the sea.

When Aonghus at last got to his feet and headed for home, the seal followed him.

He walked slowly so it could, in its awkward way, keep up with him. Every now and then he would pause and crouch down beside the animal to touch it again, with a sense of wonder, and let its tranquillity and forgiveness flow into him.

By the time he reached his village there was a light in his face that would never leave it.

Aonghus never again hunted seals. He supported himself patching boats, mending nets, building walls, whatever he could turn his hand to that utilised his skills but took no life. Without the income from the pelt and oil, he was reduced to a marginal subsistence, but he never seemed to mind. No one heard him complain.

He became the calmest and most cheerful of men, easygoing, tolerant, always willing to lend a hand when needed, so totally unselfish that as the years passed his former sin was forgiven – though not forgotten. Far from shunning him, local folk now sought him out, asking his advice.

Everyone knew he was mad, of course. 'Has been for years,' they told one another knowingly. 'But sure, is it not the madness of a saint? Like the good St Francis himself, who would never raise a hand to hurt the smallest creature. And have you not seen the seals come up out of the water when Aonghus walks on the beach, especially the white seal?'

If there were strangers about who had not heard the story before, someone would always add, 'And do you know, he calls the white seal Aidan? He had a brother called Aidan. And he talks to the seal . . . and then waits as if he can hear it reply!'

CHAPTER TWENTY-THREE

The Fairy Forts

♣

The two mounds stood, some half a mile apart, on the way to Clonmel. The grass grew green on them and gorse encircled them, but no one had disturbed them for a thousand years.

Once they had comprised two great circles of banked earth interlaced with stones, surrounding an inner hollow. Archaeologists claimed that Iron Age farmers had built wattle houses within those hollows and sheltered their domestic livestock within those banks, but local people knew better. 'Fairy forts,' they said simply, and avoided them.

The Good People, the Little People, descendants of the proud and magical Tuatha De Danann, would put a curse on anyone who disturbed one of their long-abandoned but always guarded forts.

Or so it was believed, locally.

The stranger held no such belief.

Paul Piershill was a Dutchman, broad and muscular, very good with his hands, and a lifetime of hard work had at last given him the means to retire to some peaceful land.

He chose Ireland because he knew no one there and had no relatives there, and so could be assured of peace. He bought the land between the two fairy forts because it was extraordinarily cheap and he would have enough money left over to build himself a solid house.

The local people did not tell him why the land was so inexpensive until the sale had been concluded and he had taken possession. Then, they let him know in the most circuitous manner that 'It would be foolish to build between the old fairy forts. . .'

When he demanded to know why, he was informed that the fairies still travelled between the forts from time to time, and wanted the road kept open.

'Road? I saw no road!' he cried.

The men in the pub pursed their lips and cast down their eyes, seeming almost embarrassed at the stranger's ignorance.

'No road at all!' Piershill repeated in his accentless English.

One of the older men looked up at him with an expression which might have been scorn – or amusement. 'Did you not? Perhaps you weren't looking.'

'Perhaps there was nothing to see!' the Dutchman snapped.

'As you wish. Well, build away, then.'

The Dutchman built. He was a practical man who had fought in the last war, and he was not going to be deterred by local superstition. He lived in a small caravan on the edge of the property while he built much of the house himself, basing it on the style of his homeland, and in order to keep down the costs, used much of the old cut-and-dressed stones he found lying about on his new property. Obviously someone had built here before.

When the house was done, Piershill surveyed it with satisfaction. The walls were straight, the roof was even, the doors and windows were plumb. Although tempted to move into the house immediately, he waited until a consignment of fine new Dutch furniture arrived and only when everything was in its place did he move into the house, eight weeks before Christmas.

It was close to midnight when Piershill retired to bed. After months of sleeping on the narrow cot in the caravan, he was looking forward to spending a night in the enormous wooden bed.

He had been asleep less than five minutes when a terrifying roar brought him bolt upright, heart hammering. It sounded as if the earth beneath the house were being ripped open. With a cry of horror, he leaped out of bed, and tumbled to the floor. The boards were trembling beneath his feet.

'Earthquake?' he exclaimed aloud. Then he remembered that there were no earthquakes in Ireland.

The floor heaved and bucked like a living creature.

The Dutchman ran outside. The landing buckled and twisted, and stairs turned beneath his feet and it took three pulls to wrench the hall door open. When he staggered out into the night, he discovered that it was perfectly still and silent.

Too silent.

Even the customary night noises of wind and bird and insect and small predators rustling through the under- growth were missing.

A dream? A nightmare?

The Dutchman nodded. A nightmare brought on by the many months of hard labour. The result of strain.

Piershill went back into his house. It was completely

silent, the floor lying flat and solid and immobile.

'Nightmare,' he said aloud, just to hear his voice in the silence. He made himself crawl back into bed, and lay waiting for a long time, but nothing more happened. Dawn had pearled the windows when eventually he fell asleep.

The house stood silent around him.

The grandmother clock in the hall was pinging noon when he awoke. Rolling over in the bed, he looked toward the window beside his bed . . . and sat bolt upright in the bed. The neatly sashed, shuttered and glass-paned window was now twisted on the wall, one corner inches higher than the other, the mechanism for opening the window sprung and the glass cracked. He could actually see a tiny triangle of blue sky where the frame had parted from the wall.

The Dutchman swore a terrible oath. Vandalism. The locals had to be doing this. Small-minded, xenophobic people who resented any stranger with a bit of money in his pocket, they had come in the night to try and drive him out.

But how had they done such structural damage to a window beside his bed without waking him?

He stormed into the nearby village and demanded explanations. Everyone looked at him blankly, and denied everything. He got the impression they were laughing at him behind his back, though they pretended to be sympathetic. Finally, someone murmured, 'Fairy forts,' and heads nodded in agreement.

'That is a tale you tell to frighten children!' Piershill snapped. 'And I am not a child! I bought that land. I paid good money for it. I have a right to build a house and live there. And none of you will stop me,' he added ominously.

The small knot of men gathered around the entrance to the pub smiled amongst themselves, but this only served to infuriate the Dutchman more. 'It's not ourselves,' they told him.

But he did not believe them.

He bought timber and glass in the hardware store that also doubled as a post office and returned home to repair the damaged window. As if the elements were conspiring against him, a cold, thin rain settled across the landscape, the water bubbling the new wallpaper, seeping into the expensive carpet. It also trickled down the back of his neck and chilled his spine . . . and more than once he turned, as if inimical eyes were watching him from a distance.

When the window was finally repaired, he went into his house and slammed the door. In the enormous fireplace built of local stone, he lit a roaring fire and then stood with his back to it, feeling the chill reluctantly leave his bones. He was getting too old for this. In the morning he would go into the nearest town and see about buying a shotgun. The next person who trespassed on his property would get a seatful of buckshot.

As usual, Piershill slept lying on his back, his legs straight, no pillow beneath his head, his hands crossed right over left atop the covers. Drifting to sleep, exhausted after the day's labours, he was thinking about painting the ceiling blue, with clouds. . .

The cold rain pouring down on him shocked him awake.

Appalled, he stared up at a massive hole in the roof just above his bed. It was as if a giant had taken a bite out of the house, shingles, planks, rafters, all were gone, leaving a gaping aperture almost exactly the size of his bed . . . and the edges were smooth and polished, the slate tiles gleaming, the edges of the wood looking glossy.

Shivering and swearing, Paul Piershill spent the rest of the night curled in an armchair, wild eyes fixed on the ceiling. At first light he set off to buy more building materials, a shotgun, and a large and savage Alsatian dog. Still convinced that the locals were somehow responsible, he bypassed the village and went into the town of Clonmel. The extra hour's journey did little for his humour, and it was early afternoon before he returned . . . to discover that his brand-new front door, which he had painted a crisp, bright red, was faded and splintery, sagging on rusty hinges. Piershill walked around the house in mute astonishment. Every window pane on both floors was broken, and every window frame was rotted and damp, the wood turned to waxy pulp. The mortar between the stones of his walls seemed to have failed within a day, crumbling like soft cheese. Some of the stones were already pulling free, falling away.

The house looked as if it had stood neglected for fifty years.

As they neared the house, the savage Alsatian started howling. It wasn't a normal dog's cry of anger, rage or pain, but something else, something older, something primeval that raised the hackles on his new owner's neck. As Piershill struggled to hold its leather leash, the dog suddenly pulled free and darted away, its ears flat against its head, its tail between its legs.

There was a crushing, grinding noise. Paul Piershill turned to look back at his house . . . in time to see another section of roof collapse inward, sending up a cloud of dust and splintery debris.

The sound had hardly ceased reverberating when another, deeper, stranger sound took its place. To the Dutchman's astonishment, he heard the unmistakable sound of marching feet. Tramping feet. The rhythmic thud of something very like an army on the march, heading straight towards him, the jingle of harness distinct on the damp afternoon air.

Gazing wildly around, he saw nothing. He stood on the footpath in front of a dilapidated house that had been new only that morning, a house surrounded by a neat green lawn he had carefully mown . . . and had filled with weeds in the interval he was away.

To the north he could see the rounded hill of one fairy fort, to the south the grassy mound of the second. And moving between them, he could hear an army marching.

As they drew nearer he could hear their voices, light as the hum of bees. Their footsteps were light too, unlike the thud of army boots. It was only their vast numbers that made them audible.

Now he could make out music playing, perhaps at the end of their column – a wild, free music, at once mournful and beautiful, trilling from instruments he could not identify. It seemed to blend into the very trees and air and become part of them, as if it had always been there, its rhythm in the rustles of branches, its lilting tune in the hiss of grass. And as it shivered across the countryside, another section of his roof collapsed, and several stones rolled free of his wall and fell onto the ground. The front door buckled as if it had been struck, then collapsed too.

The invisible marchers had almost reached the place where the Dutchman stood rooted to the spot. His eyes bulged, his mouth was dry, his heart pounding so loudly it almost drowned out the sounds he was hearing.

He wished it would.

He didn't want to hear the sounds. He didn't want to be anywhere in this accursed country. Images of Amsterdam flashed before his eyes, the familiar clatter of human voices in his native language, and the rows of neat houses that stood year after year, century after century, occupied by a bustling and practical race that did not believe in fairy forts.

The Dutchman even yearned for the loud voices of his sons' wives and their endless demands, and actually to hear the voices of his daughters' husbands with their endless criticisms. He yearned with all his heart to be among them again, to be among normal people in a normal world . . . and not in this accursed place. Bowing his head, he prayed to a god he had lost on the bloody battlefields of Europe.

And then the marching army reached his house and the building surrendered to them.

Like an ancient mummy disturbed by the first touch of sunlight, the fabric of the house disintegrated. The remainder of the roof went first, slates sliding off to crash on the ground, the chimney swaying to and fro, before it smashed through the attic into the bedroom below. The window frames simply fell from the walls, and then the walls themselves began to crumble.

Paul Piershill knelt on the ground and buried his head in his hands, trying to drown out the sounds of the disintegrating house, the terrible cracking and snapping as his new furniture was destroyed.

And when he looked up there was nothing left standing but a pile of rubble.

It looked like ancient rubble. It looked like the ruins of a building that had been abandoned a thousand years ago.

The marching feet came through the heap of destruction, straight towards the Dutchman. He brandished his useless shotgun in a gesture he knew was ridiculous and loosed off both barrels, the sounds flat and mocking on the air. He could hear the pellets rattling off the tumbled stones. Then he dropped the gun and ran.

The shotgun lies there still, slowly rusting and rotting, beside a tumble of stone that could have been anything, from any time. It lies between two fairy forts half a mile apart on the way to Clonmel.

CHAPTER TWENTY-FOUR

On Craglea

───────── ♣ ─────────

High above Lough Derg, alone on the grey stone crag called Craglea, Aoibheal sits. Her brooding eyes gaze out across the vast lake, seeing every ripple, watching every sailboat, equally aware of the fish below the surface and the creatures who live in the mud at the bottom, conscious of the birds in the air, the creatures that walk and creep and crawl through the woodlands. She can see them all at the same time, for her eyes are not human eyes.

Aoibheal is a bean sidhe.

Her name means 'The Lovely One,' and it suits her for, in a human guise, she is a small, slender woman with a mane of soft hair and huge, limpid eyes.

But this is not the face she always shows to the humankind.

Since the time of the Irish king, Cormac Cas, and perhaps even before, Aoibheal has occupied this crag. When the descendants of Cormac Cas became the Dalcassian tribe and settled in this part of Munster, Aoibheal took them under her protection and became their guardian spirit. There was no reason for it, it was a choice she made herself, made because it amused her. There are legends and tales told, of course, but these are fictions, created by man to belittle what they cannot understand. And Aoibheal is beyond understanding. Most *mna shee* – fairy women, banshees – are objects of fear and terror. Contradicting this image gave her pleasure, appealing to that which was most Irish in her nature.

In time she found herself the guardian spirit of the man who would one day be known to history as Brian Boru, the Lion of Ireland. From atop Craglea, Aoibheal watched his meteoric rise from obscurity to the high kingship of Ireland. With her eyes that see everything, she saw the passion in him, the dreams, the sheer force of will that refused to bow before any obstacle. It called to her, reminded her of warriors and kings she had known: men, who were more than human, but less than gods, and gods who were less than human. But they all shared a single passion, they all possessed an imagination. She discovered that imagination, that breath of vision in the boy Brian and, because it amused her to do so, she leant him her aid.

At the Battle of Clontarf in 1014, when Brian defeated the Vikings once and for all, and changed Irish history, Aoibheal wore a hideous face calculated to freeze the stoutest heart with terror. She walked the enemy camps the night before the decisive battle. Some of them deserted their leaders then, convinced that nothing could stand against Brian Boru and his supernatural guardian.

But Aoibheal paid for her devotion with pain.

When the battle was over, Brian himself was dead, and the banshee wept for him as she had never wept for anyone, and though her power was mighty, she could not raise the dead nor turn back time, the great unknown against which even the gods themselves cannot prevail.

After Clontarf, Aoibheal returned to Craglea to watch over the changing fortunes of the Dalcassians, following them down through the centuries. Then, to her horror, the wooded mantle that had always covered her mountain was cut down, leaving the knob of stone on its summit bare and unshielded. Without the trees and their bounty to feed and sustain her, and knowing she would be forced to feed off the humankind, she fled.

No one knew where she went. For generations, local people spoke of her and listened for her voice, but it never came. In time they began to forget.

Then, singly and in clumps, trees were planted once more on the slopes of Aoibheal's mountain. As they grew, they pulled the remnants of the ancient magic from the soil and spread it on the wind, and the wind found Aoibheal and told her.

One night, close to the turn of the year, when summer still lingers but winter has already made its presence felt, Tom MacMahon and his family were gathered in the kitchen of their farmhouse below the grey crag. The bulk of the mountain rising above them shielded their house from the wind, but the night was very cold, a promise of the bitter winter to come. A turf fire burned on the hearth and Tom's wife, Maureen, had just served them all mugs of piping hot cocoa – Tom had a child's passion for chocolate, which his three children had inherited. Sitting huddled before the fire, hands wrapped around the mugs, warm and safe and comfortable, they heard the sound. . .

Maureen put her mug down, untasted. 'What, in the name of all that's holy, was that?' She was city born and bred, and the sights and sounds of the countryside at night could still surprise and frighten her.

A muscle jumped in her husband's jaw. 'I never heard anything like it,' he admitted. Memories flickered, tales told by this very fire when he was a boy.

The sound shattered the stillness once again.

The children, two small boys and a rosy-cheeked little girl, ran to their mother and clustered about her, not frightened by the noise, not yet, awaiting their parents' reaction.

Transfixed between fear and fascination, the adults listened as the sound was repeated. It was something between a sob and a moan which then rose in pitch until it resonated in the very timbers of their house.

There was pain in the voice.

Fear.

Terror.

Hurt. Above all else, there was hurt.

It was the undiluted essence of grief.

'Banshee,' Tom murmured, crossing himself. 'Banshee.'

Maureen shook her head. 'You cannot be serious,' she began, beginning to smile, unsure if he were joking or not, knowing he was, because it simply couldn't be. . .

'Banshee,' Tom said quickly. 'It is. She lives up on top of the mountain, or used to. My grandfather told me the tales of the creature that haunts Craglea.' He frowned, trying to remember the creature's name. He shook his head. 'She was a banshee. But she left, a long time ago, even before my grandfather's time . . . and now she's back.'

Maureen shook her head.

'It is.'

Maureen squeezed her eyes shut. He obviously was serious and she'd been married to him long enough to know when he was serious or when he was joking with her. A banshee. Here. She wanted to deny it, but she couldn't ignore that terrible wailing. Her heart pounded in her breast. 'What does it mean?'

'Usually a banshee's wail predicts a death. They usually cry for a particular clan, one of the Macs or Os. This one was the banshee of the ancient Dalcassians and they're all long dead and gone. Perhaps she's wailing for one of their descendants. . .'

'You?' Maureen asked in a breathy whisper.

Tom forced a nervous laugh. 'Not me. My family are blow-ins. My great-grandfather bought this farm from the last of an old family who always claimed they had Dalcassian blood in them, though if they had, my grandfather said, it was thinly diluted. We have none of that ancient blood. I'm sure of it.'

The banshee cried again.

The fearful ululation rose on the night air, ringing out across the lake, rippling the water of the Shannon river below the lake, trembling off the mountains surrounding it. Tom's eyes met those of his wife. They were both pale.

Hearing the fear and uncertainty in their parents' voices, the two younger children grew upset, and their fear quickly fed each other, reducing them to hysterics. Brian, the eldest boy, heard the sounds and interpreted them as a vixen's barking. It was a sound he heard practically every night, and knew there was nothing to be frightened of. Soon he was playing happily again as if nothing had happened.

Neither Tom nor Maureen slept much that night, and when they did sleep in the thin grey hours before the dawn, their dreams were haunted by cries, moans and wails.

The next day Tom MacMahon drove into Limerick and began making some enquiries. A red-cheeked woman at the university directed him to an elderly man living out in Caherdavin who was, she assured him, the greatest expert on folklore in the area.

Lorcan Casey proved to be a wizened, suspicious man of indeterminate years who did not show any particular interest in Tom or his story until he realised Tom's surname was MacMahon. Then he brightened.

'That's your connection, then. MacMahon. You'd be descended from Brian Boru's brother Mahon, then,' he said grinning, showing toothless gums.

Tom shook his head doubtfully. 'I don't think so. But we've never had much interest in genealogy in my family,' he admitted. 'I suppose we had enough to do, just surviving, without looking back a thousand years.'

Lorcan Casey's narrow shoulders shrugged. 'It matters little if you know your genealogy or not. Blood will tell, and you bear an ancient name. An honourable name.'

Tom shook his head. He hadn't come hear to listen to an old man ramble on about names. He wanted to know about the creature that haunted the crags: how dangerous was she? Should he move his wife and children?

'What do you want me to tell you? Celtic lore is grounded in the spiral, no beginning, no end. What goes around, comes around. The trees are back, are they not, where there have been no trees for generations. And if what you tell me is true, then Aoibheal is back too.'

'Aoibheal,' Tom said slowly, nodding as he remembered the stories his grandfather had told him. Aoibheal. That was her name.

'That was her name,' Lorcan Casey continued. 'Is her name,' he amended, 'for she obviously still lives. She is the guardian of the Dalcassians, their tribal banshee.' The old man paused to suck at an empty pipe. 'And you're back, living on her mountain as Brian Boru once lived in Kincora below you there. Everything comes around again. All of us get a second chance, you see. And even a third and a fourth. . .'

'But does her cry bring death?' Tom demanded.

The old man shook his head. 'She weeps for what will be . . . the death of one of the old clan . . . especially for one who bears an ancient name. Have you children?' Lorcan Casey asked.

'Three. Two boys and a girl.'

'And does the eldest boy share your colouring?'

Tom shook his head. 'He takes after his grandfather. He had red hair and green eyes. . .'

'And the name of the boy?'

Tom MacMahon opened his mouth to speak, and suddenly realised what the old man was suggesting. Without another word, he leaped to his feet and dashed out of the cottage.

Tom drove homeward at top speed, taking awful chances on the narrow back roads. The rational part of his mind – the civilised part – told him that the whole idea was crazy, but the older, primitive part of his brain, whispered to him of something far darker. And only a fool would deny that there was magic in this land. . .

Before his eyes as he drove was a vision of his elder son, his favourite, brave and daring, a bright, bold redhead called Brian.

Young as he was, not even old enough to go to school, young Brian had an unquenchable thirst for adventure. And from the moment he could crawl he had been drawn to the mountain. Whenever his mother turned her back he was off up the mountain, exploring, no matter how many times she forbade him.

Up the mountain.

In the realm of the banshee.

A little Dalcassian, carrying the blood of kings in his veins, bearing an ancient name.

It was enough to call the banshee.

And the banshee now wailed for a death.

Tom MacMahon drove as if pursued by devils, convinced he had already heard the banshee wail to warn of the death of his son.

Sitting on her grey crag, Aoibheal gazes out over Lough Derg. Her inhuman eyes see everything, including the small boy who is scrambling up the steep slope towards her, making his way through dead bracken and lifeless heather.

Her shape . . . *shifts*.

Glancing up, the little boy spies a huge bird sitting on a rock above him silhouetted against the crisp, blue sky of late autumn. Squinting hard, he comes to the conclusion that it looks like an old woman sitting hunched and wrapped in a cloak. Staring at the bird, he tries to make out the species – he knows the names of many of the birds – but this one he cannot identify, though he knows its cruel hooked beak and fierce, yellow eyes fixed unblinking on him indicate that it is a predator.

It shifts its massive wings, then settles back on the stone.

For a moment little Brian recalls the terrible cry he and his family had heard the night before. Could it have come from that big bird up there on the rock? His parents had been frightened, he had heard it in their voices, seen it in their eyes. Had they been frightened by a silly old bird?

Laughing with sudden delight, Brian throws back his

head so that the sun blazes bloodlike on his copper hair. Holding out a hand, he scrambles towards the bird. If he can catch it, bring it back, then his mother and father will know it was only a bird cawing at night, nothing more.

Aoibheal watches the boy. Knows him, knows him for what he is . . . and what he was. The last time she saw him, his broken body was being carried from the carnage at Clontarf, and she had screamed aloud her agony because she had not been able to save him.

She had never forgiven herself that failure.

With wide, unblinking eyes, she watches him climb up to her now, up a sheer height where a single misstep would send him tumbling to certain death.

With wide, unblinking eyes, she watches him reach for the big bird, watches the stones turn beneath his small feet, watches him lose his balance, watches him sway out over the abyss, his face suddenly stricken. The wind whips the screams from his lungs.

Aoibheal opens her great wings and leaps out into the wind.

She will not wail another death.

On cold winter nights her voice still rings across the countryside, tracing a finger of ice and old memories up the spine of those with ears to hear and heart to comprehend what they are hearing.

They are listening to the last of the banshees.

CHAPTER TWENTY-FIVE

Samhain

———— ♣ ————

The Hallowe'en party the year before had been a bit of a damp squib. The same cider, the same costumes, the same all-too-familiar atmosphere. This year, the Callaghans were determined to do something different . . . something exotic.

Richard vaguely remembered reading something on holiday, something about pagan festivals in Ireland . . . no, not *on* holiday exactly, but on the plane there. It had been in Aer Lingus's in-flight magazine, *Cara*. He'd completely forgotten about it until Evelyn had brought up the subject of a Hallowe'en Party.

On the way home from the office, he picked up a book on Celtic folklore. After dinner, sitting before the simulated log fire, he found the chapter on festivals, and read aloud: 'Listen to this, Evie. Samhain is one of the four great Celtic feasts of the ancient world.'

She looked up, uninterested; her thin lips were already twisting downwards. She hated being called Evie.

'The feasts are Samhain, Beltane, Lughnasa and Imbolc. Samhain marked the beginning of the Celtic New Year, the time when the barriers between the living and the dead were lowest on the cusp of the dying year.' Evelyn's muddy brown eyes narrowed, sudden possibilities appearing . . . 'A time when the dead could mingle freely amongst the living,' Richard went on, noticing her smile. He closed the book with a snap. 'So I was thinking . . .' he began.

She nodded happily. They had been married nearly ten years, and were close enough to know what the other was thinking.

'A Hallowe'en party with a difference,' she said.

'A Samhain party. A traditional Samhain party to which we'll invite the ghosts of our dead ancestors.'

'I'll prepare the invitations,' Evelyn said quickly. 'Invitations to the living . . . and the dead.'

'Do you really think that's such a good idea?' Evelyn's closest friend, Marie Gormley, wanted to know, over coffee the following morning. 'I mean, where will you send the invitations?'

'To the cemetery, of course. Or the churchyard.'

'The parish priests aren't going to appreciate your sense of humour, Evelyn,' Marie warned her friend.

But Evelyn would not listen. 'This is the twentieth century,' she was fond of saying. 'Time to open the windows and let in a little fresh air.'

Marie sipped her coffee and kept her opinions to herself. Evelyn and Richard were yuppies, bubble-headed yuppies. She wondered if 'yuppies' was still in fashion. Or were they 'guppies', or 'puppies'?

'What do you think of the idea?' Evelyn demanded.

'Very . . . original,' Marie said.

'That's what I thought. But then, Richard is such an

original thinker. He works in advertising. You have to be original in advertising.'

Marie bit the inside of her cheek to prevent herself from saying something she'd regret.

The following day Evelyn dutifully posted the invitations to the Samhain party to all her friends and the few relatives they still kept in contact with. She took a special pleasure in posting a set of black-bordered envelopes to her and Richard's dead relatives. As she returned from the post office she suppressed a giggle, wondering what the keepers of the graveyards would make of them. It would make a delightful story to tell at her Samhain party.

As quickly as he had thought of the idea, Richard Callaghan changed his mind, and as the night of the party approached, he began to wish he had never mentioned it in the first place.

As All Hallows' Eve arrived, Evelyn was exhibiting an almost feverish gaiety, and many of her jokes were in very bad taste. She even took some chalk and drew lines on the tarmacadam drive, making them 'Coffin Parking' spaces. When she had gone back into the house, he washed off the marks. Some of his colleagues from the office, including the head of department and the chief accountant, were coming to the party, and he wanted to make sure he gave them the right impression.

At four in the afternoon, the caterers arrived and began setting up. Evelyn had locked herself in the spare bedroom, getting into her costume, which even her husband hadn't seen yet. Richard, who never wore costume for these events – 'I'm coming as a normal person, the only one here' – paced nervously downstairs, a dull migraine, like the promise of thunder, thumping at the base of his skull, an ache in the muscles of his eyes.

He was standing in the dining room, watching the clouds boil up on the horizon, aware that the garden was losing shape and definition, everything becoming grainy and ill-defined. Then the sky changed. The day seemed to fold away, and darkness flooded in. Lights twinkled on in windows up and down the Callaghans' road. Soon children with painted faces would be knocking on doors, demanding 'Trick or treat,' and giggling, while bangers and cheap fireworks sputtered and cracked in the night.

The first one to ring the doorbell was not a costumed child, however, but Marie Gormley, arriving to help her friend with the last details of the party. Richard directed her upstairs, admiring the way her gauze draperies clung to her figure, idly wondering what she was wearing underneath. Precious little.

She caught him looking. 'Net curtains,' she explained. 'I'm a ghost,' she added laughing.

'Is that what ghosts look like? It's something to look forward to,' he replied.

Marie vanished up the stairs. The caterers departed, leaving the food set up and waiting in the kitchen and dining room. Richard wandered about the house, turning on lights as the pervasive night closed in around him, bringing a damp chill that stiffened his bones and plumed his breath before his face even though the heat was on and the radiators were too hot to touch.

What was keeping Evelyn and Marie? he wondered. They should be downstairs by now, ready to greet the first guests. He was just turning to call up the stairs to them when the doorbell sounded.

Annoyed that he would have to play host on his own, Richard went to the door.

When he opened it, no one was there. 'Bloody kids,' he muttered, starting to close the door again. He shivered as an icy draught blew past him.

'Is that someone already?' Evelyn called from above.

'Just kids playing trick or treat. But come on down, will you?'

'In a minute,' his wife called. He knew her minutes. She might be up there for another half hour, even after people began arriving in numbers. Evelyn loved making an entrance. And God alone knows what she'd be wearing. Last year it had been Cleopatra: two pieces of cloth and a lot of eyeshadow.

The doorbell rang again. Richard opened the door.

No one there.

He stood on the doorstep looking up and down the road, half-expecting to see costumed children dart out of the shadows, but when he started shivering, he turned away and slammed the door.

The third time it happened he began to get angry.

By the fifth time, he was furious. 'Evelyn!' he shouted. 'Come down here right now and handle this! Some of the local kids are going too far and I'm tired of it! You answer the door for a change and I'll sneak around the back and catch them at it.'

But she didn't come. And before he could shout again, the doorbell rang again, and then again.

Eleven times in all, Richard Callaghan opened the door. And on every occasion there was no one there.

The bell was rung roughly every sixty seconds, so he never had time to leave the front door and sneak out the back. And he did not dare leave the door unguarded, in case one of the real guests showed up. Evelyn would never forgive him.

Evelyn. Where was she?

He was becoming increasingly agitated. Unless this was some sort of elaborate prank she had arranged to get at him. Evelyn had a lot of unusual ideas. Could she have rigged the doorbell. . .?

That was it! She had somehow rigged the bell and was probably controlling it from upstairs. And he suddenly knew why.

The twelfth time Richard opened the door and discovered no one there, he laughed. He had to laugh, there was nothing else to be done. 'Twelve!' he called up the stairs. 'Two sets of parents and four sets of grandparents! I guess they're all here, darling. Do you want to grace us with your presence now and start the party, or would you rather wait to make your grand entrance for the flesh-and-blood guests when they arrive?'

He waited.

There was no answer from above.

'Evelyn? Marie?' he called hesitantly. 'What are you two doing up there?'

He put one hand on the banister and stepped onto the lowest step. 'This has gone far enough,' he warned. 'If you don't come down now, I'm coming up.'

But before he began the climb, he happened to glance at the small console table in the hall, below Evelyn's favourite mirror. One of her many affectations was to keep a little silver tray on that table. When he came in from work in the evenings he would find the day's post – those letters she hadn't opened – on the tray. Tonight there was a stack of cards.

Richard was certain there had been none there an hour ago.

He took his foot off the stair, turned to the table and lifted the top card.

It was a square of pasteboard, edged in black. '*Richard &
Evelyn Callaghan request the pleasure of the company of . . .*'

He stopped, abruptly aware of the tightness at the back
of his throat, the intensity of the headache that throbbed in
his skull.

The card bore the names of his grandparents. They had
died before he was born.

Richard swallowed hard. Then with a terrible effort, he
went back and began to climb the stairs.

CHAPTER TWENTY-SIX

St Brigid's Day

———— ♣ ————

'February the first.'

Colm Fitzpatrick frowned at the calendar, a large, glossy freebie the banks were supposed to give out to the customers at Christmas, but which the clerks generally guarded as if they were money. January had been snow-locked Wicklow mountains, while February featured a scene of a thatched Irish cottage. Colm wasn't sure when he had last seen a thatched cottage.

'St Brigid's Day,' he read aloud, his voice echoing in the empty kitchen. 'In the Irish folk tradition this is the first day of spring and heralds the start of the farmer's year. The festival hearkens back to the ancient pagan festival of Imbolc.'

He swung around and gazed moodily out the window at the silver spears of rain. 'First day of Spring,' he repeated morosely.

Beyond his window, the fields of his East Galway farm were sodden and sticky with mud. The previous month the ground had been frozen iron-hard and the month before that – December – had been the mildest on record.

If anything green appeared out of the ground in the next few months, he would be more than amazed. The only things he could grow were weeds.

It had been a mistake to return to the family farm. He was no farmer; too many years in the city had allowed the boyhood callus to fall away from his hands. He no longer remembered how to coax life from the soil as his father and his father's father had done.

But times were hard, many men were being made redundant, with no jobs on the immediate horizon. When he'd lost his job, at least he had a home to go back to and work waiting, though the farm had been sadly neglected after his father and mother died.

Six months ago, coming home had seemed so *right*. As if a great wheel had turned full circle and he was back where he started, back where he always knew he'd be. He was going to get the farm up and running again, grow organic vegetables, maybe develop his own cheese. . .

Colm laughed sourly at the memory, as he glared out at the wet fields resentfully. That dream hadn't lasted long. He turned back to the kitchen to make himself a cup of tea.

Six months, and he hadn't missed Joan after the first three weeks. Coming here had allowed him to see her for what she was: a selfish. . .

'I'm not going to live on some bone-poor farm in Galway for anything,' she had told him flatly. 'I'm staying right here . . . and if you've any sense, you'll do exactly the same.' Maybe she thought she'd be able to bully him into staying in Dublin; usually she could twist him around her little finger. But not this time. He'd had just about enough of Joan and her family. Since coming here to the West, he'd been able to do a lot of thinking, and he had come to realise just what interfering busybodies they were.

'I'll send you money,' he had promised, standing on the platform as the train doors slammed up and down the platform. 'As soon as I sell the first crop, I'll send you a cheque. When you see that we can make a good living out of the farm you'll change your mind.' But even as he spoke them, he knew his words were hollow. She wasn't going to follow him. She turned away before the train had pulled out of the station and didn't even look back.

However, he had believed the dream in the beginning. Now, he knew he was never going to make a good living out of this farm.

Farming was a sort of magic, particularly in hard times.

As he put the kettle on, he noticed a small St Brigid's cross made of straw, fastened to the wallpaper above the sink with a pin. The straw was grey and old; the cross had been there a long time, and as he looked at it he had a vague sense of its always being there, part of his childhood memories. He'd never really looked at it before. His mother had put it up. She'd probably bought it some St Brigid's Eve from local youngsters who called on all the farmhouses, following the ancient tradition, with their songs and straw Brigid's crosses.

That's who had been at the door last night, he realised. He had heard children's voices out in the yard when night had fallen, but he had been sprawled in his chair in front of the telly, lost in misery, little food and just one too many whiskies inside him, and he had not bothered to go to the door. Eventually they went away.

Sipping the bitter tea – he'd run out of milk and sugar again – he looked out the window again. The tractor, rusting with disuse, sat in its shed, waiting for sunshine that rarely came . . . and when it did, the bloody tractor didn't work.

'How did Dad manage?' Colm asked aloud, simply to hear human voice in the too-quiet house. 'It must have rained when I was a kid, too, but I always remember him outside, working. And until he got sick this place prospered, even when other farms were struggling. Why? What did he do that I'm not doing?' He spilled the sour tea into the sink and stared at the murky liquid. 'What am I going to do, Dad?' he whispered hoarsely. Tears of self-pity prickled at the corners of his eyes.

Reaching out, he unpinned the straw cross from the wall and examined it curiously, marvelling for the first time at the skill of its construction. There had been a cross like this in every classroom in school, and all his friends' houses.

He thought about his friends now, suddenly wondering where they all were. Gone. All of them. Forced by circumstances and economics to work abroad, in the larger cities if they could, in England and America if they had to. Holding the cross somehow brought back all the memories of his youth. Good times. Happy times. He thought of his mother – plump, grey-haired, smiling, and never still. It used to drive his father mad. Colm smiled. He could almost hear her quick step on the kitchen floor behind him.

Wood creaked.

He did hear it.

Colm whirled around but no one was there. 'Old floorboards creaking,' he told himself, smiling self-consciously at his own stupidity.

For some reason he did not pin the cross back on the wall again, but stood holding it, stroking it almost absent-mindedly as he tried to recall the stories that went with it. His mother had been the storyteller in the family. His father, silent, had listened attentively to her until the day he died, and if she ever repeated a story, he never said, but nodded as if it were the first time he was hearing it.

Colm felt a lump rise in his throat. They had been so close, the two of them. So much in love. They had even died within months of each other. So much love. So much happiness.

Why didn't it extend to him? From the day he left the farm to try his luck in Dublin, nothing had gone right for him. He had married Joan too soon, there were too many differences between them, and he knew now – admitting it for the first time – that their marriage was at an end. Well, he was glad his mother and father hadn't lived to see that.

Rubbing the cross with his thumb, he gazed out the window at the useless tractor, sitting abandoned . . . He stopped, squinting through the misting rain. He could have sworn a shadow moved in the cabin. Startled, Colm rubbed his eyes and looked again. 'Rain and the mist,' he told himself, 'distorting things.'

But even as he looked, the figure formed again – a greyish figure that might have been mist, might have been fog, might have been just a trick of the watery light. Yet it had a certain familiar shape.

Colm knew those broad shoulders, that long torso. He even recognised the exact tilt of the head. He had seen his father sit just like that a hundred times, starting up the engine and listening to it, seeing what it needed. Colm's father had possessed the same sympathy with his farm machinery that he possessed for the land. Everything worked for him.

Colm felt his breath catch in his throat, the short hairs rising on the back of his neck.

The floorboard creaked again.

Without turning around, he was absolutely certain someone stood behind him.

'St Brigid's Day,' said his mother's soft voice, slipping easily from English into her native Irish, as she had when he was a boy. He was astonished that he still understood the words. 'It's good to have you home for it. But look at you, lad. Not a pick on you. Doesn't that wife of yours feed you?' There was a bustling sound, then the familiar creak of the oven door. A smell of soda bread wafted through the room, making Colm's stomach grumble.

He did not dare turn round. Because this was a dream, he knew it was, a hallucination brought on by poor food and not enough of it. He felt an overwhelming desire to turn around, to throw himself down and wrap his arms around her legs, and bury his face in her apron. 'Make it all right,' he wanted to cry. 'Make it all right!' But he didn't turn around, he didn't want the dream to end.

Colm stood shivering in the kitchen, smelling soda bread, watching his father who had been dead for years slowly back the tractor out from under the shed and head off towards the fields.

He could hear the tractor clatter as it crossed the paved yard, rattle off the cattle grid.

Behind him, his mother said, 'Everything begins, season after season, year after year. Your father's father tilled the field, you know. And his father before him. That man of mine out there on that tractor will work his farm until he's replaced by one of his own blood who will tend it just as lovingly.

'You brought your anger back here, lad, and your resentment. Those things won't make crops grow. See that dark sky? That came with your dark moods.

'We are the land, Colm, and the land is us. Love her. Be

joyous and generous with her, and she responds in kind. Look.'

Colm looked. And the fields towards which his spectral father was driving the tractor were no longer black with mud, but loamy and brown, and new, green shoots were appearing in neat rows, weeks before any actual planting could take place.

Yet they were there. He could see them. As he could smell his mother's soda bread.

'What you believe is real, *is* real,' said his mother's voice behind him. 'Your father always believed he would farm his land successfully. You don't believe in anything any more, do you? Look at you. The spirit is broken in you.' She sounded sad, and almost disgusted. Then her tone changed. 'And look at your father out there,' she said proudly. 'The strength in him, the faith in him! He believed he would farm this land forever, and so he is. Faith lends substance.' Her voice softened, rang with love. 'He believed he and I would always be together . . . and so we are.

'You've stopped expecting anything good and so you can't make it happen, Colm.'

'Is that all there is to it?' he asked without thinking, his voice barely above a whisper.

'Of course not!' his mother replied crisply. 'It's just the beginning, the seed, but it has to be there, as seeds have to be in that ground. There will be a day when you can plant if you believe strongly enough. Look again at your father out there; see what he's planted. See it grow.'

Through a mist in his eyes, Colm saw his father sitting tall and straight, surrounded by the richly flourishing field. 'But that can't be,' he insisted, his rational mind taking over. 'It's some sort of hallucination, too much stress, too much worry. . .'

'Och, Colm,' came his mother's voice from behind him, growing strangely weaker and far away. 'It's sorry for you I am, so sorry. . .'

The figure on the tractor seat appeared to shimmer. Colm rubbed his eyes and strained to see it more clearly, and when he opened his eyes again, the image was gone. The tractor wasn't even in the field any more, and where he had seen green corn growing a moment before, the earth was sodden and bare again.

The tractor, rusting, sat in its shed while unrelenting rain drummed on the tin roof.

'Mam!' Colm cried out in sudden anguish, feeling a greater sense of loss than on the day of her death, or his father's. He spun around. The kitchen was empty.

But on the table was a freshly baked loaf of soda bread.

CHAPTER TWENTY-SEVEN

Sun Day

———— ♣ ————

Without too much effort, Declan Costello managed to shift the stone. All it required was an iron pry-bar, sweat and a lot of determination.

Desperation would be more like it, he thought wryly. No one in Ireland needed to find the prize more than he did.

The prize was the latest gimmick thought up by the presenter of one of the popular morning radio programmes. A bar of gold – with a value of just over £20,000 – had been hidden somewhere in Ireland. Every morning another clue was given to the bar's whereabouts. Initially gold fever had swept the country, but it gradually tapered off as the clues proved almost impossible to interpret. However, as the weeks wore on and no one found the gold, the hints became clearer. The flagging interest was revived, and small ads began appearing in the newspapers as people offered to pool their knowledge and information. Soon enough, Declan knew, someone would put them all together and the prize would be lost.

Unless he was right.

And if he was ... well, £20,000 would sort out his problems with the money-lender, sort out the bank, pay off the mortgage. Christ, how had he ever got into this mess?

'Greed and stupidity,' he said aloud, his voice flat on the early-morning air.

And it wasn't entirely his fault; Sara had played her part too, pushing, pushing, always pushing, nagging at him when one neighbour added an extension to their formerly humble bungalow, and another went on a holiday to the Canaries, or when a third put in a new kitchen.

But they had had enough left over to put by to save for luxuries. It had never bothered Declan before, but now, when he saw his friends and neighbours with their small – and not so small – luxuries, he felt the first sting of jealousy.

And finally, when the man across the road – a small, insignificant, pot-bellied, bald grocer – bought an electric mower for his lawn, Declan finally gave in. The sight of the shiny machine was the last straw as he struggled to mow his own grass with the same old rusty push-mower he had used for years. But there was no extra money for an electric mower. There was no extra money at all, as his wife frequently reminded him ... though there was always enough for her to have her hair done in the expensive salon in the new shopping centre in Cork.

However, while he had always been able to ignore her nagging, he could not ignore the soft, grumbling purr of the machine across the road. The very sound seemed to mock him. So he had gone to a money-lender – without telling Sara – and borrowed a few bob to purchase a small, electric lawn mower, a rival machine, for himself.

Sara had been incredulous. 'When I think of all the

things we need around this house!' she cried, her hands on her broad hips, lips pursed, as she watched him assemble it. 'A new washing machine, for example, and a. . .'

The list was very long. His purchase of the mower had given her the thin edge of the wedge to drive under his skin, and at last he was forced to buy the new washing machine . . . and the fridge, the tumble dryer, the microwave. . .

It meant more trips to the money-lender, the interest mounting at a terrifying rate.

And when he slipped behind on the payments, the veiled – and not-so-veiled – threats, the sudden visits of large men to his home, reminding him that his interest was overdue, the late-night phone calls. And now Sara was becoming suspicious . . . though she suspected that he was having an affair! He couldn't tell her the truth: Hell would be lukewarm compared to the roasting he would get from her.

So Declan Costello simply had to find the hidden gold bar. He studied the clues assiduously, repeating them over and over, spending hours in the library going through the encyclopaedias, the dictionaries, the thesauri, working out the answers. When he came to a conclusion, he thought at first it was nothing but wishful thinking. However, when he checked the answer, he realised that he had been right the first time: everything pointed to the gold's being hidden within a mile of his own house. If he was right – and he was, he knew he was – then the gold was buried beneath a tumble of stones on the crest of a hill just beyond the last row of bungalows sprawling out from the town. The hill was windswept and barren, its stark outline against the sky relieved only by a tangle of thorn trees and a straggle of gorse. The gorse was studded with golden blooms, however, and when the wind was right their sweetness drifted down to the bungalows, though no one paused to sniff the wind and enjoy them.

Declan Costello had no time for appreciating nature's wild perfumes. The gold was there! It had to be. Had to be. He was determined not to waste a moment . . . why, even now, someone was probably making their way to the hilltop in search of the gold – his gold. He was going to look for it today, even if it was a Sunday.

The wife moaned at him, but more often it was for not going to Mass.

'You go enough for both of us,' he had growled at her as he gathered his tools.

She stood at the door of the shed and watched him. 'Where are you going, then? And why do you need a shovel and a pry-bar? What are you up to, Declan?'

He shrugged. He didn't want to tell her just yet – if he was wrong, she'd never let him forget it. 'You're always giving out to me about the garden,' he smiled slyly. 'I thought I'd go . . . uh . . . dig up some heather if I can find some, and put it in the rockery.'

Sara Costello stared at her husband, nonplussed. They had been married fifteen years and in all those years he had never offered to do anything remotely like this. Maybe she was right; maybe he was having an affair, and this was just an excuse to sneak off to his fancy piece. Well, she'd call him at his own game. 'White heather would be nice, I think. It's good luck.'

Good luck. Declan smiled inwardly. Good luck was what you made for yourself. God helped those who helped themselves.

With the shovel on his shoulder, he walked down the

road to the hill. If his calculations based on the radio hints were right, the gold was under the largest stone in the tumbled pile. During the spring, some fellow from the university had been up on this hill, measuring and photographing. Declan later heard him interviewed on the local radio. The professor claimed the stone was some sort of ritualistic maker.

'*This place was probably where the Lughnasa celebrations for this area were held. In pagan times, the people used to gather on hilltops to offer the fruits of the harvest to the sun in thanksgiving. The first of August was one of the four great festival days of the pagan Celtic year.*'

Sweating on the hilltop, in the blistering noonday sun, Declan heard those words again and smiled to himself. Today was not only Sunday, it was the first of August. Lughnasa. An important pagan festival, if you believed in such things. He didn't.

Grunting, digging, moving stones, Declan paid attention to nothing but the task at hand.

He did not notice when the sun went behind a cloud and shadows began to gather.

'*You should not disturb sites like this,*' the folklorist from the university had said.

The old people, the local people who lived here when all this was farmland, had probably said the same things, once. And they had probably used it as an excuse for not digging up the fields. But they were gone, washed away on the rising tide of modern, identical bungalows blighting the ancient landscape.

Declan continued digging. He had moved the mass of rocks surrounding the largest stone, inserted the bar beneath it, and was now gently levering it up. As he drew it free of the earth he shoved stones under it with his foot to keep it propped high enough so that he could feel under it with his hand.

The gold was here – it had to be here.

A part of his mind – coldly rational – was noting that the stone gave no sign of having been recently disturbed. Surely if the radio programme had buried the gold bar under there, there would be some indication? But maybe not; God knows how long it had been buried.

Declan went on working, oblivious to the growing darkness of the day.

'The sun was sacred to ancient farmers. We can be sure they went to great lengths to propitiate it. Perhaps they even offered sacrifices at places such as this. Perhaps the largest of these stones was a sacrificial altar long before the coming of St Patrick to Ireland.

'Even after the arrival of Christianity, the old traditions survived for centuries, almost until the present day.

'Until very recent times, games would have been held up here, races, dancing. Perhaps fires lit. Flowers laid in tribute at the summit of the hill. In Christian times this was called Fraochain Sunday in honour of the whortleberries ripening, and they would have been picked and some also offered, together with the flowers.'

Those half-forgotten words echoed in Declan Costello's mind as he got down on hands and knees and stretched a careful arm under the edge of the large stone, feeling for some roughness in the earth to indicate it had been dug recently.

Nothing.

Squinting in concentration, he lay down full length and stretched his arm further.

There had to be . . . had to be.

His fingers touched something. Something . . . cold and smooth and hard.

Declan grunted in satisfaction. He tried again, but his questing fingers just about touched the side of the object. His arm was not long enough. He would have to crawl further under the stone, and that meant lifting it higher.

He went back to work.

Around him, the shadows shifted. An observer standing off to one side might have thought they took on the near-transparent forms of dancing people. Some appeared to be carrying baskets heaped with flowers and fruit as they neared the summit where Declan worked feverishly amid the tumble of rocks.

But there was no one to observe the shadows.

The sky grew darker still, and a cold wind sprang up.

'The ultimate purpose of all these celebrations, these rituals, was the same: they were designed to invoke the sun. Christian or pagan, the Irish have always adored the sun and longed for it to come and stay, to warm their flesh and grow their crops. No people love the sun more than we do, and sites like this have ancient connections of great power. It was as if that overpowering desire for sunshine was concentrated here, permeating the landscape.'

Declan had the stone high enough now. He could crawl under it.

But before he did, he peered into a Stygian blackness one last time to make certain he was not deceiving himself, that the risk was worth the reward.

And it was.

The gold was there.

He could see it clearly now, golden and glowing, far back under the stone! They must have set the bar right down on the bare earth and then lowered the stone back in place over it!

Without any further hesitation, he lay flat on the ground and wriggled under the tilted stone.

Behind him, the shadows closed in.

The dark figures that had appeared to be dancing formed two lines facing one another, like an avenue leading towards the pile of stones.

A soft chanting began, so soft that Declan Costello, grunting and wheezing as he forced himself farther underneath the stone, did not hear it. Nor did he smell the sweet fragrance of ripe whortleberries.

But it was there.

Declan was conscious only of the golden gleam ahead of him. He reached out for it again, certain he could close his fist on it now and claim the gold bar that would change his life.

The chanting grew louder.

As his hand reached for the stone, Declan yelped in sudden dismay. Something hot had burned him!

He snatched back his hand, feeling the skin start to puff and blister immediately. The thing which he had taken to be a bar of gold was blazing hot now, shedding an increasing light that shone into his face and blinded him. The light intensified, the heat exploded from it like a sunburst as the chanting beyond the stone rose in decibel power, the flesh on his face tightened across his cheekbones, his eyelashes and sparse hair curled and crisped.

Declan tried to wriggle backward and escape the flaming fury he had unearthed beneath the stone, the miniature sun roasting his eyeballs. But it was too late.

Ghostly hands tugged, ghostly shoulders pushed, and the great stone fell back into place, crushing him beneath its ageless weight.

Completing the sacrifice.

CHAPTER TWENTY-EIGHT

The O'Sullivan Bear

♣

The touch of a human hand, warm, gentle. . .

'Oh, he's gorgeous!' Katherine Townson lifted the small, grey teddy bear off the shelf and brushed at his patchwork fur. The ball of her thumb stroked the single black bead of an eye.

Robert O'Sullivan lifted the bear from Katherine's hands and turned it around to stare into its grubby face. 'This is the O'Sullivan Bear,' he said proudly, 'named after the great sixteenth-century Irish hero, Donal Cam O'Sullivan, the last prince of Ireland, who was called the O'Sullivan Beare.' He straightened a flapping ear, and then abruptly hugged it close to his chest, resting the point on his chin on the bear's head. 'O'Sullivan here was my bear, and my father's too, and his father's. He's been in the family since around the turn of the century and, as you can see, he's had a lot of use.' Robert handed the grey-furred bear back to Katherine.

'I think there's nothing sadder than a clean bear: it means no child has played with it.' Katherine placed the bear back on the shelf behind the door, and tilted her head to one side, looking at him. 'He looks sad,' she said eventually. 'If he could talk,' she grinned, 'what tales he could tell!'

'I've often thought about having him refurbished,' Robert said, crossing the room to push open the window, breathing in the late-afternoon air, redolent of turf and wood smoke, and the faint salt hint of the distant sea.

'Oh, you couldn't,' Katherine said, 'he'd lose all his character.' She came up behind Robert, wrapped her arms around his chest and rested her cheek against his back.

'Well, I wouldn't want our children to say they grew up with a raggy old bear.' He turned quickly and caught Katherine in his arms, holding her close.

'Lets just tell your family that we're engaged first before we begin talking about children,' Katherine smiled. She lowered her voice to a whisper. 'Do you think they know?'

'I'm sure they suspect,' he grinned.

'When are you going to tell them?'

'After dinner.'

'And how do you think they'll take it?' she asked.

'They'll be delighted.' He kissed her quickly. 'Now, get some rest. I think it's going to be a long night.' He paused beside the shelf and straightened the bear which had tilted over to one side. 'You don't worry about anything: O'Sullivan will look after you.'

Katherine unpacked slowly. She hadn't wanted to come to Ireland to tell Robert's parents about their engagement. She had met Una and Michael O'Sullivan on two previous occasions, and she had come away with the distinct impression that they didn't want their son involved with an English girl – especially a coloured English girl. Maybe if they had a little more time to become accustomed to the idea, they would have found it easier to accept. It was going to come as quite a shock. Even her own parents, who had seen Robert coming and going for the past year, had been taken aback with the engagement. They had said nothing, congratulated the couple, given them their blessing, but Katherine knew they didn't really approve. It had been left up to Grandma Townson, who had retained her broad Jamaican accent though she had lived in London for more than forty of her eighty-two years, to talk to the young couple about the extra pressures that an inter-racial marriage brought with it.

But Katherine and Robert were very much in love, convinced they'd be able to weather the problems.

Katherine had known Robert for ten months. He was twenty-five, two years older than herself, charming, almost handsome, with deep-set, coal-black eyes that gave his face a perpetually hurt look. It had been his Irish brogue that first attracted her to him: a curiously flat, musical accent, not unlike the accents of her aunts and uncles, and the lilting twang she sometimes heard in her parents' voices. She'd made a point of getting to know him, and been pleasantly surprised when she discovered that he was one of the first men who hadn't immediately tried to get her into bed. Nor did he have any problems being seen with her; a previous relationship had ended when her boyfriend had discovered that his chances of advancement were considerably reduced because of his association with a coloured girl.

Almost nine months to the day after they met, Robert asked her – without warning – to marry him. She said yes, without hesitation. From that moment on, it was as if she'd stepped on a roller-coaster. Within days, they told her parents, then their colleagues in the office, then had a small party to celebrate. The final step was to come to Dublin to tell Robert's parents.

And this was the part she was dreading.

Katherine gathered up a bundle of underwear and carried it over to the chest of drawers. She pulled open the top drawer and was immediately enveloped in the slightly acrid odour of old lavender. A layer of tissue paper had been laid out in the bottom of the drawer. Gathered in the corners she could see the individual, dried, purple leaves of the lavender plant. Katherine pulled the drawer out and carried it over to the wastepaper basket, tilting it to one side to empty the remnants of the lavender into the basket. Lavender gave her a headache. She slid the drawer back into place and dropped her clothes inside; she knew they were going to reek for the rest of the weekend. When she slammed the drawer shut, O'Sullivan slid sideways and she caught him just before he tumbled to the floor. Cradling the small bear in her arms, she went to sit in the window seat, looking out over an old orchard, the trees twisted and gnarled, a few small red and green apples scattered through them. In the distance, she could just make out the blue line of the sea. Lifting the bear, Katherine stared into its single black eye. 'Well, O'Sullivan, any advice? How do you think they're going to react, eh?' She suddenly realised she was dreading Robert's parents' reaction . . . because she didn't know how he was going to react. Robert, she knew, was still very much under his mother's thumb. Katherine hugged the bear tightly, squeezing her eyes shut as the tears came, salt water soaking into the bear's ragged fur.

The touch of a human hand. Warm, gentle. The pain. The anguish.

The fear.
Somehow, there had always been fear.

Katherine lay in bed, holding the bear tightly, watching a triangular shaft of moonlight slowly inch its way across the high ceiling. Her eyes were red and swollen, and there was a burning in the back of her throat, a queasiness in her stomach, and she knew if she moved she was going to throw up again.

She had always known that telling Robert's parents was not going to be easy, and her instincts had been right. However, she hadn't realised that telling them had been far harder than she had imagined.

Katherine was watching Una, Robert's mother, when he rose to his feet after dessert and tapped his glass for silence. Even before he spoke, a look of panic, of loss, of betrayal, flashed across the woman's face, and then – as she looked from her son to Katherine – her expression turned bitter.

Robert's simple announcement of the forthcoming marriage was met with a deathly silence. Katherine bit into the soft flesh inside her cheek to prevent herself from showing any emotion.

Finally, Michael O'Sullivan cleared his throat and forced himself to smile. 'Well, this is a surprise, I'm sure. We weren't expecting this . . . I hope – we hope – you'll both be very happy together. Don't we?' he said, looking at his wife.

Una O'Sullivan said nothing, simply stared at Katherine with a fixed expression.

'I know this must come as a bit of a shock,' Robert said quickly. 'We hope to be married early in the New Year. Katherine and I love one another, and we don't see much point in waiting.'

Una O'Sullivan surged to her feet, knocking her chair

over backwards. She had gone deathly white, her lips drawn into a thin, bloodless line. For a moment it looked as if she were about to say something, then she simply turned on her heel and hurried from the room. Her husband hesitated a moment, his eyes wide and panicked, before he followed her. Robert's brother and two sisters looked at one another. With mumbled apologies, they too left the room.

'She's just a bit surprised,' Robert said quickly. He sat down heavily and reached for his wine, trying to steady his trembling fingers. He attempted to smile reassuringly, but his lips twisted into a sour grimace. He kept looking towards the door, half-expecting his mother and father to return.

'I think she's more than surprised,' Katherine said softly. She lifted her glass and sipped the cheap, bitter wine.

'Maybe we shouldn't have sprung it on her like that.'

'There was no easy way to tell her. And no matter how or where or when you told her, I think she was going to react that way,' Katherine said softly.

'What do you mean?' Robert asked, twisting in his seat to look at his fiancée.

'Nice white Catholic boys don't marry black girls. She's prejudiced.'

'Nonsense!'

'No, it's not nonsense,' Katherine said sadly. 'Did you not see the look of loathing on her face?'

'No, I did not,' he snapped.

'I did,' Katherine said forcefully.

'I'm sure you're mistaken. She's just surprised.'

'Robert,' Katherine said as gently as possible, 'I've grown up seeing that look. It's a combination of pity and contempt, mixed with just a little fear.'

'I think you're mistaken,' Robert said coldly.

'It's a look you never forget, Robert. Your mother was plainly horrified at the thought of your marrying me.'

'You're wrong!'

Katherine shook her head. 'I'm not.'

The quarrel began then, one word leading to another until, almost before either of them realised it, they were having an argument, an icily polite argument, unwilling to raise their voices, though the words were bitter and unforgiving. When Katherine finally walked away from the table, her head was pounding and she was sick to her stomach.

It was only as she lay in bed that Katherine realised that the wedding was off. Too much had been said.

Hugging O'Sullivan tighter, she closed her eyes and attempted to sleep.

It felt the pain, the hurt.

It felt the tears, and the tears awoke old memories.

It had no knowledge of time except as a vague passage of seasons; instead, it counted the passing of years in terms of tears shed. And over the years there had been many, many tears. Bitter tears cried into its fur at dead of night, tears of frustration, of sadness, of loss, of regret and fear.

So much pain.

So much fear.

The tears brought back memories.

It had a life before its spirit had been drawn to this shell, but that life was now little more than a memory of a dream. The first child had drawn it here, called it with its pain.

Its earliest memories were of a male child, small and freckled, with tumbled red hair – a lonely boy, the only child of a loveless marriage of convenience. He had named the bear, given it an identity, believed in it . . . believed in it with such fervour, such intensity, that he had called the spirit of the creature known as the pooka into the shell of the child's plaything. And once the child had named it, calling it O'Sullivan Bear, it controlled it, for there is a magic in names. O'Sullivan's awareness increased as the boy grew more dependent on it. The spirit of the pooka experienced his pain, his loneliness, and gradually it learned to absorb the pain until subconsciously the boy came to realise that respite from the constant, aching loneliness came only when he held the O'Sullivan Bear.

But the boy grew and put away his childish playthings, though the grey-furred bear was amongst the last to be left aside. Even in his teens, he could still find comfort of sorts when he held the bear.

In time there was another child, the son of the first boy. He was neither as lonely nor as fearful as his father had been, though the night held special terrors . . . creeping nightmares that slithered from beneath the bed and lurked in darkened cupboards. But the O'Sullivan Bear comforted him, and while he slept with it in his arms, his dreams were pleasant. The boy was fifteen before he gave up the bear.

In the years between owners, O'Sullivan was still dimly aware of the comings and goings in the house, of the occasional occupant of the room, an accidental touch giving it a brief respite from the greyness that threatened to overwhelm it.

The last owner had been the son of the boy who feared the night, the grandson of the red-haired, freckled youth. A shy and introverted boy, the eldest of four children, who felt that his parents cared more for his younger brother and sisters, he had lavished all his love and affection on the bear. O'Sullivan's awareness had expanded during this time. It was at its most powerful, able to detect activity throughout the house, to read the thoughts and emotions of all the occupants. It drew its strength from the boy's love. And the boy wanted nothing in return from the bear, save a little comfort. The night held no fears for the boy, and his early isolation had made him independent. The bear was a companion, a familiar weight in his arms, a comforting shape in the bed beside him at night.

O'Sullivan's consciousness grew stronger. It needed the boy to survive. And so, in a myriad subtle ways, it set about ensuring that nothing would distract the boy from him. When the boy's mother fought with him, she developed a migraine, when the boy's father argued, his ulcer troubled him, when his brother or sisters quarrelled with him, they had minor accidents that gave them something else to worry about.

The boy was fifteen when he vanished. One morning, O'Sullivan became aware that the boy was no longer in the house. Extending his consciousness through the building and out into the surrounding gardens, he discovered that the boy was gone. But he received flickering images of the boy dressed in grey clothing wearing a grey cap on his head, carrying a satchel.

In the years that followed, without the boy's love and affection to sustain it, O'Sullivan gradually lost much of his awareness. There were brief moments when he was aware that the boy – changed, altered, no longer a boy – returned to the house and his old room. But he no longer held the O'Sullivan Bear. No one had held the O'Sullivan bear with love and affection . . . until now.

*

Deep in her dreams, Katherine Townson tossed in a troubled sleep, a nightmare in which a massive shape loomed ever closer.

O'Sullivan absorbed the emotions, fed off the pain and anger, used the woman's hurt to make it stronger. Then it began to explore. . .

Through fragments of dreams and flickering images, in emotions and snatches of conversation, O'Sullivan built up a picture of the events of the past few hours. He saw the boy's face – older, harder, sharper, but still the boy who had loved without demand. The face was now twisted in anger, in rage . . . in fear. O'Sullivan saw the woman – the same woman who now held it in her arms – hurt the boy, not with blows, but with words and looks.

Once, O'Sullivan had protected the boy from words and looks like these. Now it would protect the man: payment for all those years of affection. . .

The doctor came out of the bedroom, patting at his bald head with a spotted handkerchief. He stopped before the family who had gathered on the landing. 'It's the most bizarre accident I've ever come across,' he said hoarsely. He held out the one-eyed, grey-furred bear. 'The young lady rolled over on to this teddy bear in her sleep and was smothered.'

Robert O'Sullivan clutched the bear to his chest, pressed his face into his damp fur and wept bitterly. The pooka, trapped in the body of O'Sullivan Bear, drew strength from his pain; the boy would never leave it again.

CHAPTER TWENTY-NINE

The Hitch-hiker

———— ♣ ————

Patricia Wilde smiled at the blank-faced Garda sergeant and gently eased the BMW away from the kerb. With an effort, she resisted the temptation to floor the accelerator and shower the cold-eyed bastard with gravel, but she was in enough trouble already. This was the third time this month she had been stopped for speeding. And the second time by this particular Garda.

'Are you aware that you were doing eighty-two miles-an-hour in a fifty-five mile-an-hour zone?' he had asked her patronisingly.

How were you supposed to answer that? 'Yes, I knew, that's why I was doing it,' or 'No, I didn't know, why do you think I was doing it?'

She reckoned the Gardai were jealous. They sat there behind their radar guns or whatever the hell it was they used, and they saw this fire-engine-red BMW speeding towards them with a pretty young woman behind the wheel, and even if she wasn't speeding, they were going to stop her.

And eighty-two wasn't *that* fast. The car would go a lot faster. She knew.

While she'd been speaking to the Garda, dozens of cars had sped fast, braking lights blazing as they suddenly realised there was a police car hiding in the narrow side road.

Patricia glanced in her rear-view mirror. She could still see the two cops standing on the road, watching her. She thought the younger Garda was grinning.

The young woman scowled. There was a good possibility she would lose her licence this time.

And what was she going to tell Brian?

She rounded the curve, and once out of sight of the police, changed gears and shoved the accelerator to the floor. The heavy car surged forward. The needle moved smoothly up to seventy . . . seventy-five . . . eighty. Holding the car at a steady eighty, Patricia cruised down the dual carriageway. And eighty *still* wasn't that fast; cars were still passing her.

Brian was not going to be pleased about this latest speeding ticket. Sometimes he seemed to forget that he was her husband, and not her father. He referred to her as 'the child', which made her squirm. He was nearly twenty-five years her senior, and indulged her outrageously, buying her everything she wanted . . . and lots of things she didn't. She knew that a lot of people thought she had married Brian for his money. They couldn't accept that she had genuinely loved him when she had married him four years ago.

And now?

They had been deeply in love when they married, but over the last couple of years the differences – in background, education, tastes, age – had become points of increasing friction between them. Everything he said or did seemed to get on her nerves.

As the dual carriageway ended and the road narrowed, Patricia slowed the car minimally. The reserve-tank light began flashing on the dashboard. She swore softly; she had meant to fill up the tank at the last petrol station but her encounter with the Gardai had driven the thought from her mind.

A roadsign flickered by: Balbriggan – Drogheda – Dundalk – Belfast.

Brian had been due to fly into Belfast airport earlier that morning for a meeting with the managers of the hotel group he owned. He had planned to drive down to Dublin afterwards himself, but she had insisted on going north to collect him. Belfast was less than two hours from the capital in her BMW, and she thought the long drive would do her good . . . and give them a couple of hours alone together so they could talk. They rarely seemed able to find the time to chat together any more. When they first started seeing each other five, six years ago, they'd done nothing but talk. God, the things they'd talked about! She'd been fascinated by his wealth of knowledge, his wide range of experience, the stories of his travels. Brian in turn had been entranced by her vivacity, her enthusiasm for living, her eagerness to learn about fine wines and good food and the theatre, all the things he knew about and took for granted, but which she had only dreamed of until then.

Brian and Patricia had been exact opposites; that's where the attraction lay, in the beginning.

But had they ever really been in love, she wondered now.

Was she in love with him when she had her first affair two years after their marriage? Didn't the fact that she needed an affair tell her something was very wrong with the marriage?

The bright red, orange and yellow lights of a petrol

station loomed on her left. She indicated and slowed, cutting across the road and pulling into the station with a squeal of tyres.

The young male attendant had eyes only for the car, even as she climbed out with her skirt hitched up, showing a length of tanned thigh. 'Fill it, please,' she snapped at him.

Patricia was pulling out of the station when she noticed the hitch-hiker. He was sitting on an army rucksack by the side of the road, and from his weary expression and the despondent slump of his shoulders she guessed he'd been sitting there a long time. He was young – early twenties – his long, blond hair pulled back off his face into a tight ponytail. His face was a long oval, with full lips and a pronounced jaw. He reminded her of someone, but she couldn't think who.

Her decision was made in an instant. She caught a glimpse of his expression as she slowed and pulled over: the flaring of hope, then indecision, and finally relief.

Patricia lowered the electric window as he came running up. His eyes were a vivid blue.

'Thanks for stopping,' he said. 'I'm looking for a lift north.' He had the faintest trace of some accent she couldn't identify.

'Dump your bag in the boot.' She pulled the lever that popped the boot lid open and watched as he heaved the bag inside, then brushed the dust off his clothes.

'You look like you've been waiting a long time,' she said as he climbed into the car. He exuded an earthy scent; musk and sweat, she decided. Very male.

'Not many lifts today,' he replied quietly.

'Have you come far?'

'A long way,' he told her. 'When I left school I decided to take a year off and hitch my way around the world.'

She was impressed in spite of herself, but asked, 'Why?' to see what he would say.

He shrugged and grinned. Glancing at him, she decided he was even younger than she'd thought. And very attractive. 'Why not?' he said. He swivelled towards her. 'You can call me Mark,' he volunteered.

'I'm Patricia. Pat.'

He nodded. 'Didn't you ever want to just do something crazy, Pat?'

'All the time,' she told him. Then she realised with surprise how bitter she sounded. She threw back her head and laughed. 'Oh, Mark, I wish it were that simple. I'm married; I have a husband, responsibilities. . .'

'Oh.' He glanced pointedly at her hand, aware of the absence of a wedding ring. 'I guess that would make a difference, all right.'

'I don't like wearing jewellery,' she said defensively. To an extent that was true. If she wore a lot of jewellery people were more convinced than ever that she'd married Brian for his money. But the wedding ring came off two years ago. Maybe Brian hadn't noticed; maybe he was too preoccupied with his business to notice. He never said anything, and she felt . . . more like herself . . . without it.

'I'm driving to Belfast now to pick up my husband,' she went on hurriedly. Approaching the town of Balbriggan, she slowed the car. Most of the northbound traffic out of Dublin went through Balbriggan and its narrow main street was nearly always congested. 'So you're a student,' she said, making conversation.

'A student on sabbatical,' he grinned.

'Will you continue your education, once your year of travel is over?' she wondered.

'Absolutely. You can do anything once you've an

education. And I want to do so many things. I might be a student until I'm forty!' he added with a laugh.

'That's nice,' Patricia said absently. She had never been interested in school. Sitting in a classroom hour after hour listening to teachers droning on was the most boring thing she knew. It was only when Brian began teaching her things that she got interested in learning, but that was different.

And he didn't bother, any more.

'Maybe you should take some time off,' Mark said quietly beside her. 'Go on a trip, make some time for yourself. Alone,' he added.

'Alone?'

Brian didn't like her going off alone. Older men, younger women; he thought she'd get into trouble. And she did, when she had the chance, she thought.

'Why not? What do you do for fun?'

'Fun?' She hadn't thought much about 'fun' in a long time. It seemed such a . . . a childish idea. 'I go shopping,' she told the hitch-hiker.

'That's it?'

She didn't answer him. They drove on in silence for a while. She could feel his unspoken disapproval. Was her life so obvious? Flash car, expensive clothes, businessman husband who travelled and left a dissatisfied wife at home. . .

She felt a sudden need to explain herself. 'You don't understand how it is, Mark. Life is never the way it looks from the outside.'

'You seem to be doing all right.'

'I'm not talking about material things. I'm talking about time! When I was your age – and that's not so long ago – I used to think I had all the time in the world. When I got married, though, there were always demands on my time. Now I don't seem to have a moment to myself.'

'Even when your husband's away?'

'Especially when he's away. There's a big house to run, and social engagements, and the charities I volunteer time to, and . . . and once you get on the merry-go-round, you never get off,' she finished lamely.

'Sure you can,' he said decisively. 'Just step off.'

'You're only a kid!' she flared. 'You don't know what you're talking about, you simply don't understand!'

'Maybe I understand more than you think,' he said softly.

She glanced at him again, trying to work out his age. He really was good-looking; that unlined skin, those even white teeth. Patricia felt the old restlessness stirring in her. I wish I was his age, she thought. And had just met him, and both of us as free as the wind.

At that moment he turned and looked at her, his eyes locking with hers, and she had the profound conviction he knew exactly what she was thinking.

'Just step off the merry-go-round,' Mark said again. 'It's easier than you think. Before it's too late, take something for yourself.'

'What do you mean by that?' she wanted to know. But he didn't answer, just sat staring out the window, watching the Irish countryside rush by.

They neared Belfast sooner than she had expected. Mark was quiet as they crossed the border, letting her explain about picking up someone at the airport. The border guards didn't even glance at him as Patricia did all the talking. No questions were asked. The BMW obviously belonged to someone important and they were waved through.

But as they neared the city she had to ask her passenger, 'Where do you want me to let you off?'

'You're going to the airport? That'll do me, I suppose.'

She laughed. 'You can't hitch a ride on an aeroplane.'

'No.' He continued to gaze out the window. His silence was beginning to make her uncomfortable.

She wheeled the BMW into the short-term parking lot and glanced at her watch. Brian's plane would already be down; she'd have to hurry. He hated to be kept waiting. Impatiently, she popped the lid of the boot. 'Get your bag,' she told her passenger as she got out of the car, expecting him to get out on his side.

But when she walked around the car he wasn't there. Neither was he standing beside the car, not still sitting in the seat.

He simply wasn't there.

Puzzled, Patricia glanced into the boot. His bag was still there. A lucite name tag attached to a chain was fastened to the strap. Idly, she bent down to read what it said.

Brian Mark Wilde.

Patricia gasped.

Brian never used his middle name, but it was Mark.

And the features of the young hitch-hiker were suddenly known to her, from photographs she'd seen of Brian at that age.

Why had she not recognised him before?

And how could his younger self be hitching rides on the Belfast road. . .?

Choking back a scream, she began to run towards the terminal.

But it was too late, of course, she knew that from the moment she read the name on the tag. A professionally sympathetic airline official explained gently to her, 'We tried to get in touch with you, Mrs. Wilde, but you must have been en route. Your husband took ill on the flight, and the plane turned back. There was a nurse aboard and she did all she could for him, but he had suffered a massive heart-attack, and there was nothing she could do. Nothing anyone could have done. I am very sorry. . .'

Patricia turned away. All the guilt welled up inside her . . . and then vanished, as she realised that he'd known, and forgiven her. She wept then.

At the end of the dual carriageway on the Dublin-Belfast road, a blond-haired, blue-eyed student hitches for a lift to Belfast.

☐	Image	Michael Scott	£4.99
☐	Reflection	Michael Scott	£4.99
☐	Irish Folk and Fairy Tales	Michael Scott	£6.99
☐	Irish Myths and Legends	Michael Scott	£5.99
☐	A Celtic Odyssey	Michael Scott	£5.99
☐	Imp	Michael Scott	£5.99

Warner Books now offers an exciting range of quality titles by both established and new authors. All of the books in this series are available from:

Little, Brown and Company (UK) Limited,
P.O. Box 11,
Falmouth,
Cornwall TR10 9EN.

Alternatively you may fax your order to the above address.
Fax No. 0326 376423.

Payments can be made as follows: cheque, postal order (payable to Little, Brown and Company) or by credit cards, Visa/Access. Do not send cash or currency. UK customers and B.F.P.O. please allow £1.00 for postage and packing for the first book, plus 50p for the second book, plus 30p for each additional book up to a maximum charge of £3.00 (7 books plus).

Overseas customers including Ireland, please allow £2.00 for the first book plus £1.00 for the second book, plus 50p for each additional book.

NAME (Block Letters) ....

....

ADDRESS ....

....

....

☐ I enclose my remittance for _____

☐ I wish to pay by Access/Visa Card

Number ☐☐☐☐☐☐☐☐☐☐☐☐☐☐☐☐

Card Expiry Date ☐☐☐☐